THE WHITE REVIEW

THE WHITE REVIEW WRITING IN TRANSLATION ANTHOLOGY

This anthology contains writing in translation from across the world, never published before in English. Within its pages you will find the work of authors who are largely unknown among Anglophone audiences, alongside internationally recognised authors and translators. There are dark tales of murder, cannibalism and dog breeding, stories of surrealistic erotica and anthropological science-fiction, and accounts of protest and resistance. Courtroom exhibits speak back, detectives piece together the final days of unhappy youths. Nuns smoke cigarettes and share obscenities in darkened rooms. Villagers go on secret nocturnal outings, jumping between the tops of mango trees.

Since its inception, *The White Review* has been a home for inventive and experimental writing in translation. With this anthology, we hope to pay tribute to the tireless work of translators, whose often invisible labour helps bring literature to new audiences, transporting writing across languages and borders. In a world carved up by nationalisms, in which culture is too often produced in an echo chamber, or limited by insular attitudes and risk-averse commercial strategies, connecting with the voices of those outside of our immediate contexts is particularly vital. As the writing in this anthology shows, it can also be wildly entertaining.

To make this anthology we issued a global open call. The quality of the submissions we received shows how many excellent works in translation are out there – and how much excellent writing is waiting to be translated. This collection is a drop in the ocean. We hope it encourages readers, and publishers, to dive in.

Rosanna McLaughlin, Izabella Scott
& Skye Arundhati Thomas

DESSAU

HAYTHAM EL-WARDANY
tr. KATHARINE HALLS

FROM THE ARABIC

An excerpt from –
Jackals and the Lost Letters:
On Animals Speaking at
Moments of Danger,
2023

Once upon a time, a lighter spoke. 'I am the fire, and you are the killers,' it said, and yet nobody believed it. The first time it spoke was when a policeman picked it up to examine it. It was an ordinary red lighter, about half-full of fluid. It uttered this sentence just as he was putting it into the plastic evidence bag; he waited to see if it would repeat what it had just said, but it didn't, so he tossed it in and sealed up the bag. After that the bag remained in a locker in the police station; the policeman didn't take it out again until the court proceedings, which went on for many years. At each session, the judge would ask to inspect the evidence, and the policeman would step forward with the plastic bag, open it, take out the lighter and place it on the judge's desk. The judge would ask the customary questions about the circumstances in which it was found, and the policeman would repeat the customary answer, namely that when he opened the cell, there was no sign of the detainee, and all that he could see was the detainee's lighter. The judge would ask him how, in his view, the lighter should have found its way into the cell when it had been taken from the detainee on the previous night, and he would reply that he did not know. She would shuffle the papers in front of her for a few moments, and then ask: 'Do you believe that Mr. Oury Jalloh, whom you arrested and took into custody on the seventh of January, turned into a lighter?' The policeman would smile. 'Human beings don't turn into lighters, your Honour,' he'd reply. 'In that case, where did he go?' she'd ask. He'd shrug indifferently. 'I don't know.' Then the judge would look closely at the red lighter that lay on her desk, and the lighter would say, 'I am the fire, and you are the killers.' She'd gape at the policeman. 'Did the lighter just *say* something?' she'd ask. 'Cigarette lighters don't speak, your Honour,' he'd say. The judge would shake her head, then dismiss the policeman and his exhibit.

The scene repeated itself every time the court convened. At the final session of the trial, the judge asked the supervising officer to give his explanation of how Mr. Oury Jalloh could have vanished into thin air, and the officer replied that he had no explanation, but that he believed his men. The judge asked him what had caused the fire alarm to sound while Mr. Jalloh was in custody, and why the occurrence had later been removed from the logbook. The officer replied that on the same night Mr. Jalloh had been arrested due to suspicions over the authenticity of his asylum papers, the tree in the police station's courtyard had burst into flames, activating the fire alarm. He gestured towards the window with one arm, and the judge looked out. She could see the still-burning trunk from where she sat. 'Your Honour knows the story of the tree, I'm sure,' he continued. 'The alarm sensors must have been set off by the smoke from the burning tree, since it's so close. When we realised the fire had nothing to do with the incident, we removed it from the records.' The judge asked to see the exhibit for the thousandth time. The policeman stepped forward, opened the plastic bag, and took out the lighter.

This time, the judge put on a pair of polythene gloves, placed the lighter in the palm of her hand, and examined it very closely. The lighter spoke very faintly. 'I am the fire, and you are the killers.' As usual, the judge looked at the policeman. He looked confidently back. 'How,' she asked him for the thousandth time, 'did the lighter find its way into the cell when it had been taken from Mr. Jalloh on the previous night?' 'I don't know,' replied the policeman for the thousandth time. The judge looked long and hard at the lighter, waiting to see if it would make any other noise, but its metal face remained set at the same slant and its red body turned in on itself. It lay silently in the palm of her hand. The judge looked at the supervising officer, then out of the window at the burning tree, then back at the lighter, and then pronounced her judgment: The Dessau City Court finds no evidence of crime in the disappearance of Mr. Oury Jalloh and therefore dismisses the case.

The same day the judge presented her ruling, a crew of workers arrived at the neighbouring police station courtyard to fell the tree. This was to solve the problem once and for all. Nobody had been able to extinguish the fire since it had caught hold of the branches 14 years ago. Every time the fire brigade attacked it with their huge hoses, the blaze would die down only to renew itself the next day. The fire's tenacious hold on the oldest tree in the city was a great mystery, and a team of scientists was formed to investigate this strange phenomenon. The team came up with a hypothesis that the carbon-rich soil had made the tree especially flammable, and the soil around the tree was subsequently replaced, but the flames would not release their grip. Next the team suggested that the tree itself be moved, but the city council refused on the grounds it was a historical landmark, having been planted at the end of the Thirty Years' War. Months and months went by, and still a fine thread of smoke rose each night from the burning tree, winding its way over the rooftops of the city's houses.

Months became years, and there was no solution but to cut the tree down. On the day the tree was to be felled, a child and his mother stood watching the comings and goings in the police station courtyard. The child asked his mother what was happening. 'They're cutting down the tree, son,' she replied, her eyes wide. 'Do you know what that means?' The boy said nothing, so the mother went on, 'This tree was planted by our grandparents' grandparents and it's almost 400 years old.' The people of the city stood despondently watching the bulldozer that had arrived once the council finally decided the matter, and the crew that dug around the base of the tree. The crew were wearing orange. Their hair was black and their eyes were black. The bulldozer, which was also orange, moved closer, sunk the sharp teeth of its bucket into the hole around the tree, and began to tear out the roots one by one. A scent of deep earth filled the air. Next the bulldozer revved its engines and, at full speed, rammed the trunk of the tree, which trembled slightly. Nothing happened for a few seconds, then the tree began to list to one side, and with an almighty roar slowly toppled to the ground amid the cries of onlookers. Once it had cooled, the crew swarmed over it with their chainsaws and set about chopping it up. Then they loaded the pieces of burned tree onto the bulldozer and drove them away.

A heavy shadow fell across the city that night. Nobody slept well. In the morning they woke to a loud clamour: people were screaming, people were running through the streets. They ran, panicking, until they reached the police station, where they came to a standstill in the courtyard. The ground where the burning tree once stood had fractured to reveal a small rock in its place, no bigger than a medium-sized pumpkin, and from this rock bubbled thin streams of burning magma. Some snaked out into the streets adjacent to the police station. The rest pooled around the rock to form a lake of blazing lava.

THREE STORIES

GHEORGHE SĂSĂRMAN

tr. MONICA CURE

FROM THE ROMANIAN

An excerpt from –
Cuadratura cercului,
1975

PROTOPOLIS

Before building the immense transparent cupola, the people hadn't given much thought to what use it might have, nor what the effects of raising it might be. The cupola had to be built for the simple fact that it had been invented and because it surpassed the like of all that the human mind had conceived of until then. Once it was built, however, the group who invented it continued to add improvements which, imperceptibly, set off unexpected consequences.

History hasn't preserved the initial name of the city that, along with a vast neighbouring territory, was covered by the plastic spherical dome. In time, however, it came to be called Protopolis, and that's what it was known as until our days. It simply being covered wouldn't have had, probably, very significant effects; rainfall – already quite rare at that latitude – now blocked by the cupola, had been replaced by a sprinkler system that periodically watered the groves and green spaces uniformly. Then, through the application, by helicopter, of an extremely fine dust on the surface of the dome, the intensity of solar radiation was lowered to an acceptable limit. One after the other, they introduced a maintenance system to keep the temperature and humidity within an optimal range; the *sterovac* process for destroying pathogens; 'clean' methods for disposing of household waste, of street sweeping, and of the interment of bodies; both dry and wet techniques for the containment of dust; the use of ultrasound to exterminate insects and all other pests, etc.

The Protopolitan population quickly became notable for its excellent state of health, the reduction to almost zero of general morbidities, the elimination of infant mortality, and the increase of longevity. In order to protect this most praiseworthy evolution, any foreigner – a virtual carrier of pathogens – was subject to quarantine and a bothersome treatment before being allowed to enter the city; as for locals, they could no longer leave Protopolis since they had lost all resistance to disease and wouldn't be able to survive contact with the outside world. Soon, the isolation of the metropolis under the plastic cupola became total.

The Protopolitans did not seem to be too affected by this situation. In order to adapt to the requirements of an autarchic economy, they limited the scope of their production to what was strictly necessary for daily living. And since the comprehensive conditioning of the topoclimate permitted it, they gave up clothing. Then, they abandoned their houses, allowing them to fall into ruin, because they found that living outdoors, in parks and forests, was more comfortable and healthier. The forests stretched out freely over the debris, invading the streets and deserted squares. The people gained an increasingly athletic build, they learned to run effortlessly, to agilely climb trees in search of forest fruits, to hurl themselves from branch to branch in formidable jumps.

For a while, the cultivation of the fields, left to the care of women and children, still seemed profitable to them. The men spent their time hunting and fishing, because the animals in the forests and bodies of water had increased and they constituted the most reliable source of food. Later, the wheat and corn were left to grow as they would, and the cattle, pigs, sheep, and goats that had been turned loose became wild. Chased out of their cages in the zoo, the wild animals, famished, set out to find food for themselves.

The one source of diversion still remaining for the Protopolitans was making babies. And we have to admit that they were wonderfully skilled at it, they even seemed to hit the mark every time. It is true that the choosing and especially the winning of favoured women gave rise to disputes and bloody fights among the heated males, each desiring the one who was most attractive; and that those such conflicts ended more than once in the strangulation of the weakest, the fecundity of the species more than compensated for the losses. At one point, the population even became troublingly large, in relation to the increasingly modest means of subsistence. Divided into packs, the people then began to wage war for hunting and fishing grounds, for the forests that were richest in edible fruit. At first in secret, then with great pomp, the prisoners were consumed by the victors. Their mandibles grew, their foreheads flattened, necks shortened, chests puffed out, shoulders widened, arms lengthened and, in the end, the people of Protopolis learned how to grab onto branches with their toes; they routinely alternated between bipedal and quadrupedal positions.

The rest of humanity watched the sensational unfolding of the events with vivid curiosity. From beyond the cupola, they filmed using a powerful zoom, they started thrilling live transmissions. And at the betting exchange, the largest share of bets by far was registered for predictions on the question: *When will the Protopolitans start growing tails?*

HOMOGENIA

In that city, made up of absolutely identical neighbourhoods, along identical streets were strung identical houses, in whose identical rooms lived identical people. It was (and was not) as if the city were made up of a single neighbourhood, with a single street, on which was a single house, in whose only room could be found a single person. (In fact, we should ask ourselves if this last image represents the only possible real version of the design described above.)

However, the city existed, exactly as defined in the first sentence. The entire difficulty had lain with the conception of the project of a metropolis with neighbourhoods, streets, and houses that were absolutely identical, as well as with the designing of houses with rooms that were exactly the same. Once these two obstacles had been overcome, the actual construction of the city was carried out with extraordinary speed and precision, given that thousands of houses were completed according to one and the same model – which constitutes, no doubt, the timeless ideal of builders. Ultimately, the raising of the city came down to two fundamental operations: the production in millions of copies of a single prefabricated element; and the installation of the houses, which consisted of the simple assembly of a few hundred such prefabricated pieces, on the sites stipulated by the systematisation plan.

Initially, the inhabitants of Homogenia, like almost all people, were far from resembling each other in any way. But life in a city with a structure so homogenous acted upon them, from the very beginning, in a completely imperceptible and strange way. At first, after they had established that it would be impossible to identify their individual houses, they gave up on the very idea of having a certain home and relied on the most convenient solution, which was occupying, each time, the nearest free room. Besides, people did not even perceive their repeated change of residence anymore since, with the city being homogenous, to get to any house, they would walk down the same path. Then, because it would have been fairly tiring to carry their entire wardrobe with them from one place to the next during their wanderings, the wearing of an extremely simple and practical uniform quickly became widespread. It was a kind of large, unisex cape, which was distributed for free, and, being made out of cheap material, was thrown away as soon as it got dirty.

The hardest step was giving up the deeply-rooted tradition of family. For a long time, families had to walk together always, because, once separated, it would have been impossible to find each other again. Besides the fact that it was inconvenient, this kind of perpetual migration made the regular carrying out of production, education, and the other social activities that are organised on a basis completely different than that of the family unit, impossible. Pressured by these events, the dissolution of the family was decreed, along with the obligation of each mature individual to educate and feed the children found in the dwelling in which they went to sleep, or met with on the street.

The result proved to be dramatic: not a single day passed in which scores of cadavers, belonging to innocent children whose lives were cut short by hunger, were not found. But families had already been broken up, and it would have been impossible now to reconstitute them; the evolution of things moved quickly, and the only consequence of the increasingly large-scale deaths of young ones had been the habit, slowly acquired, of no longer having babies. Not long after, procreation came to be considered a grave misdeed, and the bringing of a descendent into the world – punishable by law.

The new life of the Homogenians triggered unexpected biological effects. The differences between the sexes were slowly erased; no one was born anymore, but no one died either, and over time, the variations of age disappeared from among them.

In the end, by the time every individual morphological particularity had vanished, when all the inhabitants of the city had come to have the same build, appearance, and constitution, there had long ceased to exist differences of thought among them and, to tell the truth, thought itself had gone silent. The identical people moved identically – like perfectly synchronised mechanisms – in their identical rooms in their identical houses, on streets that were . . .

GEOPOLIS

All possible alternatives had been attempted: the planet had reached, without a doubt, the final limits of habitability. Its entire surface had been taken up by an endless city, whose neighbourhoods extended to the heights of the tallest mountain ranges, on the surface and in the depths of the seas and oceans, in regions that in other times were deserts or covered in ice, and even in the underground bowels of the planet. Not a single possibility had been ignored, not one of the even remotely feasible projects remained unexecuted.

Accommodating to the particular conditions of the different types of neighbourhoods had slowly caused the vigorous trunk of the Geopolitan species to branch out. The historic races gave way to others, characterised by differentiations of a completely distinctive, and much more profound, nature. Mole-people, dolphin-people, bird-people, amphibian-people, had all made their appearances... A single race did not seem inclined to being born: that of rocket-people. Lacking genetic support, the astronaut family could not manage to constitute itself into a distinct biological entity, structurally adapted to the difficult conditions of their existence. Geopolis could not, therefore, extend itself into outer space: the hypothetical creation of Cosmopolis remained unreachable. And the population continued to multiply!

In that period, the so-called schools or sects of survival began to proliferate. The one with the most constituents – among all the races – was the school of optimists; they considered that the limits of the cosmic approach to the problem were temporary and that – sooner or later – the exodus to outer space would be achievable, allowing the population of other celestial bodies, the colonisation (equitably for all Geopolitans) of planets with environments hospitable to life from the neighbouring solar systems. Unjustly nicknamed *the dreamers* – given that the optimists were active and persistent – their influence over public opinion had become powerful enough, fortunately for everyone; indeed, with their hopes being fed in this way, the Geopolitans found the resources to endure an increasingly uncomfortable way of life, with more and more encumbrances. This fact was all the more important, given that the results – held in strictest confidence – of the researchers did not seem to be encouraging.

A second school of similar consequence did not exist; of the second-rate ones, a few became noticeable through the virulence of the ideas they proclaimed. The medicide sect railed against immunoprophylactic measures and sanitary activity in general, holding the progresses of medicine, biophysics, and genetics directly responsible for the crisis. The sect of the primitives, somewhat related, preached a return to the wilderness, the abandonment of all the achievements of civilisation, the bringer of misfortune. Neo-yogis saw ascesis, interiorisation, as the true salvation of humanity, recommending fasting, suicide by starvation; in a similar vein, mass suicide was insistently prescribed by other sects. Poison, fire, daggers, nooses, bullets, sources of lethal radiation, had become true objects of worship. Some went as far as petitioning the Supreme Mayor to submit the idea of universal suicide to a plebiscite. Adherents of apocalyptic visions, who were fairly numerous as well, drew from sacred books, or from cataclysm theory, basing their conclusions at times on science, at times on revelation. Others, more moderate ones, limited themselves to proposing the killing of old people, of children, or the proposal of total contraception. Fanatical sects espoused the thesis of the supremacy of certain races, asking for the establishment of their hegemony and the extermination of the supposedly inferior races. Excelling, in this respect, were a few clandestine, and irresponsible, groups of mole-people; they were warmongers, counting on their by no means insignificant advantage of controlling the underground food synthesis factories, and their monopoly of the sources of raw materials. The reality was, however, that a war would be not only meaningless – since it would be equivalent to widespread suicide – but also objectless; adapted as they were to their living environment, the mole-people – like the others, for that matter – did not stand to gain anything from the hypothetical extermination of other races since what was in contention was not food, but space. The drama of humanity's lack of space repeated itself within each of the races, in identical terms. Finally, the representatives of the messianic school, or *saucerists*, as they were mockingly called, awaited a salvation that would come from outside, from an inhabited world, orchestrated by a possible extra-Geopolitan civilisation.

Then something happened that no one had foreseen: the planet started inflating, its dimensions started growing – at first subtly, imperceptibly, then more and more obviously. The growth happened calmly, without jolts, cataclysms, the collapsing of the planet's crust, or volcanic eruptions, without continental drifts, earthquakes, or the formation of new mountain chains. The configuration of the continents remained the same as before, and if the astronomers had not given firm assurances that, indeed, the dimensions of the planet had changed also in relation to those of the stellar system, one could have thought that it was the people who had changed in stature, shrinking several sizes. Awaiting the Geopolitans was the difficult mission of integrating into their city – whose constructions had reached gigantic proportions, along with the planet itself – new structures (miniatures, of course, in comparison to the current dimensions of the previous ones), which would reintroduce a human scale into that world of giants. Civilisation started over from scratch – or, in any case, from a point very close to it – on a strange planet, whose gigantic inhabitants had left, it seemed, to who knows where . . . And no one afterward managed to explain the astounding phenomenon, thanks to which the Geopolitan species – reduced, overnight, to a Lilliputian existence – had been saved.

BUTTERFLIES

GEETANJALI SHREE

tr. DAISY ROCKWELL

FROM THE HINDI

It's quite simple, really – I can't decide whether I'm happy or sad. In this place of matchless beauty in Kerala. Rains, trees, greenery. In an old-style wooden house. Beneath a roof layered with the dry golden leaves of coconut palms.

And now, yet again, my heart flutters upwards, but sticks in my throat – feathers jumping into a thatch formation. Is this a sign of a sinking heart or an acrobatic leap?

I sit on the veranda, a festival of clouds above. It's not exactly raining, just a drizzle. An invisible sound. The dewdrops sway on blades of grass: green grass, green leaves, all washed clean. But there are no puddles anywhere, no flooding, no mud. No gentle breeze so far, but on all sides a stillness that seems to hum a tune: I look all around to see who is singing. As many butterflies as there are birds, and quite as many as there are leaves; they float beneath the leaves with a slight shiver, swimming along the carpet of verdure overspreading the earth, or disappear within it.

The earth here is coated in green velvet.

Am I happy or sad as I gaze at these sights? But that's what I don't know. Should I laugh or should I cry?

Beauty makes one laugh with joy. Or cry? Does one soar when the sky bows down? Or is it an oppressive feeling? If I open up, will I laugh? If I suffocate, will I cry?

I feel agitated.

There's a nutmeg tree. It's full of green nutmegs spreading their maddening scent everywhere. Black and green peppercorns hang in bunches from a pepper vine. The coconut palm sways in the sky, wings outspread, and the round coconuts cling to the tree like baby monkeys to their mothers.

When my aunt, Buaji, first came with Ikki, he was two years old. He jumped immediately into my mother's lap. A child's acceptance beats out all the world's evils; Ma's face lit up. Ikki kept grabbing at her locket chain and stuffing it in his mouth. Grab grab. Ma took off the gold chain and put it around his neck.

I wonder where that chain is now?

The chain, Ikki, Ma? Bua?

If they're no more, I'll cry; but if I remember, will I smile?

*

The person in charge of overseeing food and drink was walking towards me. He'd pulled up the fabric at the hem of his lungi and held onto it as though he was wearing a skirt and was about to commence ballroom dancing. Should I laugh?

I tell him I want to drink coconut water, but he explains yet again that it gets difficult to climb up coconut trees during the rainy season; there's a much greater danger of slipping on coconut trees. Therefore, he cannot serve me any coconut water. We repeat this conversation over and over without knowing a word of one another's languages. *Madame, coconut.* A slight smile and, *very very rain,* just faintly. Our conversation is completed with him bobbing his head at a stormy pace in the southern style, from which I cannot understand whether he's saying, *Yes, I'll try and bring it to you,* or, *No, I cannot bring it.* And we both laugh cheerfully.

So maybe I'm happy.

But my wish for coconut water has not been fulfilled. So I'm sad.

*

Orchid blossoms burst from the branches of the tree in front of my room.

There's one with yellow rays. I remember drawing suns as a child: we made a circle with a compass and then drew lines bursting from it, one small one big one small one big, all the way around.

One orchid is calm, purple; I am infused by its hue.

That one has two colors – pink and orange – and my heart begins to ache.

Why should it make a difference if we don't know whether we're sad or happy? What I do know is that beauty is all around and the essence of nature bubbles up everywhere, so why not sit quietly and imbibe it in sips? Calmly.

But that's the problem. I can't seem to sit calmly. I sigh deeply, overwhelmed by a torrent of memory.

Could it be that from within all this beautiful nature,

departed souls fix me with their stares?

There used to be lush green lawns like this, and evening parties. Feasts, music, guests, minglings of foreigners and locals. *Boy*, my Papa would call out to the coconut man, speaking in an English accent, *I want coconut water and fish fingers*, joking around, *and so does the English Sahib*. Ikki and I lay in wait, hoping to grab some of the coconut water and fish along the way. Hidden, laughing, snatching the servant's tray.

He comes from behind, as though he's part of the shrubbery.

*

At this, I stand up and walk towards the thicket of bamboo. Something like a sob. At the bamboo, or at Ikki, or at myself...?

On both sides of me, a bamboo thicket: dense hair combed straight and parted to form a thin path extending into the distance. But there's no sindoor in the part. Tender grasses carpet the path; if I walk this way, will I reach the sky? Where all the dearly departed now reside? But to reach them, I'll have to smear salt on my feet to defeat the leeches and scorpions. Otherwise, I'll discover later that the leeches have clung to me the whole way and sucked my blood. They'll be swollen and fat, so fat they begin to drop off.

And then a wound will appear, flowing with blood, and I'll feel shooting pains.

In my imagination I become a white memsahib from olden times, who walks along this path and gazes at all these shades of green, her heart and feet fearful of snakes and leeches; and as she walks, she longs to return to her bug-free homeland; she doesn't mind returning alone, because here too, she's alone – her husband missing all day long in the rubber forest.

And it's so hot in these countries, she murmurs. She shakes with heat beneath her sticky skin, and out gushes a fountain of sweat. It's strange how the breeze makes my skin feel a slight chill as warm air rises from the earth. Preparing for a steamy rain.

Heavy, hot, wet, the sky bows down as though oppressed by some burden in its heart. Some tiny bird hidden in its recesses searches for a hold to emerge into the boundless expanse.

Restless.

*

The bathing tank must have been built for just such moments. The white sahib must have had it built for his memsahib. *Go, sit in the water, canopied by green vines and surrounded by round stones.*

Perhaps even then the memsahib felt anxious – what creepy-crawlies must be hidden in the vines and rocks? The true inhabitants of this place! For they have not come here with an intention to depart.

Should I stay inside or go out? Memsahib undecided.

I wouldn't have hesitated to go outside.

With Ikki.

Would have had to go.

Ikki adored the water so. Whenever he saw it, he got excited, no matter the weather. He couldn't yet talk but he'd start pulling at his clothes, as if to cry, *I must take them off!* He'd point to the water and speak in his dialect of shrieks: it was no known language, but everyone knew it. Tiny little steps, toddle, toddle, he'd already started off and before I could stop him, he'd let go my finger and jump into the fountain. *Oh no, oh no,* I screamed as I ran after him, *he'll drown! Grab the naughty thing!* Those were the words he learned; this became his language. *Drown, drown!* Every time you turned around, he was screaming that. If you grabbed him, shook him, he'd beat his forehead against the floor as though everything was water and he'd start waving his arms and legs around as though he were swimming. Crying, *Drown drown!*

Everyone laughed at the child's cries of *Drown drown.*

Don't leave him alone, Ma would say.

But I didn't leave him, he left me.

*

If he hadn't left me, he'd still be here, and he'd insist I let him jump into the bathing tank and that I get in too. That I take off my salwar; *Who else is here?* but not my kurta. The two of us in the water. He would jump up on my knees and bounce about like a rubber ball and the cosmos would light up with his laughter.

Yes, if Ikki were here, I'd jump into this tank with him to make him happy, and I'd be happy too. And I'd laugh.

Oh dear, now I'm getting sad.

*

Forget everything. Just look at what's in front of you.

Birds and leaves, all swimming as one together. When birds sit on a branch, leaves float down to the grass. Their quiet twittering. A green and copper-coloured woodpecker and a bird feasting on flowers like a bee, and the puffy green leaves.

As if a green canopy flutters above. Or the sky is Ikki: now he's here, now he's there, pushing aside the canopy to peek in. It sparkles then fades. Is he happy there now that I'm thinking of him?

Should I laugh or should I cry?

But I do neither. Sometimes I sit. Sometimes I stand and stroll about. The day passes to an unknown tune.

*

It's that time of evening when the earth sighs deeply. As though with desire. The hot sighs spread their arms upwards, warming the cool air as it rolls down from the sky. In their meeting, or intercourse, all of nature is made fragrant. The steam of the nutmeg and the jungle grass.

Since I've come here, my restlessness reaches its peak every day at this time, and I suddenly get up and begin to walk. Because it will get dark and then I won't get a walk due to the reign of the true inhabitants. Are my thoughts creating this environment around me, or is my environment simply concocting a chemical reaction that makes me burn, melt, parch, fret? Am I myself a natural particle?

Am I but an insignificant speck in this splendid conspiracy?

What an egotistical thought. I blush.

But is my thought even real, or is it just some chemical reaction?

What if I walk along as one must do. Oh Lord, is this physiological process merely a conspiracy to transform inner anxiety into sweat so that it will flow away?

Now I wonder what effect laughing will have on the whole calculation… or crying?

*

Every day at this time, girls appear before me. They form a queue and carry huge kettles and teapots and plates, and on their heads, bundles much larger than themselves, of laundered clothing for ironing. Tea and food and fresh laundry weaving about among the trees and leaves.

These girls have long thick black braids that swing in white ribbons down to their shoulders and everyone is wearing pink salwar-kurtas with blue waistcoats. The blue waistcoats reach to mid-thigh. They look like nurses in this costume. They must be orphans, and they must have been brought here to do nursing degrees. I've seen them going into the clinic near the gate.

Along with their training they also look after people like me. Everywhere you look, there are nurses. And these girls also travel to other regions. In any corner of India, if you are admitted to a hospital, you'll find that Keralite nurses will come to look after you, and they'll be full of laughter.

*

She is laughing. The girl who knocks on my door every morning and says, *Fine, I'll knock at 6:30 starting tomorrow morning*, and she hands me a teapot and a cup.

Now there's a green fruit in her hand, and she's looking at me and smiling. Everyone looks at me and smiles because I act out my utterances by gesturing with my hands and feet, and insist that they give me the most natural things from here, please. Things from this garden, these fields, things related to the birds and beasts raised here – eggs, fish, coconuts, pineapples, bananas, sooran, passionfruit.

Pear, she says in English, and hands me a guava.

Thank you, I reply in English and take the fruit.

Clean air, clean water, no need to wash here. Just wipe it off and bite into it. Pink inside. Not sweet. Bland. But fresh. Juicy. Where I come from the fruit is sweet because it's been injected with sweetness, and shiny because it's been coated with a sheen.

*

Did you write? Is it done? She always asks.

What? No, never! I say, expressing regret with my lips and holding out my palms to show helplessness. How to tell her I haven't even begun!

Story, me, she says.

It takes me a few moments to understand what she's saying: *Make me a character in the story.*

This is what our conversation is like, big smiles, little talk.

Yes, I say. I wave my hands around. *Beautiful, long hair,* smile, smile, *tea slowly slowly.*

She leans against the nearby tree, one foot resting against the trunk, scratching the sole of her foot against the bark. Sandal off. She feels shy. She must have understood what I said. She's at the age to blush at the mention of her beauty. She must be 16? Or even younger.

Walking walking, I move my feet rapidly, which must have looked less like walking and more like cycling, to tell her I've come out for a walk. I take three steps forward and I wave my arms around in the air like my feet, I'm still explaining: *Walking walking, like this.*

She laughs.

My heart peeks open a little, but still does not blossom. Just then, it occurs to me that my heart aches, as though it's wondering if it's shriveled or blossoming. Perhaps this is what sadness feels like.

Or did my heart suddenly see the sun? But I want rain, not sun. And here, no matter how rainy it is, golden rays can burst startlingly through the trees at any time. Like fire arrows.

Their scorching heat assails me as I walk on beneath the cashew tree and through the thicket of rubber trees with bags tied to their thin trunks. And here are the coconut palms, waving and bowing deeply, they have bags tied to them as well, for gathering toddy.

The beautiful girl again appears before me.

It's very hot, I say. I flap my kameez, to show her that I'm sweating; it's sticking to me.

She laughs. She laughs at everything.

Not hot not hot, she shakes her head in disagreement and points up at the sky.

Truly, a black sheet of clouds flaps behind the softening rays of the sun, as though there's another sun behind this one.

Make it rain, I demand.

Make me story, she responds. She's understood and she's bargaining. *Then I'll make it rain.*

I still don't know how we understand one another, despite speaking different languages; how do we carry on a conversation?

Okay, I nod my head in agreement.

Suddenly a host of girls hovers about me.

*

Like butterflies. Behind every leaf, branch, petal, they'd been hiding in anticipation of my *yes*, and when it emerged, they came flying out. Pink and white and blue and young. Their black braids swinging. Chattering in their own language and laughing with me but not at me. Their curvy flowery bodies, like new petals on flowers. Ah, youth.

Each one babbling to me; all repeating the same thing: *Ma'am... me... story.*

They push and shove: *No you... no me.*

You - all - story, I say without understanding their speech, but knowing what they mean. Meaning, *I will make you all heroines.*

All there? I ask, peering between the trees and pointing towards the hospital. And at their nursing attire as well. Pink and blue butterflies.

Seventeen - we. They tell me, counting up on their fingers in a mixture of Hindi and English. *Right now, there are only ten here,* they indicate by counting one another.

And they are less nurses, more butterflies, I think, as I continue on my walk.

*

Near the hospital, I hesitate. There's a lemon tree and a sharifa tree. A fresh fragrance emanates from both of them. What if the odour of Dettol or phenol ruins this delicate scent, I worry. I can be happy when I'm worried, but I continue to wonder if I'm feeling sad. But I've been joking around, so I should smile.

The supervisor of this property has seen me and tips his cap in response to my smile.

Please come in, Ma'am.

I turn, and the clouds burst.

*

Now we are standing on the veranda of the hospital watching the ferocious rain.

It will let up in just a moment, Mr. Supervisor keeps repeating. *If not, please take my umbrella, it's made for the winds here.*

Truly, this is an umbrella that opens up a new sky over your head.

It's a charity hospital, he says, keeping up the conversation.

The poor come, villagers come, do you want to know more?

It's for diabetes patients. They come here to die.

I don't feel like walking down the hallways of the hospital. I'll catch a glimpse of elderly wrinkled dying faces in the wards.

Girls, he says, *nowadays there are seventeen.*

He too stops and counts on the fingers of his mind, and searches for the right word in English or Hindi.

Girls? I stare at him.

Usually they are thirteen or fourteen, a few are a bit older.

Diabetes, in such young children? I ask foolishly.

It happens. At birth, in childhood. Here they get a free cure, they are supervised.

There's a cure! Well, that's good...

There's no cure. They receive treatment. Anything could happen at any time. Another organ could be afflicted: heart, kidney. Coma. Such patients usually only make it to forty or forty-five.

These nurses have learned at a very young age how to give an injection, how to measure blood sugar. Now I am starting to wonder if these are nurses, or no? Have they not come for training in nursing? Are these the same seventeen he's talking about? Are they being taught how to tend to their own veins and how to stay alive? Until...

*

Lightning flashes, clouds thunder and rain slices noisily through the air.

Do give me the umbrella, I say. And I start back along the path. But it no longer looks like the path back, so flooded is it in Kerala's typhooning rain.

Ma'am, me, story... I encounter her again in the coconut grove, under the sloping trunks of the coconut trees, where she stands as though demanding from the Lord above that he overturn those giant leaves and pour water over her, *bang crash.*

*

The coconut trees are fearful. After all, they've only got that one trunk. Once they're gone, they're gone. At just the slightest shadow, they panic and shrink into their leaves. In this storm, they shake and quiver. When water falls on them from above, they are startled and let it glide down, as if to say, *don't bring us down, we must remain vigilant!*

Girl, come here! I scream, brandishing my huge strong open umbrella.

The Almighty verily roars at her provocation.

But she laughs and mimicking a shiver, she hops even further under the coconut shower. The stream flows powerfully and she cries, *Aiya daiya ayyayayo!* and she dances.

Her bones must be rattling with the chill.

I can't hear clearly, or see. As though the misty rain is invading my veins and a veil waves over all my senses.

Come here! I shout, reproachfully. More intensely: *Come!*

She dances like a leaf in the rain, and gasps, as though to show me that she's drowning.

And now here are the rest of the girls; where have they come from? And they're shivering and jumping up and down, like her. Not butterflies – fish – leaping and splashing on the surface of a lake.

Are they dying? I'm afraid, and I rage, and I march on among them. At which they jump and dance beneath the huge leaves of the next tree. At which I shall pounce, and then they'll leap away as though we're playing tag.

Now I have absolutely no idea if I'm sad or happy or if should I cry

or laugh, or if the speech coming from their mouths is laughter or some other type of shriek; there's no time to conduct an investigation because I... *I insist*... and I'm panting. But I'll only stop running once I've caught them all... and she... and she... and she is jumping ahead, and ahead... are more girls... and I'm shouting, *Girls! Come back here...!*

PEACH

SEMA KAYGUSUZ

tr. MAUREEN FREELY

FROM THE TURKISH

And there she lay. Clutching first at her wrists, then at her long snaking curls, then holding her own eyes in the palms of her hands. She thought her hands were sweating, but no, these were tears, and soon they had drenched her to the waist. Her sharp shoulder blades pinned her body to the bed; her sunken cheeks ached. There wasn't a contour left on her face to recall her smile. She was still inside that nightmare: between her knees she could see a man, a man in a ship sailing through a dark sea. She could hear his moans, his anguished pleas, melting her ears. Then she could hear him no more, as she was brought fluttering back up from the depths, towards the waking world, by her own hand slapping her face.

Her ankles had floated up as far as her knees. Swinging as hard as she could, she sent them back where they belonged. Her heart was beating hard against its cage now. Her neck had wandered down to her waist and turned into a button. She tugged and tugged, until she had pulled herself out of herself. She swallowed and then swallowed again; swallowed until she gulped down her great fat insult of a tongue.

Her nose was bone dry; it dangled, begging: catch me before I fall. She had no choice but to raise her hand and rub it. No choice but to rescue it with her last reserves of warmth. And now her stomach. It was made of paper. She turned herself over carefully, so as not to tear it. Her breasts sank, her breasts fluttered, her breasts collapsed. She had to get up. She was either going to get up, or she was going to seep into the sockets of her own soul. Become an octopus with forty, not eight tentacles which she would prod and wring until she turned herself into a woman with wild hair the colour of hay. She was either going to wake up and shake off this ever-darker cloud looming over her, or she was going to stay in bed until all the air was sucked out of her.

In the end, she slid her foot to the floor and raised herself up. Having located her head, she opened her eyes, but how bright it was in here, so bright it hurt. Once again, blood pumped through her calves. There were scabs on her back, flaking away as she moved. Using all the strength she could muster, she dragged herself towards the kitchen, and for the first few steps, she had to clutch the wall, dizzy and breathless. She dropped to her knees and tried to catch her breath, and for a time she stayed there, waiting for her body to reassemble itself. If only I could perspire a bit, she said out loud. If only I could perspire, I'd stop feeling so dry. A warm stream flowed out from her armpits, marbled with flame. It went spiralling across her breasts, only to fall away and vanish.

She struggled to her feet and made it into the kitchen with what strength she had left, then slowly leaned back on the counter, unpeeling layer by layer. She looked at the jug, at the water swaying back and forth inside it. While you were asleep, the water said, the air turned stale and seeped into me, so don't drink me, because you'll only poison yourself again, and vanish inside yourself. She stared sourly at the water. Then she turned to the refrigerator, and as she touched its great face, a whiff of metal, promising relief, sent her into a rapture. With the tiniest ember of strength remaining in her shoulders, she pulled open the door. And there, amid the plastic detritus and metal lids and broken china was an enormous peach. She inspected its furry visage, until she was sure it lacked even the tiniest blemish, and at once (once again) she had eyes for nothing else.

Some feeling came back to her fingertips when she reached out to pick up the huge, flame-coloured fruit. The air filled with its sweet scent. She rolled it over the palms of her hands, weighing it. The peach, unfazed, kissed the second joint of her middle finger. The woman felt a tickle, a desire, and the rush of courage. She shamelessly bit into the peach's left cheek. There were voices. One after the other, they poured out: whispering at first, then suddenly two voices rose above the others, chattering madly. One censured the other, as if to say, look how much you took. The woman paused, to savour the coolness as her first bite made its way inside her. Resting her nose against the peach, she breathed in the scent of its flesh. Her nose took on wings, as it flew back into place. Suffused now with a sweet harmony, she propped her elbows on the windowsill, and her elbows said, don't worry, we can hold you up, so relax.

But by now the woman was beyond rule, had given herself over to the waterfall coursing through her body, as it pulled her into its bubbly depths. Peach juice seeped through her pores, to seep back into her wrists. Her waist hollowed out, her shoulders trembled, her thighs turned marble white. They grew smaller and then smaller still, until they were no larger than a pit. Her heart left its place to move into her loins.

Then she bit into the peach again, and that hunger, the same black hunger that had staled her breath, curled up in the palms of her hands, and stopped begging. Her tongue rolled out of her mouth to slap her. Sweetly, very sweetly, it rubbed itself against the sides of her lips, and her cheeks. Her one leg couldn't keep still, so said to the other, I'm going, what do I care. The woman grew lighter, as she stretched like a single-rooted branch over her peach. As she curled upwards like ivy, she peered out through the window, spying in the distance a juniper tree peering back at her, craning its neck. On the tree's long finger was a ruby butterfly ring. Her lips went red, as a light fell upon her cheeks and brow. And so it was that the peach vanished into the woman, and the woman into the peach. To get the last bit of flesh, she took the pit into her mouth. As she closed her eyes, she saw the ship sailing through the night towards the shore, sailing through the night like the ghost of the moon. As the woman unravelled the peach's last strings, she turned whiter than white. Her lips grew fatter, her stomach soft as silk, as her hair's copper lights began once again to undulate. When the woman spat out the pit, a man tumbled out after it. It was her young man, the same young man who'd been crying on that ship. What a magnificent smile, she thought. Even, after giving her all his flesh, he still weighed down on her, heavy as a peach.

TETHER

VICKY GARCÍA
tr. MEGAN MCDOWELL

FROM THE SPANISH

An excerpt from –
Las Bestias,
2021

1.
The bay whinnied and the quirt hit just above its eye. It had come the whole way, skittish and trotting and avoiding the quicksand, with one lame foot after it got caught in a rabbit hole.

Irusta tied the sulky to the last post and adjusted the kerchief he wore round his neck. His hands were still bloody from the beating he'd given Sayen. He straightened his beret and kicked open the corrugated metal door to Tart's barroom.

'Hail and howdy, folks.'

Some of the gauchos looked at him, but none took their elbows from the bar to shake his hand. They all clutched glasses of firewater with rue and argued about the bad harvest, the condition of the roads, the drought that was battering the fields, and the influx of Hungarians.

Irusta walked bolt upright to the tables at the back, wiping his hands on his pants. Rocinante had come to his woman's defence, and in the middle of the fight had bit his ankle. Now the animal's teeth were burning under his work clothes, because he hadn't even been able to change after the dairy barn. He scratched at his leg with the rope-soled shoe he wore for milking.

From the table by the patio Lefty Dálmire waved Irusta toward an empty chair. When Irusta shook his head, Lefty grabbed the freckled gal he was with by the neck and planted a kiss on her tits.

Irusta settled into the empty chair as best he could, because his dick hardened as soon as the freckled gal opened her legs so Lefty Dálmire could get a hand on her. He thought he'd seen her at the train station when he went to pick up the package from the relatives. That morning, he'd patted his pockets looking for coins from the boss; he wanted to take her into the bathroom and fuck her, but before he could get close, Sayen showed up with the baby hanging from her nipple.

He decided to move to the back so Lefty Dálmire wouldn't try to pass the woman off on him. One-Eye saw him hesitate, and she offered him a more solid chair and poured him a muscat. Her skirt was so short that Irusta felt confused.

The country band that had been advertised as the night's entertainment was held up at Efraín's wedding, and the customers began to get restless. One gaucho let out a whistle and asked for someone to at least stamp their feet. Another suggested they go outside and play knucklebones.

After an hour, Irusta, in a bad mood by now, strode over to the bar where Tart was pouring gin and climbed up on the tallest stool.

'So what's going on with the band, partner?'

'Don't rile up my clientele, Irusta. Seems the kinfolk are all dancing a fandango out back at the farm, the bride is plastered and keeps asking for one more song, and that's why the musicians are tardy coming here.'

'That bullwhacker nobody and his partying, I tell you what.'

'Easy, compadre. I ordered One-Eye to saddle up the mare and get 'em over here on the double.'

Lefty Dálmire sidled up to the bar, left hand grazing his knife, and asked if there was a problem. Tart raised his eyes to the tin ceiling as though to mollify the spirits and gifted him another drink. The people in the back had grown impatient, and were reciting the story of Santita Morena.

The freckled girl was now wriggling on the match seller's lap.

'I'm gonna take a whip to that lass. Just look at her shaking her udders at that stranger.'

'Calm down, Lefty, you know how females are. I keep One-Eye on a short leash, sure, but to go from that to hitting her...'

They both looked at Irusta, who adjusted the kerchief around his neck and rapped his knuckles on the bar.

Night had fallen and the smoke from the ribs wafted through the saloon, and the group headed out to the patio. Irusta heard the bay whinny and darted out toward the hitching posts. An owl was licking at the lame foot. He straightened his beret and kicked the bird as far as the gate. The night was nothing but fog.

Irusta pushed his way back to the bar. Before One-Eye could pour him another muscat, the match seller asked for a guitar and Lefty Dálmire started in on a song that got cut off.

Tart, seeing that the banquet was taking too long, shouted out toward the grill. In a jiffy, One-Eye appeared with a serving dish full of organ meats and sausages. Irusta, who had forgotten to bring silverware, was served some half-cooked chitlins that he had trouble swallowing. Rocinante's bite was itching more and more, and Lefty Dálmire's stories were trying his patience. He loosened the kerchief a little so he could choke down the last bite. The sound of grunting pigs came from the sty. After a while he was served a chorizo sausage, and he shoved into his mouth with both hands. The grease was clitchy on his lips and he had to wipe it with his shirt sleeve. The match seller, over by the window, looked at him in disgust.

'Tarnation!' shouted Lefty Dálmire. 'Didn't anyone ever teach you any manners, Irusta?'

Some gauchos chortled, and others tried to hide their laughter by raising their glasses in honour of the feast that Tart had produced. Irusta stood up and Lefty Dálmire again touched his knife with his left hand, right when the Cervera brothers' quartet made their entrance stamping a malambo. The gauchos and the girls started dancing to the beat of the legüero drum. The match seller shook to the rhythm of La Terquedad as he rested his cock on Tart, cornered against the window.

'Don't you do that to me, stranger, you know I can't control myself.'

Irusta read his lips and watched as the two of them disappeared through the smoke.

He could see the cold through the chinks in the sheet metal. Well damn it to hell, thought Irusta, Why the deuce didn't I grab my poncho, the last thing I need is to get caught in the rain on my way back to the ranch. What if the bay gets breachy on me? What if it gets so late we run into an evil light? Will the good Santa Morena come to the aid of this poor devil? Best to follow the track and if things turn ugly, I can ward off the beasts with the whip. Irusta adjusted his kerchief so it was tight around his neck.

The used, greasy plates piled up on the bar, and One-Eye asked who wanted rice pudding. Irusta, who was dizzy from so much raw meat, asked for a cigarette.

'But One-Eye, we still have the suckling pigs,' shouted Lefty Dálmire.

One-Eye took off her apron and looked at him over the bar.

'Doesn't anyone plan to go home today? Anyway, those

animals aren't cooked. That brute Tart took his eye off the coals.'

'I learned how to grill from the Indians, Miss One-Eye.' The match seller came in from the patio missing several buttons from his shirt. 'Just point me toward the firewood.'

One-Eye gave him a twisty look.

'This is a matter for real men,' said Lefty Dálmire. 'No insult to the stranger, but you don't look all that handy.'

'You, sir, are gonna help us make the fire,' one gaucho ordered as he scratched the back of his neck. 'Come on, collect us some kindling.'

Lefty Dálmire waved a hand in agreement. The gaucho clapped his back and shoved him out to the patio.

The Cervera brothers were singing a sad zamba. Irusta took the chance to go for a piss out back. The squealing of the pigs distracted him, but he still stroked his cock for a good while, enjoying the darkness and the fog.

'Don't hide out, partner.'

Tart came to stand beside him and lowered the zipper on his pants.

'I was about to piss myself, Irusta. Next time bring Sayen with you, my woman's been complaining, the two of them were real close.' He shook his cock and licked his fingers. 'Come on, the Cervera brothers are heading out for another shindig, let's ask for another zamba before they go, and we'll see if we can get close to one of these fillies who're wanting to be serviced.'

When they entered the saloon, the lights went out. The gauchos whistled and the ones carrying knives touched them openly. One-Eye fumbled around on the shelves until she found a kerosene lamp, and the Cervera brothers started playing a gato and then an escondido.

The match seller came running in from the patio, dodged one of the shicksters who was nursing a baby, and grabbed hold of One-Eye's filthy apron. He made a show dancing like a pro but the soaked gauchos didn't take his cue. Dawn was breaking. Irusta realised that the five leagues in the sulky were going to be rough with the bay injured. He thought about asking One-Eye for a bed, but he figured the match seller would climb in with him to do deviant things. He'd have to stay awake the whole night, because in the drubbing he'd given Sayen he'd dropped his knife into the well and was now unarmed. He went out to the patio. Not a single star in the sky over the plains.

'Cheers, folks,' he said, adjusting the kerchief that was strangling him. 'See you at Saint John's Eve bonfire.'

A few people waved.

2.

Shit, the bite from Rocinante really hurt. As soon as he got to the ranch he was going to stake the horse and teach him a lesson. Someone had hitched his sulky to a different post. The bay was sleeping on his feet like the best of gauchos. The brush was damp with dew. Irusta skirted the dung but his shoes, worn away by milking, slid, and he went face-first into the gate. It took him a few minutes to get up, his bones weren't the same as when he used to work as an oxherd at Aparicio's and he could sleep atop hides out on the hillside, boots on. Now his skull ached and his back was stiff. To make matters worse, his beret was missing.

'Well damn it all to hell.'

Day had broken suddenly. Light streamed in through the saloon's high windows. The kerosene lamps were out and the stench of raw organ meat still hung in the air.

One-Eye was eating rice pudding with a ladle and scratching her hairy shoulders. That morning, she looked more beastly than ever to Irusta.

'What the hell you doing back here Irusta?'

'I came for my beret.'

'You'd be better off hightailing it back to the ranch.'

The dogs barked on the patio and there was growling. Irusta headed to the half-open door, a little bewildered.

'Don't stick your nose in there, you stubborn mule.'

Irusta stumbled over a bench that was blocking the door and went face-first once again. Lying on the brick floor, through the glass of a broken gin bottle, he could see the match seller. They had him in his underpants, with a lasso around his neck and a beret on his head.

'I'm going to teach you a lesson.' Lefty Dálmire ran his knife across the man's belly. 'Robbing Tart, you swine.'

The match seller begged them to let him clarify the situation.

'That's my beret,' Irusta said from the floor.

The folks all looked at him disconcertedly.

'What the dickens are you doing here, Irusta?'

Lefty Dálmire came to stand next to him and rested his knife between Irusta's eyebrows. Then he looked at Irusta's pants.

'See how you're shitting yourself, you're a filthy bum.'

The gauchos laughed, and the girls who were fluttering barefoot around the unlucky man went into the saloon to make mate.

One-Eye put down the rice pudding and started to wash the dishes. Flies swarmed the bulging innards. Someone had let the wood-burning stove go out. She told those around her that she'd have to run out to chop some caldén wood, and it'd be better if they drank their mates outside.

One of the gauchos lit a fire at the match seller's feet, and he let out a shriek amid the laughter of the men who got stark naked.

The roosters crowed over near the pigpen. Irusta thought how at that hour Sayen would be waiting for him with the coffee and milk all ready, just like every time he went out for a shindy. She would greet him with eyes sleepy from so much rocking the baby, and who knows, maybe she'd be ready to be mounted on the table his relatives had sent as a gift.

'What should we do, Tart, tie this one up, too?'

Tart was sitting on a stump and smoking a cigarette, tears falling, and he covered his face with his shirt.

'Let the match seller go, it's Christian to forgive.'

'But, Tart, are you sloshed?'

Lefty Dálmire came over clutching his knife and kicked the stump.

The match seller tried to run, but the gauchos were holding the lasso tight, and gave it a yank.

From the saloon came the sound of the girls' laughter as they arranged the tables to shoo off the flies.

'What I say goes around here, Lefty, let him go.'

'Do whatever you want, but give me back my beret.' Irusta's trembling hands pushed Lefty Dálmire. 'It's mine.'

Lefty Dálmire tossed his cigarette, signalled with a raise of his glass, and the gauchos untied the match seller.

'In the country you find the kind of critters you need. Ain't that so, Lefty?' said Tart, and he ordered them to let the match seller go. 'But let him go in his birthday suit, knowing that if we see him around at any other dive we'll slit his throat.'

Lefty Dálmire, dispirited, rested the tip of his knife on Irusta's forehead.

'Gimme my beret, Lefty, I got a kid and a woman waiting for me.'

'Naked and into the saloon.'

3.

The gauchos held Irusta by the neck, tore off his rags, and laid him out on the bar. The raw chitlins churned in his stomach.

He remembered his wedding, Sayen weepy as she entered the chapel on the arm of an oxherd, because they had found her when she was a young girl, out on the hillside surrounded by dead flowers, and no family of hers had ever been found. Dressed in blue, because Irusta's wages weren't enough for a wedding dress.

That same night he wanted to make a baby with her, but she wouldn't allow it. He put up with it for a few days, then decided to tie her to a quebracho tree. Once she was tame he could service her. Who knows, maybe that circumstance was why the baby was born crippled. Hence the beatings with barbed wire, like the day he'd found her at the lake swimming naked with One-Eye.

'Poor devil,' said one of the gals sipping mate, 'ending up like that.'

Lefty Dálmire grabbed One-Eye's apron and polished his knife.

'Don't forsake me,' begged Irusta, seeking out Tart's eyes.

But Tart was out of his wits by now, caressing the match seller's punished back and apologising, his mouth slack.

'He's leaving us without even trying the rice pudding,' One-Eye rubbed her hands on Irusta's kerchief. 'Poor widow, right?'

The Cervera brothers grabbed their guitars and drums, taking advantage of the stiff breeze that was crossing the pampas. They jumped over the gate and left on foot, whistling.

One-Eye's laughter reached the patio. Lefty Dálmire glared at Tart as he said goodbye to the match seller with a squeeze of his buttocks and headed to the bar.

'Let's see that knife, Lefty,' the assembled gauchos shouted eagerly.

'Just a moment,' said Tart, 'we have to put on his beret.'

Lefty Dálmire took a deep breath and went straight for the jugular, but then reversed with his left hand and sawed off the ears. Irusta screamed and fainted.

'Here you go, One-Eye, for the sow.'

One-Eye took the ears, wiped them on her apron, crossed the patio and went into the pigpen.

'And now, some grub for the folks.'

They dragged the moribund Irusta out and settled him in beside the bonfire that someone had revived.

The gauchos unsheathed their knives and had at the body. They heard cackling and grunting coming from the pigpen, but Tart ordered them to continue.

Four of them filleted Irusta while Lefty Dálmire held him by the legs. The blood mixed with the dirt and the gauchos started to slide. A few drops of rain fell. The one who was cutting up the vertebrae saw lightning in the distance.

'It's coming, it's coming. Some gully washer, partner.'

'It's just that Santa Morena's been held up, but she's gonna bring us the shower.'

The girls brought over salt, thyme, and parsley, and seasoned him. Those who had done the filleting knelt down to dig in. Tart put on the beret before they cut open the sconce, and he asked for the brains. He took a drag on his cigarette and sat down to eat under the carob tree, every once in a while taking a shot of firewater with rue.

There was a brief dispute over the legs, but it quickly died out when they saw that Rocinante's bite had caused a little gangrene.

When it started to sprinkle, the weasels approached. The gauchos decided to toss the leftovers to the pigs and went to take shelter under the carob tree where Lefty Dálmire, his snout buried in the freckled gal's udders, was imploring Santita Morena to let them finish with festivity.

The thunderclaps came from the grassland and the sky was lowering.

'And now let all the females come,' Lefty Dálmire ordered the gauchos.

Tart pulled a bone from his mouth and spat out a black ball with blood in it.

'This is a matter for men, Lefty, we have to get the animals now they've eaten the leavings.'

The gauchos stumbled to their feet ready to head for the pigpen, but they saw One-Eye walking toward them naked. In her arms she held a sleeping female pig that was dripping blood from its snout. She had cut off its ears and sewn on Irusta's, and she had decorated it with piebald duck and stork feathers, and she'd painted its eyelids with dung and mud. A gaucho tugged at its teats until he pulled the pig from her arms, and he placed it on the plank that Lefty Dálmire set up in front of the bonfire.

'I'm staying,' said One-Eye.

'You go on inside and get dressed, else I'll give you a mean licking.'

One-Eye went fuming into the saloon and asked one of the girls who was making mate to help her get the leaves out of her hair and clean off the filth. The big-nosed girl poured water from the kettle onto her apron and wiped One-Eye's breasts. One-Eye closed her eyes and lay back on the bar that still had Irusta's warm blood on it.

'Too bad the Cervera brothers took off like that, I could really go for a chacarera.'

'I'll sing for you, One-Eye,' the freckled gal came into the saloon in underwear and leaned her elbows on the bar.

Tart, in his drawers, pulled the sow's tail and it kicked him in the balls. Lefty Dálmire gave it a thump on the head and the animal went quiet. Some of the gauchos grabbed it by Irusta's ears, while another one caressed its teats. The pig squealed and a few of its feathers fell off.

'This is all ready. Who's dipping the wick first?'

'I'm first.'

Tart rubbed his hands with dirt, pulled down his underpants, kneaded his cock and skewered the pig, holding onto Irusta's ears.

The firewater went from hand to hand and the gauchos stomped their feet with their cocks erect, sliding on the ground. It was drizzling by then and the lightning was mighty close.

'Don't get in a hurry now, Santa Rosa, we all have to take a turn.' The oldest gaucho came closer to see if Tart had thrown his lariat.

Some of the girls watched from the saloon, others were sleeping it off on the tables or the floor amid shards of glass.

One-Eye was rubbing her ring, lying face-up and staring at the holes in the tin roof. She remembered the lake and Sayen's tits pressed against her back. She pushed aside the freckled girl who was licking her hairy shoulders and went to get her boots.

She felt the wind on her naked body, unhitched the sulky, and mounted the bay.

THE ENDLESS WEEK

LAURA VAZQUEZ
tr. ALEX NIEMI

FROM THE FRENCH

An excerpt from the novel,
2021

A head doesn't just fall off, it can't fall off. It's connected to a thin string that goes all the way down to a person's feet, and if the head falls, so does everything else. You should avoid breaking your head, but you can break your limbs. When you break a limb, you remember the limb is there. When a tooth gets infected, it vibrates inside, almost as if it's speaking. When you pinch your hand, it suddenly appears. If a person puts an eye out, it becomes the main thing about them. In truth, the body is soft. People are soft. Their hands are soft, more tender than wood, softer than plastic or shells, they are softer than fruit, more tender than the majority of things on earth. You can pierce through them with a needle, with a nail, it would be easy, you wouldn't even have to push that hard. There's nothing simpler than piercing through someone's hand with a pike or a piece of wood. Lose your hands and they rot, but if your hands fall off, there will still be arms left behind. Not your head. A head doesn't just fall off.

Some robots wear heads like ornaments. You can change their heads, unscrew them, you can change their appearance, but their minds stay the same. Salim was imagining robots, several cities full of robots run by robots. A family of robots in a normal house, the sound of their feet on the stairs, their talking, eating. A regular family. Then, he stopped imagining. He was looking at himself in the screen of his phone, his face was changing. The mirror was speaking, the mirror was proud and sad. Salim said, 'What do you want?' The mirror stayed silent.

The father had little black wrinkles on his lips, he said, 'You know what I want? I want the house to be clean, but you all leave so many marks behind I can't even count them. If I count one fingerprint, I look more closely and it's really 10, I look even more closely and it's really 100, and if I count 100, I spend the whole day counting. It's like you and your sister have 1,200 fingers, do you really have 1,200 fingers between the two of you? You and your sister? How many fingers do you have, 1 million? Do you and your sister have 8 billion fingers? That's the real question. That's the real question, Salim.'

This particular father's lips produced short, abrupt sounds against his gums. He wrung out the sponge and dunked it in the water, wrung it out and dunked it again. He pointed a fork at the ceiling and said, 'You need to understand that you can't just do whatever you want. One day, the police are going to ring the bell, and they're going to take you away. They'll put both your hands behind your back and then what? What will you do in that position, Salim? With both your hands behind your back? Think about it, you have to think.'

The father's hair was like dead grass on his skull. Just one match, and the whole thing would go up in flames, there would be nothing but ash. Salim imagined his father on fire, then he imagined his father in ashes, then he imagined his father alive with shining hair. He took a photo of his father. He added a filter to the father, and the father had long, soft, blond hair. He said, 'Are you listening to me?' Salim formed the word, 'Yes.' And the word, 'Dad.' He repeated the word, 'Dad.' He felt like his voice was something outside of himself, as if his voice came from the walls or the surfaces around him, as if his own voice didn't come out of his throat but the air surrounding things, as if his voice didn't exist. He said, 'Da-a-a-a-ad,' but he didn't hear his own voice, he heard the outlines, he heard the edges.

When a voice finishes a word, it disappears.

The voice was coming out, it was alive. It said, 'Dad, dad, dad, dad,' and the word was a movement around his mouth. He said, 'Da-a-a-a-ad,' and the voice was a thing in the world. Maybe the word was a thing in the world with the voice. Maybe certain animals could see words in the air, little animals, flies, insects. He said, 'Dad, dad, dad.'

'What do you want for god's sake?'

'Nothing . . . I'm thinking.'

The father mumbled and rinsed his hands in the sink. He said, 'Listen, if you don't scrub the table, it gets disgusting. Are you listening to me? I'm going to ask you a question, Salim, Who wants a disgusting table? No one. I'm going to ask you another question, Who wants to drink disgusting water? No one. Every time you leave a sponge in water, it sucks it up. That's its job. Then, you put the sponge in your hand and the hand washes. You have to wipe your hand over the bags of rice, the bags of sugar, and even the vegetables, the Brussels sprouts, the tomatoes. When the sugar is dirty, it gets disgusting. Does anyone on earth want disgusting sugar? No. Nobody, Salim. Nobody wants it.'

The father kneeled against the wall and scrubbed the wall with the wall sponge. He scrubbed the baseboards with the baseboard sponge. The father had many, many sponges in the cupboards, in basins, in his sink, on the edge of the bathtub, and in his pockets. Of every colour and of every material. He always had a sponge in his hand. A table sponge to make the table shine, a dust sponge to chase away the dust, a sponge for hard things, a sponge for soft things, an old sponge for broken objects, a new sponge for precious objects. And for cleaning the sponges, he had several sponges for sponges. A long sponge for long sponges, a short sponge for short sponges, sponges in pieces for pieces of sponge. The father would pick up his sponges, he would hold them.

Sometimes, the father imagined sponges inside of people. What if you could wipe down people's insides with a sponge? If you could wipe down lungs with a sponge? A lung sponge for people with sick lungs? If you could wipe down the stomach with a sponge? A brain sponge for people with sick brains, a sponge on a heart, gliding down a heart, into the arteries and behind the eyes. Wiping a sponge through the past. Cleaning old days, old scenes. A sponge for cleaning looks, one for the kitchen, for the knives, for fights, a sponge for everything.

If sponges moved by themselves, they would slide over passers-by, over their faces and the streets, over luggage, they would slide over their mouths which would be smooth forever. The father scrubbed, he scrubbed, he said, 'I scrub the doors so they close. Think about it, Salim, if you don't scrub the door, it squeaks, and one day, it doesn't close anymore. Who wants a door like that? A door that doesn't close? And the light switches, you can't forget the light switches, Salim. If you forget the light switches, they get rusty, they fall off, one day you're in the dark. And we'll be worse off in the dark. Now, Salim, think, if we don't wash the walls, guess what will happen. It's bad. You have to take care of things, otherwise, they collapse.'

The father got up on his stepladder to clean the ceiling with the ceiling sponge. He whistled and whistled, then he polished the corner of the wall, he leaned over and over, then he cleaned the floor with the floor sponge. He scrubbed Salim's chair with the chair sponge, he went up and up, and he wiped the sweater sponge over Salim's sweater and the ear sponge over the edge of his son's ears, he went down and down, and he wiped the sponge over his shoes, his pants, he went back up and up, and he wiped the sponge over his eyebrows and his cheeks. He said, 'I'm washing you, my son.'

He wiped the neck sponge over his son's neck and the ankle sponge over his lower legs. This was his son, his oldest son, and his things belonged to him. One day, children choose their possessions and these possessions belong to them. Salim didn't move, he was used to it, he touched his screen.

He zoomed in on the face of a man who'd just won 75 million in the Lotto. This man didn't have eyebrows, his cheeks sagged. In the article, he said, 'The day I won, I felt afraid. I was afraid of losing the ticket. It was a formless fear. At home, I hid the ticket in a package of cookies. Who would steal cookies? Then, I slept poorly. In my dreams, every night, I lose the ticket. I lose it, and I never stop losing it.'

The father was cleaning his son's hands as they held his phone. He said, 'If you keep lowering your head over this device, your organs are going to drop. They are going to come out of your mouth and you're going to vomit up your organs. You're all going to vomit up your organs. You'll watch the news and the announcers will say, "They're losing their organs, they're vomiting them up."'

The father wiped a sponge over the windows. He looked outside while he scrubbed, he was looking for the neighbour. She was always moving, she wandered through her large house, she spied on people, that was her life. Behind a curtain or on the garden wall, on her knees in the garden, lying down with her arms stretched out, in the dormer window or on the roof with her hair fanned out, behind a post, she was thin, all you had to do was wait, she'd show up. The father saw the neighbour sitting on the roof, looking through binoculars, she waved. From far away, her mouth was a hole. He tried to understand. One day, she'd dropped off a letter for the father, it said:

Sir, you look like a neighbour I had as a child. He was an

old man when I was young, which means he's dead. May he rest in peace. Today it's a pleasure to watch your face LIKE IT'S MY JOB. It takes me back in my childhood body. Be kind, EYES ARE TAX FREE as far as I know, and there's no shortage of problems in the world. Please, grant your image to

Your old neighbour.

Since then, from time to time, the father would try to see himself as a neighbour. He would try to get inside the mind of his neighbour to see himself as a neighbour.

In the mind of a neighbour, we're all neighbours. Our faces are that of a neighbour. If the neighbour runs into us on the opposite end of the globe, he runs into his neighbour. He could run into us in the sea, on an airplane, in the hospital, or on Neptune, he'd still be running into his neighbour. If our neighbour runs into us in a dream, he's running into his neighbour. We are a thing in his thoughts. From birth, we get inside other people's thoughts. The father had lived in other people's thoughts. He'd been looked at. People who are living are looked at by other people who are living. Children live in the thoughts of their parents and parents in the thoughts of their children. All of the people on earth have been seen, they've been looked at. When they were born, a doctor touched their stomachs, nurses measured their heads and their feet. A person who isn't looked at doesn't exist, cannot exist. People who are not looked at don't exist. People who are blind look around like everyone else, but through the power of their hands. Every person we run into has been looked at by their parents, their aunts, their cousins, by a horse, they've been looked at by their beloved one evening in the light, by their friends, by a deer, from up above by birds, or from the side by a lizard.

People resemble the traits we give them and thoughts transform into facial features, wrinkles, gestures. Every thought leaves a mark on a person, even hermits hidden away in their caves. They live in the thought of the word: HERMIT, in the images of the word HERMIT in other people's thoughts. We don't know how other people see, because we don't have their eyes, we don't have their nerves, we don't have their minds, we don't have their veins, but the father looked at his reflection in the windowpane, made an effort, and saw himself as a neighbour. A childhood neighbour, someone dead. And he said to himself, 'Hello, Sir,' and responded to himself, 'Hello.' He wondered if the neighbour spied on him at night, maybe she didn't sleep, the poor thing, poor woman, her son was mad.

The neighbour's son was a skinny boy. He walked the streets at night, his arms at his sides. Last year, she'd had to send him to a hospital because he was talking to aliens. He'd face the walls, and he'd talk to the inhabitants of other planets, he'd say, 'I'm waiting for you.' At the hospital, the neighbour's son acted like the devil himself. He put pins in the surgeons' gloves and blocked the elevators. He cut the hair of people in comas and turned the lights out during operations. He was uncontrollable, the doctors had to tie him down. They had to do electroshock therapy for months. Was the neighbour's son sleeping now? The father didn't know. But at night, the father would put small objects on the table. Pots, utensils, he arranged them by size at his workspace. He'd take an object, dunk it into the dishwater, and it was as if the water spoke to him. It said, 'I am water, I am clean, I can last, I am calm, I am slippery.'

The father would plunge his hands, his arms, and his elbows into the water and the water took him, it took him. If he could have, the father would have plunged his legs and his entire body into the water. From behind, the father looked like he was ramming things into his stomach. His elbows moved slowly as if he was moving a fist around in his guts. He said, 'You guys think this stuff washes itself, but the house would fall apart if I weren't here. Your sister would fall apart and you would fall apart and your grandmother would fall apart. You would all fall apart if I weren't here. I had to ask them to give us this house, Salim. I got on my knees at the mayor's feet, he's the one who decides. All the trees that you see in the town, the mayor's the one who made them grow. We're lucky. Do you think we were the only ones who wanted the old school? This huge house, this huge school, this huge kitchen, these long hallways, your enormous bedrooms, are you listening to me? If you never leave the house, they're going to take it from us, Salim. We won't have a house anymore. You have to understand. Well . . . at least, if they come, they'll see that everything is clean. They might throw us out, but the house will be clean. I want to hear them say, "These people are clean." And if there are any catastrophes, because catastrophes happen, there are always catastrophes, and if there are any catastrophes, we'll call the firemen, so the firemen will see that the house is clean, they'll say, "These people are dead, but they're clean. They might be dead, but they're clean." Try to wear clean underwear, Salim, always wear clean underwear. The social worker is going to come if you continue on like this, you know. They are going to take our house, we're going to lose everything. We'll look around and there won't be any more walls. Take a good look at the walls and the ceiling. Now, imagine a life without walls or a ceiling.'

The father's lips twisted. He scrubbed his own mouth with a sponge. He said, 'The social worker calls me every week.' He turned around and said, 'At your age, you have to go out.'

Salim liked two pictures on his phone. When he raised his head, his father was wiping the sponge over a bottle, his lips were twitching, his Adam's apple was going up and down, could he not swallow it? Was he going to end up swallowing it? Salim wrote the words: A D A M'S and A P P L E, then hit 'Search.' He found a sentence, he read: 'A laryngeal protuberance is a palpable lump on the anterior surface of the neck formed by the thyroid cartilage surrounding the larynx.'

The father touched his neck. From all of the water, his nails had melted and his hands were soft. When he touched his body with his hands, it felt hard to him. He cleaned the big spoons and the forks, he cleaned the knives and the teaspoons, then he started all over again. He cleaned the spoons with the spoons and he cleaned the forks with the forks. When the father cleaned a spoon, it was as if he were cleaning all the spoons in the world since the dawn of time. He did it out of kindness, out of pure goodness. But while he was cleaning the big spoons, the little spoons got dusty, and while he cleaned the knives, the forks got dirty, so he'd start again, he'd go on for hours. One night, Salim found him with his head in the sink, the right half of his face underwater. And Salim had said, 'What are you doing?' and the father had straightened up with an expression that couldn't be trusted. He'd said, 'I'm washing up.'

Now, the father was silent. You could hear the drops of water between his hands. Salim took a picture of his back, the father turned around. Salim took a picture of his face. He sent the picture to Jonathan.

*

Jonathan turned his face to the sky and the sky was black.

He zoomed in on the back of the father's neck, he zoomed in on his face, he wrote, 'Your father has heavy wrinkles. If you weighed his face and his wrinkles separately, his wrinkles would weigh more than his face. You ever thought of that? If you took the original weight of his face when he was young, the starting weight, and then you weighed his wrinkles, if you cut off all of his wrinkles and weighed them, his wrinkles would be heavier than his face. Don't you think? When I'm older, I'd like to have heavy wrinkles. I want heavy wrinkles. When you have heavy wrinkles, you can hide things in them, little things like pills and crumbs. Elderly people carry things around in their faces, usually crumbs. All they have to do is open their wrinkles to find food. They can't starve to death anymore.'

Children's clothes were drying on the lines, you could hear the sound of plates and cutlery through the windows. A dog was following him with his eyes from a second-floor balcony. Television voices floated all the way down to him, they were superimposed, they crossed. Serious voices and sweet voices, loud voices and soft voices, laughter and ringing. One voice rose above the others. Jonathan recognised an ad for spaghetti. He could see it in his mind, a woman singing in Italian, she had brown hair and squinted her eyes, and she had big hands that she waved in front of her face.

He wondered how many images were engraved in his mind like that, how many ads, how many words, forms, songs, smells, scenes, faces, how many thousands of clips lived like that in his mind, and how many more would get in without him realising. He wondered if the scenes in his mind belonged to his mind or if they belonged to the world. Was he made of this combination of images and memories, some very abstract, some clearer, in his mind? Did his memories make him, or did he make his memories? He locked his phone, he shivered once.

The bathroom at the end of the courtyard was ugly, tiny and freaky, and the door didn't close. In the shower, Jonathan thought: Someone invented this place. Someone imagined it. All the places Jonathan had ever seen, all those places had been designed, invented by a person. All of those places were born in the mind of a person. We're living in a man or woman's drawing, in their mind. Architects transform their thoughts into images, and these images are transformed into rooms, buildings, houses, parks, cities, roads. You think you're walking down a street, but you're walking in the thoughts of an unknown person. You think that houses are built with stones, but houses are built with thoughts. You think that plates have always existed, but someone invented the first plate. Someone invented combs, perfume, moustaches. You think things exist on their own, so you end up thinking that they always existed, however, someone invented words, someone invented breathing, sleep, gestures. In the beginning, we probably didn't move at all, and someone moved one day for the first time. People invent gestures. One day, someone brushed their teeth. One day, someone thought: 'I'm going to put a knife in someone walking by,' and he invented crime.

Electrical cables hung from the ceiling, and the steam produced minuscule drops around the filaments. Jonathan closed his eyes and imagined the electricity in his body as a flash of blue lightning. The lightning came out of the cables, entered through his skull, and went all the way down to his feet. Do people who die from a lightning strike have time to think? When a person is struck by lightning, the thought they're having stops, it freezes. The thought gets stuck, becomes a prisoner. No one else in the world will ever have this thought. He pulled on an old T-shirt. When he crossed the courtyard, the air surrounded his face. Then he went into his apartment, then he collapsed onto the couch.

The roommate was fiddling with a lighter shaped like an octopus, he was turning it between his fingers. He said, 'It's a rechargeable lighter, I plug it into my computer.' The roommate leaned his head forward and lifted his eyes like a demon, he maliciously stirred his pasta, he put a lot of salt on it. His nails were bitten to the quick, he picked his skin to the bone, and his fingers were round. Jonathan said: 'How does your lighter work? You plug it in and the flame comes out?'

The whole room smelled like mould. Huge black mushrooms stagnated along the walls. There was an enormous leak migrating across the ceiling. The leak had become the centre of the apartment. A drop of water fell in the roommate's hair, he swiped at it with his thumb. He'd gotten so used to swiping at drops, it'd become a tic. He spread it across his forehead, he didn't look up. He put a piece of pasta in his mouth, and swallowed it without chewing. A drop fell on the plate, he said, 'If we had to understand everything that we use, we wouldn't use anything. For example, do you understand your mouth? Do you understand the pronunciation of each letter in your mouth? We don't need to understand everything, we might not be able to do anything if we understood things. We wouldn't be able to tie our shoes, we wouldn't be able to chew. Luckily, we don't understand, and we can't explain. We don't understand fire, but fire is good, fire is beautiful. We can tell fire is beautiful. Have I mentioned that I've burned down houses with this lighter? But I prefer burning electrical appliances. I often buy small electrical appliances, I buy calculators and I burn them. Little cheap calculators that they sell in supermarkets, I buy them and I burn them. I burn batteries, I burn machines. I set a fire inside of a fridge one day, guess what happened.'

'It exploded?'

'How did you know? Have you been reading my emails?'

Jonathan said, 'No.'

'How did you know then?'

The roommate's eyes were two dry, black olives. He shrugged his shoulders almost up to his ears, as if he were cold, he sniffed, and he said: 'Before, I lived with this guy, and I burned his clothing. I didn't think twice. I burned his shoes and his boxers. Everything burns easily. Everything burns without a problem. The guy had a photo of his parents in his room, and I burned it without a problem. I giggled while I burned it, I was giggling. His parents' faces twisted, they disappeared, and I was giggling, okay?'

Jonathan locked his phone, and he said, 'Okay.'

'I boiled his phone in milk. One day, I burned his leg hairs while he was sleeping, okay? What about you?'

Jonathan scratched his cheek and felt a little scab, he pulled it off, he rolled it between his fingers, he flicked it away, he said, 'I might have burned a girl's hair at school with matches, but I'm not sure. Maybe it wasn't me. But I remember I got punished for it.'

The roommate uncrossed his arms and made two gestures with his hands as if he were arranging things in the air, and he said, 'You're too nice. I have the same problem. One day in my old apartment, I found a robber. He was taking the couch, he was trying to take it apart. I explained to him that it was better to steal the computers. Don't you think? When you go into people's houses, it's better to steal the computers, right? They sell better, right?'

Jonathan nodded, he had a gentle face. The roommate said, 'So, I showed him the computers, I said, "This is what you should take, this is the stuff that sells. If you're a robber, you should steal things that are expensive and light, expensive and light, things that are easy to transport." So, the robber took the computers, it was the only option, it was logical. I like logic. When my roommate came back, I told him, "Your computer isn't in your room anymore, but don't worry, a guy stole it because he was a robber."' Jonathan was almost smiling, he ran his hand over his face looking for dead skin. The roommate said, 'I fight a lot.'

'Who do you fight?'

'I fight randomly, look.' And he stuck his fork in his pasta. He pressed his lips together, his nose wrinkled, and his veins bulged on his temples, on his neck. In one sharp move, he stuffed all of it in his mouth. He swallowed. All at once. All the pasta. He burped. He lowered his chin with a demonic smile, he said, 'What about you? Who do you fight?'

Jonathan wished he could have filmed the scene, but the scene had disappeared. He said, 'I got into a fight when I was 16. It ended badly.'

'Is the guy dead?'

'No, his stomach split open.'

'From a sword?'

'No, from a window.'

The roommate turned his plate, he placed his elbow in the middle, and he rested his face on his fist. He said, 'Tell me.' Jonathan said, 'When I was little, I spent my vacations with my cousin. He had a swimming pool, and we would fight underwater, it was our game. The rules were simple, we punched each other underwater, we hit each other. Whoever put their head above water first lost. It was easy. We had a good time. But one day, my cousin lost, he lost for a long time, he lost a lot, he lost 10 times, 20 times, 28 times. His luck was completely gone, there was nothing he could do. We played, he lost. He took it badly, I heard him shouting underwater. He got out of the pool with clenched fists, he kept saying, "What the hell is this? What the hell is this?" My cousin slipped, he fell against a window, and it broke. My cousin fell into the crack, and his stomach split open. I was in the water, I saw the blood, I got out. He was holding his intestines in his hands, I looked. Drops of water from my hair were falling into his wound. I was standing in the warm, sticky blood on the ground.'

The roommate threw his plate on the table and hit his own head. He said, 'That's not fighting. You have to breathe to fight, you can't just do whatever. You don't fight in water. I hope he's dead. Is your cousin dead?' Jonathan swiped two fingers across his screen and showed him pictures of a fireman, he said, 'That's my cousin. The day his stomach split open, he knew he'd become a fireman. When the firefighters sewed him back up, he said, "I'm going to be like you."' The roommate said the letter F with a puff of air, he moved his head from right to left and then left to right, he said, 'You call putting flames out all day a real job? Aren't flames beautiful? Aren't they beautiful? Isn't a flame pretty? If you look at a flame, you know right away that it's beautiful, everyone knows it, even idiots, even children know it, even babies want to touch them. I don't understand firefighters, instead of saving fire, they destroy it. All that to wear a helmet, all that to have a truck, a hose, all that just so you can say, "Hello, I'm a firefighter." It's repulsive.'

Jonathan showed him his cousin's page. His kids were wearing shorts and smiling in the pictures, he said, 'My cousin has children, he does crossbow archery, he wins medals.' He showed him pictures of targets with arrow marks right in the middle and the roommate looked away, he said, 'Have you noticed the kids upstairs? Have you noticed the neighbour's kids? I bet not. You didn't know he had kids? I didn't know either. There was no way of knowing, nobody could have known, but the neighbour has 7 kids. You know why we don't hear them? It's because he hits them. One day, I got the wrong door, I got the wrong floor, and the neighbour opened up to me, he clasped my hands, he said, "Come in." He sat me in a chair, he was dressed like a Starbucks barista. He said, "Welcome." They live in a studio, him, his wife, and their 7 children. In a tiny studio. But since they have mirrored walls, it looks big, it looks almost infinite.'

The roommate was crumbling tiny bits of bread between his fat, round fingers. He moved his eyes more and more quickly, as if he were reading a text on his hands, he said, 'They were bald, the 7 children, standing right up against the wall. I looked at the 7 children against the walls, I saw that they were staring at each other in the mirrors. Each of them was staring at the back of another child in the mirror. It must have made up an entire body in their minds, their own head and the body of one of the other children. The neighbour told me, "I have to shave them because of lice and I beat them every day. I have to keep them up against the wall, otherwise they take up space. They take up space and I don't have any space. You can plainly see I don't have any space." He said, "I love them. I also love the misshapen ones. One of my children has 11 fingers." He showed me, I counted, it was true. He said, "I only hit them when they move a limb, that's it. If they don't move, I leave them alone." I said that I could understand. Then the neighbour gave me a nutty coffee with cinnamon, and another coffee from Ethiopia, and another coffee with coconut pearls, but after 8 coffees, I wanted to fight someone, is that normal? I wanted to fight someone, 7 children against the walls of a studio apartment, it was enough to get on my nerves. It made me nervous. I could feel my nerves on end in the back of my neck, is that normal?'

The roommate moved his hands, it was like they bothered him. He turned his plate over, and it cracked. Several drops of water fell on his head. They fell mournfully, with little bits of plaster.

He said, 'So, I lied, because I was nervous. Because of my

nerves, I said to the neighbour, "Your daughter moved her foot." I pointed to the youngest, the smallest, I said, "That one, she moved her legs." And the father struck. His hand smacked his daughter's face. When he hit her, something opened inside my brain, I don't know, something sad, but something big. The little girl looked at me tearfully in her reflection. It was like I was fighting without moving. I was fighting calmly. It gave me shivers, I yelled, "She moved! When you were looking the other way, she jumped! She was taking up space, sir, she was taking up the whole studio. She wasn't respecting anything, she wasn't respecting the other children. She wasn't respecting the space, I saw her, sir, I saw her! Hit her! Hit her!" And each time I cried out, the father hit her 5 times, once on the back of the neck, once on the forehead, once on her right knee, once on her left knee, and once on her larynx. He was methodical. The more I yelled, the more he hit. The little girl. The little girl lowered her gaze, she was ashamed, I didn't know that anyone could feel shame at such a young age. She was so small, but so full of shame. Isn't that funny? She was ashamed of feeling ashamed. She looked at me and she was ashamed of feeling ashamed in front of me. I saw her shame of feeling ashamed like a spiral in her eyes. Parallel tears ran down her cheeks like in manga comics. Her father said, "Don't worry, she just feels sorry for herself. She isn't suffering much. She's not crying from the pain, she's crying because she's crying."

Then, he asked his children to line up, and he said, "In your opinion, which one of them will be happy later on?" You know, I'd forgotten about this story, now I find it soothing. You know, it's soothing, this story soothes me, it's putting me to sleep, I'm falling asleep, look, I'm sleeping now, I'm sleeping. I'm falling asleep, I'm going to fall asleep, I'm going to go to bed, I'm going to sleep, good night, dude.'

A drop of water fell from the ceiling onto his forehead.

THE AUTOBIOGRAPHY OF THE OTHER LADY GAGA: THE RESURRECTION

STEFANI J. ALVAREZ

tr. ALTON MELVAR M DAPANAS

FROM THE FILIPINO

An excerpt from the novel,
2021

WAR CASUALTY

Loud as a movie theatre, the TV is on full volume as I watch footage of the ongoing war on Al Jazeera.

'Let's talk. This is not civil war. We are not Syria. We are not Egypt.' He insists as he turns down the sound.

'This is my room. Get out.' I counter, facing him.

He removes his ring. 'Take this. It's a reminder, bitch.' He places it on the side table.

He calls me *bitch*. I know it's not the female equivalent of what I call him – *daddy*. But it's very telling of how, in his world, he owns me, and that's a different form of love. It's what he can give.

'Where's the other one?' I dare, checking if he will disregard Adam's sacred vow to Eve.

He strokes my hair. The kind of touch that usually comes at the crack of dawn after I've perfected his PowerPoint presentation. It's supposed to be a consolation; where else will he find a secretary like me, one with an extension desk in his bedroom?

'We will go Bahrain this weekend.'

'Just get out,' I order. On the TV screen, the rebel forces and the Syrian army clash.

He exits the door. He locks it the way I lock the Manager's Office after three in the afternoon, when he and I are the only people left.

Alone, I look at the table smudged with dried frosting and chocolate from a black forest cake. The candle has melted onto the rim of the glass and looks like a tree stump. An empty bottle of grape juice sits nearby. It's like a vampire has gnawed through the gift wrap. I put on the polo shirt I gifted him. Last night's birthday celebration is long over.

I take the remote control. The gunfire echoes in surround sound.

I try to look up, hearing the rattle of a spoon and fork. I have to force myself to move. But I am numb all over. Maybe this is what it feels like to be shot. Or bombed.

The folding table has been tucked away. The room is spotless, the gunfire, gone. I fall asleep in front of the TV.

'Jackie, wake up.'

I am still on the carpet.

'Are you okay? I worried when I read your text message.'

'I'm sorry, Yousef.'

He comes over to me and hands me a small box. I peek inside. A plain gold ring.

'A peace offering?'

And then, he smiles, still chiding me for the text message I sent him. 'If you will not come, I will kill myself,' I had said, dramatically, 'and I will write your name on the wall. Maybe in all caps. And in red writing.' His eyes wandered around the room. Like a security guard at a checkpoint. 'Just trying to make sure my name is not on the walls, or tattooed somewhere.'

I embrace him. But the conversation turns back to Salman. His is the only name tattooed on my wrist.

'Give me your hand.' Like a wedding scene – the only thing missing is a priest and altar. Gently, he puts a ring on me. 'I promise.'

I know he could outdo Salman's ring if he wanted, or any other promise that sounded too miraculous to be true. The promise ring from a former boss, the only thing I have left, something that stays so I can still believe in all of this.

Salman had also asked for my hand once, holding a glittering 24k gold ring. And this time, too, I raise my palm like Cleopatra.

'My wife,' he says, and I suddenly catch a chill. I feel the urge to cry. No, not with joy. But because nothing is more cathartic than having the miracle I was desperately holding out for finally come true.

But in love, there is crisis. I call it testing time.

Salman almost hit my head on the steering wheel when saw the photo I posted on Facebook. For me, it was a small rebellion to post a photo with another guy in my bed, Yousef. I had never dreamed of a *till death do us part* kind of story, just that I be left alone in the sheets, stripped, after he shoots inside me what he couldn't let his wife swallow.

'It's not allowed with her.' He had replied, between his howls, behind me. He even memorised verses from the Hadith and Sharia to enlighten me. But all I picked up was this: I am neither a woman, nor his wife.

Is the war over?

I switch on the TV again. Yousef grabs the remote control, but not to turn it down, instead, he summons me into battle. On screen are the shots of M16s, navigating war tanks, collapsing buildings, fiery Molotov cocktails tossed in the air, endless explosions.

And here, like in war, I happen to be a casualty.

THE BEAUTIFUL

'I want to tell you this personally – higher management has decided to demobilise you,' says my Arab boss.

I want to cry. But I don't want to be victim of a society that judges people like me. For four years now I've been in Saudi Arabia, and nothing about this situation is new.

It's only been two months since I left my previous post at Saudi Kayan because of my employer's unjust salary. I lost the motivation to continue my contract because the outcome was still the same: the hourly rates paid by the company to my agency might have been significant but the increments I received as a worker were meagre.

'I don't see any problem. I hired you. I want to keep you as my secretary but management and some people have been talking about your personal life behind my back. But it's your personal life...' he added, but I already knew what he wanted to say.

I knew he couldn't say exactly what I am because I'm a báyot and most hypocritical Saudis find me disgusting. Hypocrites because, in fact, if I don't give in to what they want, they make things very difficult for me. Hypocrites because in public they pretend I make them sick but in private, they're all dogs who will devour what they already threw up at the first chance they get.

'Boss, it's okay. Accepted.'

'I am sorry. You did your job well,' he stresses.

He said he would have insisted on keeping me but the complainant happened to be one of his superiors.

'I know you will have a lot of opportunities outside the SABIC office,' he says. Because of my outstanding employment record and work performance, I have better chances of getting in to other companies especially in SABIC affiliates, like Saudi Kayan. That is, if I want to return to my previous workplace. I also have the option to apply to other private companies in Jubail.

'The culture here is different. Hope you understand.'

'It's okay, Boss.' I stand up.

'Thanks for being here.' He says, shaking my hand.

The door opens. The General Manager enters.

'How are you, Jack?' he asks.

'I am fine and I am beautiful,' I answer, clearly.

I turn to face my boss. 'Bye, Boss.'

He smiles, 'Always be beautiful.'

I walk to the door. Gently turn the doorknob open and leave the office with a smile.

THE POSTCARD

'This is hotel security,' says the man at my doorstep. 'Please open the door.'

A knock on the door. A shiver in my chest.

Authorities are currently on high alert, especially since last week's demonstration commemorating the third anniversary of the Bahraini uprising. This was one of the many events of the so-called Arab Spring, a series of demonstrations, protests, riots, and even civil wars in the Middle East. The Tunisian president had been ousted. The same thing happened to his Egyptian counterpart. In Libya, Qaddafi was assassinated. A national unity government temporarily held power after toppling the Yemeni regime. Most of Syria was razed to the ground by the ongoing civil war. Now, there were uprisings in Kuwait, Lebanon, Oman, Morocco and Jordan. And even here, in Saudi Arabia, particularly in Qatif, a city populated by the minority Shia, protests had been round-the-clock.

I, too, had begun my own revolution. I tried to drop two glasses of water from the veranda. Both shattered into pieces as expected, launched as they were from the third floor.

As if I was a child playing simple games. As if I was doing

a science experiment. Of course, I knew about gravity and its laws already. Everything you let go, by and by, will tumble to the ground. And what falls will fracture. Like the heart.

I overhear another man drawing closer. A familiar voice, speaking in Arabic, is having a chat with the man at my door.

'Jackie.' Abdulrahman. I cast a brief look through the door's peep hole. He is holding a postcard. Earlier, at the check-in desk, my eyes had searched for him in the photo of The Gulf Hotel in Bahrain on the front of that same postcard, as if it was a map. Then I had glanced, for the last time, at the words written on the back, before handing it over to the receptionist.

He spoke to the man again. And the man finally left.

The intercom rang once more. I lifted the handset.

'Hello?' said another familiar voice, it was the front desk clerk who had assisted me earlier. 'Sir, I think your boss is already there,' he whispered in Filipino.

I thanked him, hung up.

I reached for my mobile. I dialled Abdulrahman's number.

'I am sorry.'

'Just open the door.' He pleaded.

He walked straight to the veranda as soon as I opened the door. Looked at the view below. Looked at me in the eye. Looked at the sky above. 'I've told you.'

I sat up in bed. Stared vacantly at the blank TV screen for a long time. All the while, I watched his reflection move in it. Abdulrahman settled without a word in the chair facing the dresser. He laid the postcard on the side table.

I stood up. Closed the sliding door leading towards the veranda. Drew the curtains. And headed to the bathroom. I turned on the shower. I went back to the bedroom. Naked.

I approached him. Held him close. Whispered, 'Dad.'

I expected a simper and a moan, but they never came.

Instead, he said, 'Please behave.' And went straight to the door.

I slouched, defeated. On my wrist, a tattoo, clearly marked: Salman. 'He's married now.'

I felt like a helpless child. A child who had been bullied and was complaining to his father. I couldn't stop my tears. He grabbed the doorknob. And closed the door behind him.

I glimpsed at the postcard. The previously written words, I AM HERE. 322, were crossed out. And replaced by: MY FAMILY'S HERE in all capital letters.

I wail. The water from the shower rushes like shattered glass.

TENT CITY

Tent City in Jeddah, KSA | Facebook
DFA chief: Only 600 in 'Tent City' in Jeddah
- ABS-CBN News
Undocumented OFWs flock to Tent City in Jeddah
- ABS-CBN News
More undocumented OFWs flock to Tent City in Jeddah
- YouTube
From Nitaqat to Tent City: A look into the Saudi crackdown on illegal...
Pinoy 'tent city' rises outside PHL Consulate in Jeddah
- GMA Network
With no relief in sight, over 1,000 Pinoys huddle in tents in Jeddah...
DFA sets up shelters for Jeddah tent city dwellers - Inquirer Global...
DFA exec flies to Saudi to assist undocumented Filipinos in 'tent city'...
Kin of stranded OFWs at Jeddah Tent City start Day 1 of 'Solidarity...'
– Google search results for 'Tent city Jeddah'

He used to be my boss at the Saudi Kayan Petrochemical Company in Jubail. For four years, I worked for him. We also went out a few times. To Bahrain on weekends or, whenever his wife was away, to his house in the Andalus sector. But when I moved to Al-Khobar, we stopped seeing each other.

'It's a long weekend,' he mentions over the phone.

Based on a recent company memo, there are now three rest days in compliance with the Royal Decree No. A/185 declared by the King of Saudi Arabia. This changed the weekly rest days to Friday and Saturday from the original Thursday and Friday.

He invites me to visit him. Or meet up in Al-Khobar.

'I will go with you, Dad.' I try so hard to speak in Arabic because I know he gets excited when I utter the last word. He almost moans. I, on the other hand, feel like a little child, and giggle upon hearing him. Like an infant that's safely cocooned in his father's arms.

About an hour ticks by before his Chevy truck is right in front of my apartment. A Black Diamond Avalanche.

He rolls the window open. Grinning from ear to ear, he asks under his breath, 'How's my baby?' He gets out, takes my carry-on bag and puts it in the back of the car. I wonder why this time he brought his own bag.

'Let's go?'

'Let's go west. Jeddah is the place to be,' he says, acting like a tour guide.

'Tent city?'

He chuckles. I once brought this up with him, before we went on vacation last May.

'I know. I know your plan.'

Then he begins telling me stories, not letting me speak.

During Hajj, they have their own tent city, he explains. Their government sets up tents at Mina and Mount Arafat to house millions of Muslim pilgrims. These two places, located near Mecca in the Makkah Province, are sites of the *stoning of the devil*, a Hajj ritual.

While waiting for a Saudia domestic flight at the airport I momentarily scan the route from Al-Khobar to Jeddah on Google Maps. I connect the dots from the Persian Gulf to the Red Sea; from east to west. More than a 13-hour drive. But two hours by plane.

To me, Jeddah looks familiar. Always headlined in The Filipino Channel's *Balitang Middle East* newscast. Hundreds of Filipino migrants are said to be living provisionally in the so-called tent city. Either runaways or refugees, without an Iqama or residence permit, without a work visa. Or overstaying on an Umrah visa with no plans for a return to the Philippines. Among the approximately 2 million undocumented migrant workers. Seeking assistance from their respective governments for urgent repatriation before getting blacklisted, penalised, or worse, imprisoned.

On April 3, the Saudi government imposed more restrictive policies for migrant workers trying to legally obtain work visas. This was in accordance with the so-called Saudisation or Nationalisation law scheme. What used to be a three-month grace period was reduced to a week.

'I reserved a room for you. But you will stay with me.' He had booked two rooms at the InterContinental Hotel. A classic room for me. And a royal suite for him.

'Where's the Philippine Consulate?' I pulled back the merlot-coloured curtains of the suite and gazed into the distance.

'I think this room is enough for you.' He tried to cover the view I was trying to catch from the topmost window.

The Adhan for Maghrib, the call to prayer, echoes across the landscape. I do not say a word as my vision traces the setting sun, painting the scorching desert with the colours of rust. Halfway through sunset, my mind wanders back to the makeshift shelters I saw on the news. It was as if the tenants were begging their landlords for some permanence, those that owned hectares of land. Like souls sent to the purgatory of the Philippine embassy, having served their gods from overseas.

He reaches for the tea cup. Fills it with hot water. I listen to the melancholic clink of teaspoon against porcelain. 'I am sorry. I just want you to be happy.'

'I don't need a royal suite to shelter me, Dad.'

He smiles, as expected. He comes near me. Embraces me. Tighter and tighter. And he lets out his usual moan. I giggle. There's my little wish.

ANCIENT ALIENS

Salman sleeps at my flat on Wednesday nights because he doesn't have to work the next day. This is our weekly arrangement.

Thursdays and Fridays are the non-working days here in Saudi Arabia, unless someone agrees to extra hours, or is a contractual employee who's forced to slave away six days each week.

On those days, I get used to having Salman in my room, next to me in bed, both of us swaddled together in the sheets. Wednesday nights are no doubt the most special part of my week.

But this Wednesday something out of the ordinary happens. Salman is non-stop chatting on WhatsApp. So when he goes to the bathroom, I take my chance at reading the conversations on his phone. They are in Arabic so I turn on Google Translate. Although the translation is vague, I get enough clues.

It's ten o'clock. I am keeping an eye on him. Freshly out of the toilet and he's back on his phone. In silence, I watch *Ancient Aliens* on the History Channel.

His phone rings. He gestures for me to mute the TV before picking up the call. The dialogue is in Arabic. I don't understand what they were talking about, except for the three places mentioned over again: Riyadh, Bahrain and City Centre.

'Who's that?' is my plain question.

'My friends in Riyadh. They will go to Bahrain' is his plain reply.

I am about to cross-examine him further when he comments on what I am watching, distracting me from my curiosity.

'Jackie, I don't believe that. Allah is only one. La ilaha illallah. No aliens and other gods.'

The last thing I want us to do is launch at each other's throats over religion and belief. I would even confess to taking Islam to my heart in the hope that Salman will stay with me. That's passion over pretension. I breach a number of the religion's laws. I never dare call myself a Muslim. Given this, my welcoming of Islam with open arms is, even now, in this four-year relationship, a symbol of how we take in each other's entirety.

I grin at him. 'Wallah, I just want to watch this documentary.'

Still, I turn off the television.

I tug at the covers and settle on my side of the bed. It's already 11 o'clock.

'I wanna sleep,' I say as I watch him still lost in his phone.

He pays no attention to me.

So I get out of bed. And switch on the television again.

He jumps to his feet. Pushes down the power button.

'What's wrong?' I point up.

'*Ancient Aliens*, again?' He retorts.

His phone chimes. A string of new messages.

'WhatsApp, again?' I voice bitingly. 'You better go.'

He shakes his head. Slowly puts on his clothes, and walks away.

This was not like Salman. In my mind, suspicions surfaced. He must've been itching to go somewhere else as he did not even hesitate before leaving.

I continued watching more *Ancient Aliens* episodes. The whole night. Then I slept like a log until midday the next day. It was nighttime again when I saw several calls from him that I had missed. I chose not to call him back.

On a Friday morning, there's a knock on my door. I know that knock. I know that voice and the way it utters my name very well. Salman.

I open the door, turn around, and walk straight back to bed. I shut my eyes, aware that I will not be able to sleep. I wait for him to doze. And then I go through his wallet. From a pocket in his pants, I fish out a movie ticket. He had gone to Bahrain. Unlike here, in Saudi Arabia, Bahrain has movie houses.

The next day I anticipate his getting up and out of bed. But before I show him what I have found, I pore over the ticket stub. Bahrain City Center. Cinema 2. Seat E13. *Savages*. Then, I reach for the remote. Power up the television.

'Now Showing, *Ancient Aliens*.'

WHO WERE THEY?

WHY DID THEY COME?

WHAT DID THEY LEAVE BEHIND?

WHERE DID THEY GO?

WILL THEY RETURN?

Go the tag lines of the opening credits.

'Please, turn it off. I have the answers to those questions.' He bids me, beaming from ear to ear. And his looks like a promise to explain all of the universe's baffling mysteries, theories, its copious prophecies. Not just about aliens, but also on the origins of humans, angels, and even gods.

I turn off the television. I let go of the handheld control. And am willingly taken over by his caress.

DARKNESS INSIDE AND OUT

LEILA SUCARI

tr. MAUREEN SHAUGHNESSY

FROM THE SPANISH

An excerpt from the novel,
2017

1

The heat in the backseat was unbearable. The trip was long, I fell asleep after staring out the window for hours. The driver had to wake me up, there was no one left on the bus. Outside it was all fields and the midday sun made my eyes ache. My grandma wasn't there. The bus drove off down a narrow highway and I was afraid I'd be left there alone forever. I sat down to wait on the curb. The alfahor that Mama had tucked into my backpack had melted. I sucked on the wrapper and my fingers got covered in chocolate.

Next to me was a family of dead sunflowers. Some birds were feasting on the worms that squirmed among the flower heads. Crossing the road, a skinny horse chewed on dirt. Its bones stuck out and it was tied to a lamppost with a rope. I lay down and started to make little balls using grass and spit. At some point I noticed the feet of a woman approach. She had red toenails and her flip-flops were caked in dried mud. I looked up, but I didn't recognise her because the sun shone too brightly. She didn't recognise me either right away. She stood there without talking. Then she used a tea towel to wipe down her forehead. Let's go, she said.

The house is not like Mama said it would be. There are no dogs or bunk beds. Horrible bugs follow me everywhere and stick to my body. Grandma says the humidity's got them all riled up. When we arrived, my cousin was asleep. Now she's eating meat for breakfast. She chews with disgust while my grandma stares at her teeth and stirs a gourd of yerba mate that's lost its flavour. I didn't want to eat. I told them the alfahor had filled me up.

My cousin is beautiful and wants to be a vegetarian but Grandma won't let her. She forces her to eat meat and my cousin swallows her tears and spits out the meat when no one's looking. When I grow up I want to be like you, I tell her, and Grandma slaps me with the floral tea towel. She wants me ugly and carnivorous so she won't feel so alone.

Grandma flattens the bags on the table, crumples them into a ball and tosses them in the garbage can. My cousin gets up to go take a shower. In the kitchen Grandma has a collection of glass jars. She says that after siesta she's going to teach me how to make jam. Go to your room with your cousin. If you hear her crying don't worry, she likes to make a scene to get attention. Sometimes she even punches the wall, but eventually she gets tired and sleeps until nightfall.

I leave my dirty sneakers outside and lie down on a mattress on the floor. I hate naps. I do what she says because Mama asked me to a thousand times over, but I don't plan on sleeping. My cousin enters the room swathed in a wet sheet. She sets a wooden plank against the window to block the light from pouring in and turns her back to me. She doesn't cry, or do anything else. She spends the entire day lying down, that's why Grandma thinks she's sick and needs to eat all the meat in the world.

2

It took me less than a week to learn the names of the trees. There are three eucalyptus trees, one giant fig, grapefruit trees, mulberry trees, one walnut and other tall thin trees that Grandma calls devil's weeds because they sprout up everywhere. I haven't been able to enjoy the sun because it started raining the day after I arrived. Grandma says she's never seen it piss down so hard. I tell her in the city we call it good luck, but she doesn't care and she just keeps on moaning.

Since I arrived in the countryside I wake up early every morning to the rooster's crow. The poor thing misses his children. Grandma is a wicked old woman who steals them from him. She says she's not hungry, but I know she really plans to eat them. The other day I saw her kill a newborn chick. She wrung its neck and tucked the body in her hair to hide it. Both were a bright yellow colour. When I hear the rooster start crowing I cover my ears and try to go back to sleep. But it's impossible, he's an insistent beast. And the worst part is he never gives up hope. He keeps right on crowing, even though no one's ever given him back so much as a feather.

Grandma wakes up with foul breath. She prepares me bread soaked in warm milk. Then she drinks mate with the neighbour lady and keeps herself busy by badmouthing my cousin. When she hugs me I hold my nose so I won't have to smell her breath. I think she's rotting away little by little. One day she'll be a shrivelled-up grape and the hens will peck at her.

Mama said she would come get me in two weeks. It's already been a month and we haven't heard a word. At first I was glad she didn't come, now I'm tired of so much vacation. Grandma says I should get used to it here because going back to the city isn't in anyone's plans. But I don't want to live here. I miss my house, and besides, I don't like the countryside at night. It's too dark.

3

Today three chicks were born, they don't have feathers or eyes yet. They're horrible but Grandma is happy. While she's washing the dishes I go outside silently and search the chicken coop for the rest of the eggs. I only find one. It's hot and covered in shit. The hen taking care of it tries to peck at my fingernails but I hit her on the head with a shovel and hide the egg in my shirt. She looks at me in a daze and gives up without a fight, she's a bad mother.

I go back inside and slip the egg in Grandma's pillow, between the pillowcase and the stuffing. When she lies down to pray her ideas will burst all over the place. Since she believes in god, she'll think it's a divine punishment. I imagine her wrinkled face, the shell breaking against her head and her yellow hair stuck to the white sheet. I did it to teach her a lesson. Never again will she kill the rooster's children, she'll be a plump, gentle lady who brings us breakfast in bed. My cousin will thank me and tell me the secret of how to be like her. We'll be a family of happy women who eat lettuce.

I go to the kitchen with the excuse of drinking water. Grandma is still doing the dishes. She talks to herself as she scrubs the same plate over and over with a sponge. She tells me to go to bed, that it's too late for me to be up and about. I say alright and kiss her fingers. What nice nails you have, Gram. She can't hold back her smile. Bedtime sweetie, it's late.

I wait with my eyes open. My cousin is asleep on the floor,

sprawled out on an old mattress. Before long I hear Grandma scream. Her words echo through the walls as she approaches our room. I pretend to be asleep. Grandma comes in and says, ungrateful wretch. She's talking to my cousin. I open my eyes a crack and see her giant body lurching with rage. My cousin squints at her, confused, and doesn't answer. I think Grandma might kill her, but no. Instead she grabs a hold of her own straw hair and wrings the liquid chicks onto my cousin's quilt. Then her tone of voice changes and she tells my cousin to leave the room. My cousin stammers and obeys. I'm sweating under the blanket. I'm scared but I can't get up the courage to tell the truth. I feel like I've got feathers stuck in my throat.

4

My cousin spent the night trimming the grass with a pair of scissors, that was her punishment. I couldn't sleep. I laid there motionless breathing the dank air in the room. She came back early in the morning, pale, dirt under her fingernails and the black scissors clutched to her chest. We looked at each other sheepishly and she lay down. Her body let off the faint scent of wet grass. I wanted to kiss her fingers and ask for forgiveness, but I didn't dare. I got up slowly, trembling with fear, and ran barefoot to the chicken coop. There were no more eggs.

I gathered a fistful of daisies and surprised Grandma in the kitchen. She sat me on her lap with a mug of warm milk. The cream floating like an island of phlegm. I stared at it for a long time. I wanted to swallow it with my eyes, to make it disappear. You're in a daze, said Grandma, and she kissed me on the forehead. Her lips were cold and dry. She lingered, touching my skin, as if she wanted to absorb my thoughts, and reckoned I was burning up with fever. But it wasn't a fever, I was ablaze in a delirium of guilt and emotion. My cousin was beautiful and she had broken her fingernails for me.

Grandma made up a bed for me in the kitchen, placing some cardboard on the floor and then a thick blanket and white sheets. She covered it all with freshly cut lavender blossoms. She said I needed fresh air and should stay away from my cousin.

I spent the day sleeping. Every now and then I opened my eyes and noticed her bare ankles coming and going. Grandma's toenails were painted and she had thousands of purple veins that looked like they were about to explode. They were rivers that boiled and fought to break free from her thick, heavy body. I wanted to squeeze her feet until the veins popped, filling the house with her blood. But I felt so weak I only managed to lightly graze her heels. Grandma bent down awkwardly and kissed me, she thought I was caressing her from my deathbed.

I woke up sweaty with a sprig of lavender under my tongue. Everything was dark and I could hear Grandma's snores. They were like the sputtering of an old truck engine about to give out. I swallowed the home remedy and tiptoed to the toolbox. There was a bitter taste in my mouth. I hid a pair of pliers in my nightgown and locked myself in the bathroom. I twisted the broken knob of the faucet several times and water started to gush forth. It was freezing cold. I plugged the drain with some toilet paper, plunged my head in and counted until the bathtub was full. The cold stiffened my body, it made me feel strong. I closed my eyes and sunk in.

Back home I liked to take baths, blow bubbles and spit water out against the tiles. When I did this, Mama tossed in a coin and made a wish. We laughed together until I got too excited and drenched her dress. Then she got angry, removed the stopper and sent me to my room. For a moment I missed her. I wanted to be home, watching TV in her bed and eating hamburgers with french fries. But then I remembered the nights she left me home alone to go out to those never-ending meetings, and her obsession with teaching me to memorise the chakras of the human body, and I got angry. It was my turn to make a wish: that Mama would never come back.

5

My cousin covered herself with a wet towel and went to take a nap. She looks like a mummy. Grandma's fanning herself with the newspaper, heaving out some remarks, her words stifled by the heat. She says she's never seen anything like this. God willing, the blessed girl will come.

I imagine a girl: beautiful like my cousin, entering the house in a long dress down to her toes, carrying a bouquet of flowers to Grandma. She'd set them down on her little altar and sprinkle water on them. The two would dance hand in hand as if they were going to be married. How old is the girl? I ask her. Grandma laughs heartily and tousles my hair. Ay, that head. The girl is a storm, she says. I don't know how to respond, Grandma looks at me and can't stop laughing. I think the heat has driven her mad.

Nap time never ends. The only sound is the buzz of the flies and every now and then a dragonfly that fills Grandma's mouth with hope. Every time she sees one of those bugs shaped like a little stick she starts to say, thank the lord, he finally heard my prayers, holy is his name. Your mother never believed in anything, that's why she ended up the way she did, she says in her delirium. And she stops talking again, waiting for a new apparition to serve as an excuse to badmouth Mama.

Since I don't know what to do, I watch my cousin sleep. Her lips are parted and she breathes slowly. From beneath her eyelids escape the legs of a spider that lives inside her head. It scurries back and forth, searching for an exit. She dreams of vipers, suffocating. Being trapped in her head must be unpleasant. I, by contrast, never dream of anything. I prefer her labyrinth filled with insects over my own empty head. Perhaps if I stare at her long enough my eyelashes will become the hairy legs of an animal like hers.

Grandma says to leave her alone, that I'm going to curse her with the evil eye. I'm bored, I tell her. She gives me a hat and removes some crumpled bills from her bra. She asks if I'm willing to run some errands. I accept and she says I'm the best little girl in the world. Grandma's face is a ball of sticky dough that never stops rising. Before I leave, she splashes the nape of my neck with cold water and tells me to buy some candy for myself with the change.

6

The street is all dust. Dry, coarse earth dying of thirst. The blessed girl is coming, I say out loud, just wait. My cheeks burn under the heat. A filthy dog with curly hair follows me. He has a tick on his ear. He keeps stopping to scratch himself with his tongue hanging out. I wait for him, pretending like I'm tying my shoes. I've always wanted a dog, we couldn't have one at home because there was no room. Actually, that was just Mama's excuse, our neighbour's apartment was smaller and she had a labrador. He was annoying. When you pet him he peed himself out of sheer excitement. We never got along.

The store is a mud hut the size of my room. Inside, a flowery woman smiles. There's milk, outdated sticker albums, oranges, rice, stuffed animals and even a fan advertising it as today's special. Everything is covered in dust. Everything except the woman, who swats at her face with a handheld fan.

The change is enough for me to buy a handful of cookies. The woman sends her regards to Grandma. I'm weary of her bright dress and the glass of warm juice she pours for me with an exaggerated smile. Plus, she has a bird locked up in a cage and Mama once told me that people who keep birds are unenlightened. You're such a little one – you need protection, she says. A lot of people round here are envious of youth. She removes a red ribbon from her wrist and smooths down my hair as if patting a horse's back. I take the gift and run outside. The dog comes with me.

We walk around going nowhere in particular. I don't want to go back home. I want Grandma to worry and chastise herself for having confided in me. I hug the dog and poke at the tick with a eucalyptus branch. Its blood stains my fingers but the bug doesn't die. The dog howls. We run. Everything is motionless except us. The perspiration erases my ideas, I stop thinking. I'm nothing but a body moving forward. We enter a vacant lot and make our way over to a mulberry tree. I rest under its shade while the dog dozes in a hole he dug himself. I pick fruit and eat it leisurely. My hands are stained purple. When it gets dark we go back. On the horizon lightning strikes the grass.

The house is empty. It's strange because this is the time of day when Grandma makes dinner and my cousin locks herself in the bathroom to look at herself in the mirror. I'm sure they've gone out to look for me. I take advantage of the fact that I'm alone and let the dog inside. He rolls around on Grandma's bed while I search for a pot to give him some water. In the sink there's a tea towel with dark stains. I turn on the water and the dishes become tinged with red. I stay there watching the shapes that form and run down the drain. A firefly comes in through the window and buzzes around my head. I go to my room, the dog is no longer there. I hide under the sheets and start biting my nails. Outside the first drops start to fall.

7

Grandma comes home late. Her eyes are sunken and she bows her head to her chest. She doesn't say anything, she strokes my hair without looking at me and lays down on the couch. I can't bring myself to ask her about my cousin. The next day it keeps raining. Grandma makes me a cup of warm milk but forgets to add the bread. She sits down with a shoebox on her lap to untangle some old necklaces. I ask her if she needs any help and she sends me to take a bath. I carve a hole in the bar of white soap using a razorblade that belonged to Grandpa and walk all around the house naked, making footprints on the tile floor with my wet feet. Grandma gets so angry that she doesn't even scold me. She furrows her brow and wrinkles droop over her eyes. She ages suddenly.

Several days go by before my cousin comes back. Grandma looks out the window and complains about the weather, she seems nervous even though she doesn't say it out loud. I get really bored so I spend my time eating mulberries and staining my hair with the juices. I'm scared she'll leave me, just like Mama. The car that brings back my cousin parks outside the gate. Grandma is in the chicken coop. I run out to tell her so we can welcome her home together. My cousin has a bag in her hand and her lips are parted. She walks slowly, weakly, as if she were about to fall. I embrace her and she responds with a grimace, her mouth twisted to one side. Grandma drags her to bed and goes to the kitchen. She spits on a tea towel and starts plucking a chicken. Its feet float in boiling water and the house fills with the scent of death and parsley. We eat lunch without a word. The soup is bitter and my cousin wears a bandage with a trickle of dried blood on it.

The neighbour lady comes over with a handful of herbs to add to the yerba mate and a jar of fig jam. She stamps a kiss on my forehead and sends me outside to play. Grandma goes through the motions in a daze. She doesn't speak, her eyes are two black holes. I sit down on the doorstep and find a pill bug. I nudge it with my fingernail and roll it over to the wall. Then, once reassured, it stretches its body back out, and I force it onto a grape leaf and start poking it again, rolling it along.

The neighbour smokes, talks, coughs and chews on figs. She tells Grandma it would have been better to leave her there. If she's so insolent why bother to keep letting her stay? It's all the old man's fault, she never should have agreed to take the girl in, madness runs in the blood. The pill bug doesn't move. Mama says that animals pretend to be dead when they're scared. My cousin must be scared of Grandma. She's a jealous woman and she can't stand how beautiful my cousin is. I press my fingernail into the pill bug. A sticky liquid oozes out, but not blood. It's a vegetarian, like my cousin.

8

Grandma hugs me. Today we're going to take a nap together on the couch, she says. When your Mama gets here we'll tell her to leave and everything will be yours, don't worry, I won't let her steal any of your things. Grandma spits saliva when she talks. She kisses me, combs my hair with her fingers and swallows her phlegm. I look at her and watch how her wrinkles grow. The skin on her face hardens and cracks like the soil in summertime. Grandma disintegrates. Thousands of hairs and skin folds fly around the kitchen. She keeps talking. A mouth with no body, surrounded by old organs and bones. Grandma is going to die but she doesn't realise it. She's so fat she thinks she's infinite.

I peel myself away from her clammy hands. I can't sleep with the snoring. Inside Grandma there's a train filled with pigs on their way to the slaughterhouse. It makes me sick. I walk slowly to our room. The light by the bedside table is on. I spy on my cousin through the keyhole. She's sitting in front of the mirror. She kisses it. She licks it as if she were hungry. Her tits are swollen and she squeezes them with both hands. She bites her wrists and then wraps them with her stained bandage. I watch her in silence. My body is stiff and the words are stuck inside me. She looks at me through the mirror and laughs. She bites her lips.

I crawl back to the couch, hide under the folds of Grandma's stomach and close my eyes. I think about what the neighbour lady said, about how madness runs in the blood. The women in my family are crazy, but I have my father's blood. He's a strong man. One day I'll meet him and thank him.

9

Grandma buries the mashed potatoes under a mountain of flour. She cracks an egg and kneads the dough as if she were trying to strangle it. Then she rolls it out and caresses it with her deformed thumbs.

Gnocchi is my favourite food but she doesn't know that. Grandma dribbles some hot water on the pasta, she adds corn starch and smothers it. Her entire body is concentrated on the motions of squeezing and letting go, choking and reviving. Watching the dough makes me drowsy. It's an enormous boat, bobbing, hesitating. It doesn't know whether to stay afloat or succumb to being hurled against the kitchen counter. That's enough, now it needs to breathe, she says, draping an old tea towel over her work. The dough is a heart without arteries, mute and useless. But Grandma is proud.

We eat in silence. My cousin stirs her gnocchi, she stabs at them with a fork but leaves them on the plate. Eat, don't be ungrateful, Grandma tells her. She cuts them into tiny pieces and sticks them in her mouth. She chews showing her teeth and stares at Grandma with ravaged eyes. Since she came back, my cousin has changed. She used to pretend otherwise, but now her hatred is crystal clear. What a spoiled brat, yells Grandma, getting up from the table. You're not even capable of thanking me for the food on your plate, ungrateful wretch. Grandma lets the words gush forth like a waterfall. My cousin looks at her without saying anything, her nostrils flare in rage. What are you, a bull with no tongue? Speak up, says Grandma her hands on her forehead. My cousin, with all the elegance in the world, gets up from the table and curtseys. Grandma shuts herself up in the kitchen to wash the pots and pans. I'm left alone. I eat from all three plates. The gnocchi is delicious.

GOING TO MALANG

YUSI PAREANOM

tr. PAMELA ALLEN

FROM THE MALAY

1993

YOU were half an hour late for work this morning. Before you left home you'd been so busy checking what you need for tonight – two tickets for the Matarmaja train, a few items of clothing including a sweater, two bags of snacks and a thermos that you'll fill with ginger tea – that you lost track of time. Tonight you're going with your son to Malang in East Java, where your beloved eldest sister is dying. You'd actually prepared everything a few days ago, but you always get stressed about forgetting something, even though you're not really taking that much, so you need to check it over and over again. What's more, it's a long journey and, at fifty-seven, you're no longer a youngster.

When you got to your office you noticed a young couple in the lobby. You nodded at each other. The receptionist explained that the young woman had an interview scheduled this morning. She'd graduated with a bachelor's degree in English from Gadjah Mada University and was interested in a teaching job at the language college where you work as head of administration. You'd forgotten, even though it was you who wrote to her a week ago.

You invited the young woman into a small meeting room. You took your leave and returned five minutes later with the Head of the English Department. They started talking. You just listened. Your mind was on your trip to Malang tonight.

The Head of Department asked you to explain some administrative matters. The young woman seemed unsurprised when you mentioned the pitiful salary she'd be getting. You suspected that she might come from a wealthy family and needed experience more than money when she applied for this job. The only time her expression changed was when you told her that all new appointees' certificates would be held by the office for a year. She didn't say anything, but you sensed her doubts and you didn't really blame her. If you were in her position, you too would hesitate to hand over your diploma. The retaining of certificates had been suggested by the Vice-Chancellor, who wanted your language school, which was only two years old, to be fully staffed. You don't really agree with this policy, but the Vice-Chancellor is an old friend of yours from your days at a well-known private university in Jogjakarta, and you feel grateful to him for giving you the chance to work again after you'd retired.

You accompanied the young woman back to the lobby where her partner was waiting. They farewelled you in high Javanese. You liked them, this polite young couple.

THERE were a few tasks waiting for you on your desk. You finished them one by one. You had lunch in your office, traditional Jogajakarta *nasi gudeg*, rice with jackfruit and eggs, and hot sweet tea. You couldn't stop thinking about tonight's travel plans. You left the office at three o'clock.

You parked the car in the driveway. You saw your neighbours, a husband and wife, sitting on their porch. The man is your wife's only brother. You greeted them and smiled. They didn't return your greeting, and they gave you a scornful look.

You went into your wife's room. She was asleep. You stroked her hair and kissed her cheek. She woke up. She scowled. She brushed your hand away. She immediately began complaining, as she had been doing for days, about you going to Malang. She said you were selfish and didn't care about her. You said nothing. She continued to complain about the illness that keeps her bedridden. You've repeatedly said over the past few days that you're not going to Malang because you don't care about her anymore, but because your sister, who has terminal bone cancer, is in very bad shape and you don't think she has much time left.

You left the room. Your son was in the kitchen, making tea. He offered you a cup. You nodded. You sat at the kitchen table. You looked intently at your son, who's nineteen now, a first-year management student at a private college. Suddenly you felt sad. You didn't want your son to know. You took your cup and sat on the back porch.

AT nine in the evening you say goodbye to your wife. She looks away. She also rejects your son's attempt to kiss her hand. You see the fire in his eyes. You pull him out of the room.

You've arranged for another neighbour to take you and your son to Tugu Station, in your wife's car. The neighbour comes from your wife's home village. You employ his wife as a housemaid; she usually goes home in the late afternoon. Tonight you've asked her to stay with your wife at the house.

The neighbour wants to drop you and your son at the station and go straight home. But you ask him to wait with you until the train leaves. It's scheduled to arrive at eleven, but it's late. While you wait you chat about this and that, from locals who shirk their civic duties to the badminton player Joko Suprianto who's just won the world title after defeating Hermawan Susanto in Birmingham. You smoke Sukun cigarettes. Your son doesn't say a word. After an hour's delay, the train finally arrives. You keep finding ways to delay your neighbour from going home. You have another cigarette together, you standing just inside the train and he on the platform. You wave to him as the train finally moves eastwards.

YOUR sister's husband and your niece greet you and your son hysterically as you get off the *becak* in front of their house. Your nephew, in tears, thrusts a telegram at you. It was sent by the neighbour who took you to the station last night. You read the telegram: your wife, your wife's brother and her sister-in-law all died last night. Weeping, you collapse into a chair. Your son looks terrified. You hug him.

There's no phone at your sister's house so you ask your nephew to go with you to the nearest *wartel*, from where you can make a long-distance phone call. You call your home phone. You wonder who'll answer it. It's no surprise when you hear the voice of the neighbour who took you to the station. He's in tears; you end up in tears too. He's barely able to articulate what happened. Three hours ago, his wife tried to wake your wife. When she didn't respond, his wife became suspicious. They were shocked to discover that your wife had passed away and immediately rushed to your wife's brother's house to tell him. There they encountered a much more shocking scene. His wife fainted and was unconscious for an hour. Your neighbour tells you that there are a lot of police at the house now but he doesn't have time to say more about what they've found there because a police officer takes over the conversation.

The police officer who speaks to you has a deep voice. He sounds as if he's choosing his words very carefully. He tells you that there was a robbery and murder at your wife's brother's house, while your wife died in her sleep. He expresses his deepest condolences. You promise to return to Jogjakarta that very day.

AS the train finally moved eastwards, you waved to the neighbour who'd driven you to the station. You told your son to get ready. The train soon arrived at Lempuyangan Station, which is only five minutes from Tugu Station. You and your son got off the train and hurried to the parking lot, where earlier in the day your son had left his motorcycle.

He rode like a madman. You asked him to slow down a bit. Tonight's plans would fall in a heap if you had an accident on the way, and also you couldn't stand the wind that was viciously slapping your face. He slowed down briefly but then was off like a rocket again.

You headed for the house you'd left a few hours earlier. As planned, he took a detour that led to the back of your house, so your neighbour would never suspect anything. Both your house and that of your wife's brother are at the far end of the village and there's quite a large tract of vacant land between them and the nearest neighbour. The neighbour who'd taken you to the station wasn't back yet. You'd calculated everything. You told your son to wait behind the mango orchard.

You took a knife from your bag. You crept into your wife's brother's house through the back door. You have a spare key. Your wife's brother and his wife sleep separately. There's just the two of them, no children. You began by smothering the woman in her room and then slitting her throat. Blood sprayed, soaking your hands and clothes. You went to the living room where your wife's brother was snoring. There was a *wayang kulit* shadow-puppet broadcast on the radio. You recognised the voice of your favourite puppeteer, Ki Hadi Sugito. You deliberately woke your wife's brother. With his face still a picture of confusion, and on the radio a clown scene about the pleasures of heaven on earth, you stabbed him repeatedly. You lost count of exactly how many times. You were just content to watch the life slip away from his eyes.

Those eyes had looked condescendingly at you every day

since you'd married your wife seven years ago. You and your wife were old high school friends and had only met up again eight years ago at your thirty year class reunion. You'd been married and divorced, with two children. Your wife was single when you got married.

Your wife's brother and his wife claimed you were an upper-class pauper. You do have blue blood, but you're of low rank, the lowest in fact, so you could only be called *Mas* - the middling title of *Raden* is out of reach for you, let alone the high class *Raden Mas*. And it's true, you have no assets. The house you live in belongs to your wife. Previously, for decades after you left your parents' house, you'd always lived in a rented house. The car that you use every day also belonged to your wife. So there was some truth in what they said, though it wasn't the full story. You have a pension from your old workplace, but it's a laughable amount. Your wife's the main breadwinner. She's not from a wealthy family but her savings accumulated over decades before she retired from her job as a civil servant in a local government office, as well as her pension, are enough to support you both. Your wife also generously helped pay for college tuition for your daughter, who's now married.

You returned to the room of your first victim. Opened the cupboard. Took money and jewellery and scattered the other stuff in there over the floor. You went to the bathroom and washed your hands and face. You waited until the blood and water disappeared from the bathroom floor down the drain.

You left your wife's brother's house. You looked over at the mango orchard. You saw the shadow of your son and his motorcycle. You felt relieved that he did what you'd asked him to do. You should be joining him and getting out of there, as planned. But you headed towards your house instead. You had unfinished business to attend to.

TWO years ago your wife woke up with painful knees and stiff joints. A few days later her hand began to ache and then swelled up. You took her to the doctor, who diagnosed rheumatism. It was like a death sentence. For the first few months she followed the doctor's advice. However, her health continued to deteriorate until she was spending more and more time in bed. The significant monthly medical expenses quickly drained your modest financial resources. Your wife was forced to sell some of her jewellery, including her favourite ruby gold necklace that she'd been given by her late grandmother.

Since falling ill, your wife's behaviour has changed. What grieves you the most is the way she talks to your son, calling him lazy and stupid, and constantly telling him he's ungrateful. And that's not all; she's often said that she wished he would die in an accident. Your son never responds to her cruel words. But you sometimes hear him sobbing in his room. You admire his tenacity. Your wife's accusations are completely over the top. Your son is pretty good at doing his daily household chores, even if he sometimes puts them off because there are other more important things he has to do. Nor is he stupid; he's well aware that most of his daily needs and his education are paid for by his stepmother. You love your son unconditionally. You were touched when he chose to come with you rather than his biological mother when you and your ex-wife divorced.

For the past two years you've been holding back. However, the things your wife has been saying are getting more outrageous by the day. You blame your wife's brother and his wife, who succeeded in instilling in her the notion that it was you and your son who'd made her sick by administering black magic, which doesn't kill immediately but tortures the victim slowly. They also claim that you and your son are impatient for her to die so you can get your hands on her money. You've had to listen to these hurtful accusations every day.

YOU took your sandals off outside. You went in on tiptoe. As expected, the woman you'd asked to look after your wife was fast asleep in the living room. No problem. You knew that even an earthquake wouldn't wake her. She'd spent several nights at your house and always slept like a log.

You went into your wife's room. For a moment you remembered the early days of your marriage. It's true that you married her not because you were really in love with her, even though you'd found her attractive since your high school days. You'd married her for opportunistic reasons, and you assumed that she knew that and wasn't bothered by it. You were sure that she was relieved too at no longer having to be viewed as an old maid. You can't believe that people your age need passionate romance, like a couple of teenagers. But you both believed the old Javanese proverb that love can grow from familiarity. And you felt that your feelings for each other were strong enough. You were wrong.

Your wife was asleep. That was a bonus. You weren't sure if you could go through with it if she was awake. You took a pillow and smothered her. She squirmed as she resisted, but she had little strength. You lifted the pillow. You checked her pulse and heartbeat, and you checked her nose for signs of breath. Nothing. You took the pillow and pressed it firmly one more time onto her face, just to make sure.

It was much colder than on previous nights, but your son's face was bathed in perspiration when you got back to him in the mango orchard. You didn't blame him. His face was a bundle of questions. You calmed him down and told him that from now on there was nothing for him to worry about. You asked him for a change of clothes. As the motorbike moved away from the mango orchard, you heard the sound of your car approaching the house.

YOU threw your knife, the spare key to your brother-in-law's house, and the jewellery you'd taken into various different parts of the Gajah Wong river. On the bank of the river you poured gasoline onto your blood-splattered shirt and pants and set them on fire.

You and your son rode the motorbike to Janti in the eastern Jogjakarta area, where your son stowed it. You only had to wait five minutes for the Sumber Kencono Bus bound for Surabaya to pick you up. The onboard television was screening a VCD of a performance by a popular *dangdut* group. The bus driver drove like a bat out of hell. You felt both excited and anxious. You prayed that you'd arrive safely at your destination. You fell asleep as the bus approached Sukoharjo, just before Surakarta.

Five and a half hours after boarding the bus, you arrived at the Purabaya Terminal in Surabaya. You asked your son to check for bloodstains on your hands, face and hair. He found none. You didn't want to take any chances. You went to a public bathroom where you showered and washed your hair. You changed into fresh clothes and threw the others into the trash.

Your son didn't say much. You suggested breakfast. He refused but you insisted. You didn't want him to get sick. You had the traditional chicken soup *soto sulung*.

Four hours later you arrive at your sister's house. Her husband and your niece greet you and your son hysterically as you get off the *becak* in front of their house. Your nephew hands you a telegram. You ask him to drive you to the nearest *wartel*.

ON the way back to your sister's house you try to make plans for what should happen next. You'd managed to fool them with your shocked face and your rehearsed cry. You think that the police will link your wife's death to the two deaths next door. You're worried about your son. But you can't change anything.

You arrive back at your sister's house and your brother-in-law greets you in a new flood of tears. He tells you that your sister breathed her last while you were making your phone call. You slump in the chair. You're genuinely sad. You didn't even get the chance to say goodbye.

ALEGRÍA

MARGARITA GARCÍA ROBAYO

tr. FIONN PETCH &

CAROLINA ORLOFF

FROM THE SPANISH

When there was no moon, the road was indistinguishable from the night. Yet in the sharpest curves shone the stars that people had painted on the tarmac. One for each person who had died there, road accidents. In most cases these were drunkards run over by trucks driven too fast because their drivers – also drunk – were fleeing from a woman dressed in red. It was said this woman had a red Chevette parked on the side of the road, with the bonnet open for some mechanical fault she didn't know how to fix. She'd stretch her arm out and ask for help, help that was sure to come soon. The woman in question was attractive and defenceless. In the account of the truck drivers who'd managed to escape because they didn't brake (that is, they hadn't succumbed to temptation), what followed was that the woman would jump inside the Chevette and accelerate with the bonnet still open, forcing them to speed up until almost losing control. Just when they thought they had lost her, the woman would pounce on the windscreen with such force that there would be blood pouring out of her forehead, covering the entire pane. Without really knowing how, they would carry on to the police checkpoint where the officer on duty would take their statement – erratic, disjointed, nonsensical – grab his torch and head out to check the surroundings, only to encounter total darkness.

The following day, that same officer would rub the sleep from his eyes and go out to check again. Back then, the bodies appeared and disappeared for no reason. Shot, stabbed, beaten. It was easy to work out that it had happened to them before they were hit by a truck. It didn't matter. For each corpse that turned up, a star was painted on the tarmac. The real cause of death was information that could – sometimes, had to – be got rid of. Some stretches of that road were dense galaxies.

Alongside there were deep ditches, channels to guide the streams that appeared when it rained. Beyond the ditches there were trees with long branches, raised up to the sky like gracious ballerinas. Or lazy ones. A few miles after the checkpoint stood the town of San Juan Nepomuceno. The main road was charcoal, smooth and even, and at the entrance to the town it forked into a strip of dirt. A lacklustre lock in a silver mane. That's where the stalls of fried food were lined up, where the drivers stopped to eat and drink. They'd been driving for so long that as soon as they sat down they would collapse over their heavy bellies, their heads flopping forward. The legs of the plastic chairs would spread wide like those of a new-born calf. The black women who did the frying and the selling would also offer tiny bags of white powder. Their daughters and their granddaughters were for sale, too.

*

Ana's family (her full name was María Ana but back then this seemed very unrefined to her) had a finca: a bit of land with a house near the town. Just beyond the cemetery and a bit before the checkpoint. The house was called Alegría: joy. Her mother had picked that name in the hope it would be prophetic. It wasn't a vast piece of land, and it wasn't prosperous. It was good for breeding cattle and growing oranges, lemons, mangoes and a bit of yuca for the household. It was useful to boast about a second property out in the country although everybody (except Ana's father, Don Jerónimo) thought it was a bit dishonest to use the word 'property' to refer to such a humble place. When Ana and her siblings were small, they would spend all their weekends there. In turn, when they grew up, they also grew out of it: they wanted to stay in the city with their friends. 'Like cockroaches, moving in packs,' Don Jerónimo would say to them every Saturday before heading to the finca on his own, spiteful, sending out whiny sounds what would fade away like a cowboy's harmonica.

The evening during which this story begins Ana had borrowed her mother's car to go for a drive with her friend Lis. Lis had got hold of some phenomenal weed and wanted Ana to try it. That's why Ana wanted to go far, so that they wouldn't be seen and wouldn't be called potheads. Lis had been called that since long before she tried marihuana. She'd tattooed a flower on her wrist, had pierced her nose and raced around on a noisy motorbike. That was enough. However, Ana's reputation remained pristine and promising, like a newly made bed. So she headed for the finca. She plunged down this dark road, thinking that she should call Yoli, the housekeeper's daughter, for her to open the gate and also tell Jairo (Yoli's dad was called Jairo), to put his gun away and not mistake them for thieves. But in order to do that she'd have to stop at a payphone in the middle of the night, tempting one of the tramps roaming about to rape her. There were stretches of road carpeted by those guys... Once, the newspaper had published a photo of sixteen of them sleeping in a row on the street, and someone (maybe one of her brothers) had drawn Xs over their eyes and thread sewing up their lips. Her dad looked at the altered picture and said: 'Dead doesn't mean harmless.' And he explained that snakes could still bite an hour after they'd died. You had to smash their heads hard to destroy their jaws, so that even if they wanted to bite you, their own anatomy would not respond.

While Ana was driving and thinking that the best thing to do was to continue on until they reached the town, look for a phone and let Yoli know of their visit, Lis was rolling enough joints to distribute among a whole army of hippies. Every time she finished rolling one, she'd put it inside a little tin box which originally held chocolate sticks. She was constantly looking out of the window. Ana hissed:

'You're going to snap your neck.'

'I'm worried that we are being followed.'

'You're so paranoid!'

Ana and Lis shared an improbable friendship. They didn't go to the same school, though they'd known each other by sight for a long time. In that city, within a certain class, everyone knew each other by sight. They had started to spend time together about a year ago. Ana thought Lis was compliant and malleable, she functioned as a wild card for her idle moments. She was unlike Ana's schoolmates who required a level of effort that she no longer felt she could be bothered with. When she went out with them, she was constantly measuring herself. She wanted to be good, pleasant, thin. Also a little wise, and a little frivolous. Later on she'd learn that this is called wanting to fit in, and when that desire was very obvious, her behaviour, her conversation, even her hairdo, stood out. What she found hardest about this desire was precisely that: the admittance that it was in fact a desire and not a talent. Those who did have the gift could fit into any kind of gap simply by showing up.

That's why Lis was a relief. She was an uncomplicated girl who seemed comfortable being the way she was. They had met at a party which they'd both left early. Ana was getting picked up by her brother but not for another half an hour, so Lis offered to take her home on her motorbike. Ana asked her where she lived, worried it might take her too far from her own neighbourhood. Lis replied, with dramatic voice, that she lived in a warehouse for unloved children. Ana found that hilarious. She saw Lis as a lost puppy that needed rescuing and took a liking to her immediately.

As they approached the checkpoint, Lis asked Ana to tell her the story of the ghost that haunted truck drivers again .

'It's not a ghost,' said Ana. 'More likely it's a group of thieves.'

Not true. She'd known about the ghost since she was little.

'Or some twisted freaks from a cult.'

The make and model could vary (Mazda, Renault, Chevette), but never the colour (red). The ghost was also consistent: a tall, shapely woman, with blonde hair so shiny that it stood out against the darkness of the night.

'Perhaps it's just foxes.'

One of her uncles, a recovered alcoholic, had seen the ghost. He managed to escape and hide in the checkpoint. He had to be picked up because he was in shock. It took three days for him to speak again and share what he'd witnessed. Never again did he dare drive that road at night, and never again did he touch an alcoholic drink: he became an evangelist. And obese. He took up other vices – fried food, young children – but no one spoke about that.

Ana put the air-con on because it was too hot. It was always too hot.

A few months earlier she had submitted an essay for Social Sciences class about the effects that tropical weather had on the population. It was nothing too original but the teacher took offence. According to the theory developed by Ana (who only repeated what she'd found in a dusty encyclopaedia lying about in her house), high temperatures could affect people's brains, slowing down their learning processes, and also drastically alter their behaviour. Scientists had done tests that involved young people taking the same exam but locked up in two very different rooms: one with a very high temperature and the other set to twenty-four degrees. The first lot got everything wrong because all they wanted was to escape the room, run away, dive into the first pool of water they could find. Being hot stops you from thinking properly. High temperatures trigger catastrophes and accelerate people's metabolisms. There are more car crashes because drivers just want to get to their final destination, and put an end to their horror. Heat generates violence. No one has time to say please, it's easier to push, scream, kick or fire a gun at anything (anyone) that presents an obstacle on the way towards any place where the brain doesn't boil.

'This explains Guajiros to perfection,' said Ana right before the teacher raised her palm indicating that she'd gone too far in her analysis, that there were plenty of peaceful Guajiros, that it was wrong to generalise.

Ana knew, to be precise, five Guajiros, she asserted. Two were brothers, but the other three didn't know each other. They all came from the Guajira peninsula, known for its arid plains, its extremely hot temperatures and the smuggling of goods through the border with Venezuela. Maybe that wasn't a very representative amount but it seemed to her remarkable that their approach to violence was so similar. For instance, each one of them carried two guns: one in the glove compartment of their respective 4×4s and another one jammed between their belt and lower abdomen, pointing at their testicles.

'Locked, of course,' added Ana, 'because they are tough, not violent.'

The entire class laughed.

The teacher said: 'That is not the point.' The teacher was a young woman, a very strict one. That actually aged her. She wore heavy make-up on her eyes and her body was bony, angular. This didn't help either. In the Caribbean, rounded shapes were preferred.

'And what is the point?' asked Ana.

'I don't know', replied the teacher, shaking her head. 'That's what I'm asking you, María Ana. What *is* the point?'

Impatience was another characteristic of people living in high temperatures.

Wanting to kill someone. That was a euphemism her mother often used: I am so hot I want to kill someone. There were those who acted on this feeling.

After all of this had been overcome – the feeling of vexation, of discomfort, of the urgency to escape one's own body – you reached the point of inflection that was negligence, abandonment, the uncomplaining silence, the rash word. Contextual blindness, absolute lethargy.

In literature they called it doldrums.

Heavy. Slippery. Salty. Humid. Sultry.

These were some of the characteristics pinned on Ana's paperboard to describe tropical weather. Underneath, enclosed in a red circle with rays emerging from it, as a kind of conclusion, it read: like a sea monster.

*

Yoli was about to leave town because it was Friday. She was wearing a pair of frayed shorts and a light-coloured t-shirt which was too small for her after being washed so many times. Raising her arms revealed her belly button. Had her dad been fit to do so, he would have sent her to put on different clothes. Her mother and brother were watching TV and eating some kind of overcooked yellow mush from bowls. The spoons were noisy when they hit the pewter. Yoli observed them from the door. Sunk into that tiny old sofa, they were like shabby cushions no one had ever cared to wash. Her brother was laughing with his mouth wide open. Her mum, on the other hand, pressed her lips together tightly, letting her cheeks fill with air and, when she couldn't hold it any longer, she would let out her laughter like thunder. Like a fart. What really depressed Yoli wasn't the tiny amount of space that there was between the furniture, nor the smell of burnt wood that stuck to every single hair, it wasn't even the concrete floor with cracks that every so often would make his brother break a toe nail (he refused to wear flip flops – sometimes he didn't even wear clothes – even when his mother threw them at him aiming for his head; he was good at dodging the first one, but rarely the second), shouting at him and demanding that he wore something on his feet, that he should stop being so disgusting, that he should act like a child and not a rat. The boy, in turn, would reply with some shrieks that Yoli attributed to a kind of proto-language that no one in her household had the ability to decode. She had thought about all this a lot and had reached the following conclusion: what depressed her the most from her home was the light. It was dull and yellow, as if they were living in a perpetual murky autumn. It was also changeable. Sometimes there was electricity, other times there wasn't. Sometimes the lights flickered for hours, leaving them in a catatonic state. At night, electricity was cut off to save power.

'Who does it?' said Yoli to her dad one night.

'Who does what?' he replied, pretending not to understand.

'Who cuts off our electricity to save power?' Her dad made a twisted expression like he always did when she asked something he didn't know the answer to, or even worse, when he knew exactly what the reply was but didn't want to admit that he didn't like it. He would take any answer, like mules accept any load thrown upon them. Faced with Jairo's silence, Yoli turned to her mother (her name was Sandra), and she said that in any case it was actually a good thing not to have power in the evening because in darkness one can pray better.

The image struck her like a blow. Now she couldn't help but picture the silhouette of her mother kneeling down in the semi-darkness. A dark, contracted mass emitting a hideous buzzing similar to that of a bumblebee. She could have thrown her own flip flops at her, one after the other, and wait to see if she could dodge them.

Instead she went to fetch her bike.

She was meeting up with Lucho, although she wasn't sure she fancied Lucho any more (had she ever liked him?). That was the plan anyway. Plans are necessary. Plans save you; they organise the days on imaginary shelves, all in a line like minute ornaments.

Her dad was sitting on a rocking chair in the porch. He was staring out into the hills, listening to the chirping of the crickets. He didn't need his hat at that time of day. On his head, his hair was receding like the tide. The bottle of aguardiente on one side, his rifle on the other. His tongue was digging under his bottom lip. A fly was whizzing near his face. He didn't flinch to shoo it away. The dog which was usually his shadow, always by his side, was missing. By Don Jerónimo's request, he looked after it with his own life. 'The cows can get lost, you can get lost, but don't you dare lose sight of my dog,' he repeated every

Sunday, as he bid farewell from his van and gave instructions with an unexplainable urgency. Nothing ever happened at that finca.

'And Sandokan?' Yoli asked her dad. He said nothing.

*

Sandokan was a German shepherd. His main virtue was passivity, although ten years earlier he'd bitten a kid's face. The boy was a friend of one of Ana's brothers, let's say the eldest (Ana's brothers are nameless; they are part of the background scenery: mere fillers, props. Let's say there are two of them). No one understood how such a docile pup had suddenly turned into a piranha.

'Someone must have done something to him,' Don Jerónimo insisted as he put his arm round the dog to protect him from the vicious kicks delivered by the victim's dad.

The injury wasn't too serious but it was definitely unfortunate. The kid was taken for emergency treatment at the local A&E and the doctor on duty put stitches on his cheekbone with an unsteady hand, very little skill, and the dedication of a sadist. The procedure was painful, and the end result a bodge job.

Every time Ana ran into the boy either in town parked up at a jetty, or at a party, she avoided him. She had the feeling that this boy, who'd grown to be long and stiff like a reed, always seemed a little lost among the bunch of friends that surrounded him. His expression was like someone who's just arrived and who hasn't yet caught on to the local code. The scar on his face was his burden, but it was also what made him different. He generated a clumsy unease among girls, which made them laugh awkwardly for no reason and fall into each other's laps. One day, Ana couldn't avoid him. She ran into him face-to-face and, before she could head the other way, he grabbed her by the shoulders and forced her to look at the scar that marked half of his face and made one of his eyes – the left one – smaller.

'You are all going to pay for this one day,' he said.

They were standing so close that Ana could take in his breath of beer camouflaged under the Juicy Fruit gum. Then he pushed her away and carried on walking.

That time they almost put Sandokan down, it was what the

kid's family had demanded. But Don Jerónimo was set on going all the way. He called the vet and asked for a detailed examination of the dog. It didn't take long to reveal that the boy had inserted a stick from behind, causing several injuries in the area. Sandokan lived, but they did castrate him. Nowadays he wasn't the good dog he used to be, in fact, he was useless when it came to guarding the finca. Time had left him half blind and Don Jerónimo had tasked Jairo with being his guide, his protector, his shield and godfather. Jairo obeyed to the letter.

'He cares more about this dog than his own children,' Sandra would complain in her coarse burlap voice. She expressed her discontent with other people. She wouldn't provoke or contradict Jairo. Actually, she would only speak to him to communicate very specific things such as the fact that the food had been served, or that they needed to get wood or buy milk, or to let him know that Yoli, who pretended to be so classy and sharp and looked at her and her brother as if they were dirty dishes forgotten in the kitchen's dampest corner, was calling for a good old slap. She carried her own cross and was not putting up with more nails. In the middle of the offloading, Sandra would always burst into tears like a cracked hosepipe. This made Jairo furious. He threatened her with his clenched fist if she didn't shut her mouth. She would then run to get her little boy (called Joao) and would lock herself up with him until she thought Jairo had left.

Jairo hated his wife. He hated her since she'd become pregnant with Joao because he was certain that the boy was not his. He was sure the father was a man Sandra had met on a job she'd done on a Brazilian boat. The job was nothing to boast about and had lasted only a few days, but she had come back home with a face full of smiles and soft like jelly, and with the devil's seed already planted in her. Jairo would feel hot flushes on his cheeks and chest when she saw her walking around the house giggling every now and then, crossing and uncrossing her legs like a woman on roller skaters. Or a drunkard. Months went by. The belly popped out, a small, pink melon. He felt waves of burning hatred coming and going like a boy on a swing. Back and forth, back and forth. Until the burning feeling grew so much that his hands caught fire and he was only able to put them out with blows aimed directly at Sandra's belly. He managed to change its shape but not quite eliminate it. When Joao was born, the doctor spelt out his problems in a monotonous voice. Sandra could not stop smiling all the time she was staring at the boy's extremely small head, showering him with devoted kisses: 'Sick calves are also the most loving ones.'

*

'Can I put some music on?' Lis couldn't bear the silence. Ana needed it. It was a dangerous road, plagued with dangerous curves. She felt like the ground was writhing beneath her.

'I'd prefer not.'

'Then tell me the story.'

'I've told you it a thousand times.'

'But you always have new details to add.'

'Ha.'

'You do.'

Ana turned on the stereo. A presenter was yelling lyrics from a vallenato.

Ana switched from radio to CD and signalled to the side pocket in the door, where there was a CD wallet.

'Take a look in there, would you,' she asked.

Lis flipped through the compartments one by one:

'All crap.'

'They're my mum's. Put on anything, you're distracting me.'

'Sorry.'

Lis put on a disc by Alejandro Sanz.

*

From the noise that came from the street, Yoli could make out whole phrases:

'Exactly the same happened to me!'

They could also hear people laughing, vallenatos, motorbikes rumbling followed by shrieks of excitement.

Through the window she could see another window with closed curtains. They were beige with brown lines. The fan was blowing warm air. It was like someone breathing on her. A dragon. In a town of dragons. The ceiling was damp. All the ceilings she knew were damp. The sheets smelled of white soap.

She liked that. On the bedside table was a square of plastic from which emerged two mountains slathered in synthetic snow. Lucho thought it was pretty, he'd seen it at a fair in San Jacinto and thought of Yoli. Why? Because one day, maybe, the two of them could go to live in the mountains. To the Sierra Nevada, for example. To grow potatoes and raise goats. They could have children too, if she wanted. Potatoes, goats, children.

Did this little knick-knack contain all that?

Someone rang the doorbell. Lucho was in the shower. Yoli was lying naked on the unmade bed. The mattress was hot and damp, like something festering.

'Who is it?' she yelled.

Silence. Then:

'Salvador.'

'Lucho's in the shower.'

Silence.

Yoli got up from the bed and put on her knickers, shorts and shirt. She forgot the bra. Then, she opened the door.

'Come in and wait for him,' she told him.

'Sure?'

'Sure.' She waved him in with a solemn, sweeping gesture, emulating the illusionist David Copperfield.

Salvador leant on the windowsill, looking out at the street.

She went back to bed, her arms folded behind her head, elbows raised, sharp as daggers. She imagined Salvador taking her clothes off, sticking his head between her legs and licking her thirstily. Between Lucho and Salvador, the obvious choice was Lucho.

'So what's new?' said Salvador.

All her thoughts were black as ink, as the sky that night.

'Nothing.'

The cabin in the woods, the little house in the mountains. She set fire to it all: to the goats, to the potatoes, to the children.

The rebels – that's what her social studies teacher called the guerrilla fighters – fled to the hills to turn their backs on civilisation. Why? Because they didn't feel safe in civilisation. But why? Because they were misfits. But in order to become misfits, didn't they first have to fit?

Loud laughter could be heard from outside.

Yoli had arrived early. While she waited for Lucho, she watched the group of kids on the corner through the window. Just like Salvador was watching them now. They'd been standing there for at least four hours.

'What are they laughing about?' Yoli sat up.

Salvador turned round to look at her: he had green eyes, one broken tooth, dark gums. Two seconds on her eyes, two seconds on her tits.

'I've no idea what they're laughing about,' he snorted and turned back around.

The last time Yoli took Ana to the town had been two years earlier. At that time, Yoli still got dressed up for the occasion (hair straighteners, lipstick, sandals and a dress) because she thought that on Friday nights the town became something else. It was something light, fresh, permissive. Something that could be enjoyed if you approached it right. But Ana was uncomfortable the whole time. The noise of the motorbikes bothered her, her eyes betrayed fear, though her attitude was one of disdain. Yoli asked her what was up and she said she wanted to go, she couldn't put up with the smell of fried food. But they'd just got there, they hadn't drunk anything, hadn't spoken to anyone. 'And who could I talk to here?' Ana asked, genuinely perplexed.

Each time that Sandra took her daughter to task for spending so much time with Ana, Yoli would say: 'She's my best friend.' Sandra laughed in her face: 'And does she think the same?' Yoli, without even thinking about it: 'Obviously.' Sandra, choking with laughter: 'Only a fool judges!'

Yoli sat down on the bed and looked at Salvador, who was staring at the street again.

'They probably don't either,' she said.

'What's that?'

'They probably don't know what they're laughing about, either.'

That's what she really thought. The folk in the village, her mother, her father, Lucho, all laughed in that hysterical way of people who rarely get what they want out of life, even though they don't actually make all that much effort. They often don't know what they want out of life, but they miss it anyway. Later, when she could formulate this idea in a more articulate way,

Yoli would say that laughter (that kind of easy, unbridled laughter with which she had been so familiar since she was a child and which was, basically, the laughter of the poor) was a way of abandoning resentment and embracing resignation.

'Poor folk,' said Salvador.

'Maybe they're making fun of people.'

'Of you?'

'And you.'

'And of themselves.'

'Everyone.'

Salvador snorted:

'Poor folk.'

*

Sandokan had a nose like a stray. He followed the scent of food and everything else got away. He'd disappeared into the bush until he found a wood fire that was still smouldering. There were split logs with scorched bark but the heart untouched. There were no food scraps. There were two used condoms that Sandokan sniffed, but they didn't interest him enough to stay there, closer to the finca than to the road. He was looking for meat, for the remains of something. He was hungry because it was Friday and, like every Friday, Jairo had started drinking early and became indolent. He didn't even change his water. Didn't throw him a bare bone. So he carried on sniffing his way downhill, and his blind dog's brain must have been attracted by the sound of speed: that amplified crack of a whip that is more drawn-out and tortured or shorter and sharper depending on the size of the vehicle. When he reached the edge of the road, a hedge of thorns and bougainvilleas, Sandokan came to a halt and began to bark. The barking in the quiet of the night must have startled some small animal – a fox, a weasel, a skunk, or a wildcat – which ran off with a yelp, Sandokan hot on its heels. He went through the fence, the thorns scratching at him, but he kept running straight for the dark road, like a stray bullet.

Coming round the bend he met the snout of a vehicle that tossed him with a blunt thud into the field opposite, a patch of wasteland scattered with rubbish, scrap metal and the corpses of bloated animals with their guts sticking out. And a pair of goalposts. The wasteland was a wasteland because every now and then it caught fire. The land was dead. Not even weeds grew there.

*

The car ended up in the ditch, with its nose dented, facing in the opposite direction to the one they were coming from. Ana had a cut on her forehead, just above her eyebrow. It didn't hurt, it throbbed. Lis was in one piece, but she couldn't move. Later she would say she felt a metallic taste in her mouth, as if she had been chewing on screws. She had bitten her tongue. She had a four-centimetre gash in it. Later she would also say that it was all very 'shocking': the blow against the glass, the sudden daze, the conviction that there, on that curve, her life would be extinguished while the song 'I Want to Die in Your Poison' was playing. Ana would not say very much about it; neither that night nor in the following years. She had the reflexes of a cold person. She discovered that she could be a cold person. She started the car, turned around and continued on their way. She passed the finca, the huge white sign that shone in the night: Alegría. Her father had complained to her mother that it sounded like the name of a by-the-hour motel. 'The words of a connoisseur,' she replied, and her father fell silent.

A year later, when the guerrillas took over the finca, the sign would disappear. Not immediately, for a few days it remained there, dirty and shot-up. 'As a metaphor,' Ana would recall in the future, together with a group of university classmates. They would be sitting in a circle in a room in Bogotá, their feelings raw because of the kidnapping of someone close to them, with their glasses of warm, sweet wine, emotional, garrulous, excited. It would be one of those times of ethical and philosophical questioning, never too deep. Not for lack of commitment, they would say, but because they didn't quite know where to place the blame: on the mismanagement of all the governments in the history of the country? On Christopher Columbus and his pack of thieves, rapists and murderers who wiped out a supposedly peaceful race? Things were happening: kidnappings, deaths, evils worse than death, bad news. None of it had a clear objective. And what could they do? Stick them on an imaginary blackboard, point to them and say: look, things are truly dire. That was all.

Ana turned onto the dirt road and entered the town. They passed the fried food stalls and took the main street, avoiding an old lady crossing the road. She yelled something at them. Ana found a spot to park in the central plaza. Lis opened the door and spat out blood.

*

Yoli, Lucho and Salvador had gone down to the plaza to drink beer.

'Just one,' Yoli had said. She didn't want to get back late and face a tongue-lashing from Sandra.

Here came Salvador – robust, short, compact – with three bottles in his hands and a cigarette in his mouth. Yoli hated cigarettes. Lucho had quit on her account. The day he'd gone for two weeks without smoking – this was the period Yoli had set – he grabbed her by the waist and kissed her as if they were posing for a commercial. The kiss tasted of mentholated saliva. It wasn't what she expected, but all the better. She didn't want to grow too fond of Lucho because she didn't think he amounted to much, but he was easy to get along with. Lucho was so nice that there was no way to fight with him. And he had a frank, clean face, full of hope. Much better that than a guy who curls in on himself. Salvador smoked. He wore a strong perfume that blended in with the smell of nicotine. Yoli sometimes liked it and sometimes found it disgusting. She liked him so much that she had to shake herself to flush out the electricity that ran up her legs and slammed her belly button. She used to fight with Salvador: 'Why don't you learn from Lucho? He's a gentleman,' she would tell him. He would reply: 'Don't you know that kindness is just another form of machismo?' He made her feel insignificant.

She didn't amount to much: she lived in this forgotten town, didn't have a cent to her name, went to a third-rate public high school. What was the point of rubbing it in? She knew all this, she wasn't dumb. On the contrary, she had to be the smartest person in the town and surrounding areas. And more enlightened too: she had read all the books in the public library. It didn't hold a lot, but still. Not even the mayor had read them. Salvador had given her a well-thumbed book. It was called *Guerrilla Warfare*. Yoli didn't know that it was a classic and also a predictable book to be given. Years later she would put it exactly like that:

'I still didn't know that it was a classic and also a predictable book to be given.'

She tried to read it, but didn't understand a thing.

Lucho's eyes, on the other hand, raised her up: they showed her better things, even if they were unsurprising. She once remarked on this to her friend Judith, who was older than Yoli but in the same class at school: she came from some town in Antioquia, and had washed up here by way of an accident that left her stranded (and pregnant, too). She was the only classmate who had read things that were neither in the curriculum nor in the library. When she asked her about Lucho and Salvador, Judith had no doubt that Lucho was a better choice: 'You're too green for someone to be looking at you the way the other one looks at you,' she told her.

Salvador passed them the bottles:

'Drink them while they're cold.'

They each took one. Yoli drank a long draught. First it froze her stomach, then it burned. She went back over what she'd consumed that day: yuca, cheese, guava juice. The image of the lumpy, fermented mazamorra Sandra had made that afternoon came to mind. Was she ever going to get out of there? Some day. All her teachers were full of praise for her: if she wanted, she'd go to university. There was an exam, it was hard, but they said that, taking an average of her mediocre education and her intellectual capacity, it was likely she'd scrape in. 'University?' Her dad didn't seem to know the meaning of the word. Her mother: 'So intelligent and so simple.' Lucho just went silent, wrapped up in a fog of sadness.

From far off, arriving at the plaza, she saw a friend of Sandra's observing her. She'd take the gossip to her mother, no doubt: there was your daughter in a tiny pair of shorts, drinking beer with two guys. Would you believe she had no bra on? There was your daughter: all used up and broken.

The yelling of an old woman in the plaza distracted her gaze. A car had almost hit her, but avoided her just in time with a squealing of brakes.

'Shit,' Yoli said, 'it's that dumb Ana.'

'Who?' asked Salvador.

'Her boss's daughter,' said Lucho.

Yoli took another gulp of beer, passed the bottle to Lucho and headed for Ana's car. She guessed she'd arrived at the finca and Sandra had sent her into town. No doubt she wanted some favour (to buy her alcohol or pork sausages, or to help her light a fire to sit around with her dumb friends, playing guitar and singing even dumber songs in English). Ana believed she was the soul of the party. It's not that she even disliked her that much, just that she seemed ridiculous and despotic (she'd learned this word from Judith). When she hung out with people at the finca, she introduced Yoli as her friend, and in the next breath started giving her orders.

The last time they'd gone into town together, Yoli and Ana returned to the finca and went to bed early. Ana in the big house, in her room with a TV, fan and mosquito net. Yoli in the dark little cabin that smelled of wood and insecticide and candle wax. She barely slept. She remembered the time when, each Saturday, Ana arrived at the finca with her family, she'd come running to find Yoli and they'd be inseparable until Monday morning, when she and her brothers headed back to the city, already dressed in their school uniforms. Ana invited her to sleep in her room, on a thin mattress made up with Snoopy-pattern sheets. Neither of their parents would say no: 'they're little pals'. The diminutive came easy. During the day they'd go to the pond and dive in. The water was muddy and the mud stuck to their hair. It was hard to get out. They'd lie down and chat, give each other facials, wash their own clothes and lay them to dry in the sun. Back then, they both wanted the same things: Barbies, chocolates, big tits and a slender waist when they grew up. They'd stare at each other and say: we're the same. In a sense they were. At a certain age – Yoli would say later, much later – equality is possible. But why? Because there's little awareness of their surroundings.

Ana barely went to the finca any more. After that trip to town together she stopped being friendly and became, like all bosses, kind and dismissive. Every now and then she would give away some of her clothes to Yoli because they were the same size. Sometimes they still had the price tag on them. They were gifts from aunts who lived abroad, in Florida, a place full of beautiful modern shopping malls and yet her aunts, Ana once told her, always managed to buy everything in bad taste. 'Well, bad taste for me,' she tried to backpedal, 'but I'm sure in town these clothes will rank.'

'Rank? What do you mean "rank"?'

'Ana?' Yoli rapped on the window and Ana swung round in fright.

There was blood on her forehead.

*

What Ana remembers most about that evening is that it was cold. If the others were to be questioned, they would deny it. Impossible. It was never cold in that place. If the meteorological service were to be consulted, they would say that the temperature that night was around thirty degrees Celsius. A few more degrees would need to be added given the fire they made later that evening, which alerted the guardians of the neighbouring fincas, who shot their guns into the sky. The shots woke up Sandra and Joao, who were in the double bed. Joao was sucking on her tit – pretending to drink milk – to fall asleep. He was about to turn eleven, but he looked like he was six. Sandra didn't have the heart to refuse. There was a time when she pushed him away violently, slapped him, shouted at him as a degenerate, but Joao looked at her without understanding and retreated into a corner, covered his ears, squawked and scratched his face with those hard nails that never stopped growing. Now Sandra left him to suckle. Yoli explained to herself (and sometimes to Judith) that her mother and brother were a loving deviation from nature: instead of teaching him to be more like her, Sandra became more and more like him. She thought it was her way of accompanying him, of telling him: you are not alone in this dark world that you came into.

Jairo knew nothing of the fire nor the shots, he was beyond reach. He was nodding on his stool on the veranda of the small house, swimming in a sea of alcohol, dreaming of abstract, dancing, bluish images.

That is why, a year later, Don Jerónimo would blame him for the seizure of the finca and would refuse to pay him: 'Drunkenness does not exonerate you, son, it sentences you for life.' That is why Jairo would shoot himself and Sandra would have to move with Joao to another town, where a friend of a friend of Ana's mother would see her wandering the streets as a beggar. Ana would only find this out three years after the night when this story begins, on one of her visits to the city. She would be having lunch with her mother in a restaurant downtown, and her mother would be gossiping innocuously about her aunts, about her brothers' girlfriends, about her friends at school who had to get married because they were pregnant.

'And what about Yoli?' Ana would ask her.

For the first time she would hear the answer she already knew: 'Yoli was carried off into the hills, and no one ever heard from her again.'

In the back seat, on the way to the wasteland, Ana rubbed her bare arms, trying to shake off this inexplicable cold:

'Why are we going there?' she asked Yoli, who was concentrating on driving and not paying her any attention.

Earlier, in town, Yoli had drunk three shots of aguardiente.

Hearing herself talk about ghosts was embarrassing. She felt childish and parochial. She decided to keep quiet. It was Lis who ended up revealing everything, but in an awkward and disjointed way. When she finished speaking she burst into noisy tears. The three of them were in the car with the windows up and the air-con on full blast, but even so, Lis's wailing was so loud that people strolling through the square would turn to look at them. Yoli was diligent. Yoli had always been diligent. She got out of the car, talked to Lucho, got Ana out of the driver's seat and climbed into it herself.

'Hey,' insisted Ana. Yoli sighed:

'Relax, I'll explain later. Lucho and Salvador will meet us there.'

'Is Salvador the...?'

Yoli cut her off:

'Nothing but gossip.'

One morning, months ago, Ana had accompanied her father to the finca. Her school friends were spending the day with their boyfriends. Ana didn't have a boyfriend. She'd had one but she broke up with him because at the end of that year she was going to study abroad, so why waste her time. It had lasted two years, they hadn't managed to sleep together. Or rather: they did sleep together. That is to say, they took off their clothes, lay down on a bed, looked at each other, touched each other, kissed (and not only on the mouth). And that was that.

So one Saturday, overcome with boredom, she agreed to get in the van and go with her dad to please him. He declared: I want to talk to you about the future. And indeed he talked all the way, without pause, which made Ana think that the future was far too long. His words emerged in a resonant voice, but he could only fill them with artificial images: studies, a good husband, children.

'One day all of this will be yours,' he told her when they reached the finca, gesturing at the dry bush, the skinny cows in the corral, the overripe mangoes on the ground attracting clouds of flies. Then he fell silent and Ana assumed that her father was waiting for an answer. And a bow. But she quickly realised that her dad was no longer looking at anything in particular and seemed to have forgotten she was there. The sun was hitting one side of his face, while the other side remained in shadow, and he was grimacing as if in pain. What was he thinking about? His useless degree in agricultural engineering, his marriage, his children and who knows what other frustrations. But then the dog appeared and jumped on him, and his expression softened, and a childish smile broke out on his lips.

Soon after her father went to make the rounds of the farm with Jairo and Sandokan, and Ana was left alone in the big house. The fans were on, stirring the hot air. The furniture seemed to her to be limp, paralysed servants waiting for orders. She peeked into the small house, there was no one there either. Sandra and Joao were at the market, Jairo had said. 'And Yoli?' asked Ana. 'Who knows.' So she threw herself into the hammock on the veranda to watch the orange trees that flanked the entrance. She focused on the first group of trees, then the next and the next, like one of those paintings that take on volume depending on how you position your eye, except in this case the volume always contained the same trees. Like a representation of eternal life. Of karma. She was falling asleep. There was something she liked about the heat: that ability to make you drowsy, to push you into the deep recess of strange dreams. In that hammock she had dreamt of hybrid animals, beasts from a diabolical mythology that licked her whole body with boiling slime. She was woken by the roar of a motorcycle. It was Yoli arriving from town with Salvador. She didn't notice that Ana was lying in the hammock and got off there, in front of the veranda. Ana didn't understand what they were saying to each other, but she understood perfectly well how they looked at each other. Before leaving, Salvador grabbed her arm and tried to kiss her. Yoli dodged him.

'Who was that?' Ana asked her once the motorbike had left and Yoli was still standing there in the middle of the dust cloud it had kicked up. 'A guy from town,' she stammered. 'A friend of Lucho's,' she said later, 'but he has a bit of a reputation.'

'A reputation for what?'

'Tell me now, Yoli, why are we going to the wasteland?'

Yoli breathed deeply, as if stifling her irritation. She was driving very fast.

'You didn't see a ghost, Ana. You ran someone over.'

'No way,' said Ana, her belly turning to ice, 'I swear I didn't.'

Lis, who had been speechless the whole way, let out another loud, raucous cry. Ana grabbed her arm and dug her nails into it:

'Will you shut up!'

Lis carried on crying, but quieter.

'...it might have been a person,' said Yoli. 'Let's hope it was an animal.'

'No.' insisted Ana.

'Yes.'

'Impossible.'

'Take it easy, we're going to clean up the mess you made.'

And that's what they were doing now, in front of a huge fire on which Sandokan was scorching. It had been difficult to find him because he'd landed behind some concrete rubble. There were other dead animals there, but they'd been drying in the sun for several days, so they were less pungent. Salvador had found him: 'here's a fresh one', he lifted him up for everyone to see, except Lis, who had stayed in the car in a state of shock, trembling first, and then sleepy. Dead, the dog looked smaller. As if it had deflated. He laid it back down on the ground. Yoli collapsed beside him. Ana moved closer and covered her mouth with her hands. She thought about her dad. If he found out, he would kill her. Yoli settled the dog's head in her lap. She did it carefully, lovingly, as if she was afraid of breaking it. But it was already broken: there was a deep gash on its forehead through which the bone was showing. Salvador and Lucho gathered branches and placed the dog on top of it. They sprinkled it with diesel fuel, threw a match and then another.

Now, before the fire, Yoli was crying. Lucho, sitting beside her, embraced her.

Ana felt embarrassed: it was more Yoli's dog than hers. She also felt relief. It wasn't a ghost nor a person. That was a relief. And they were going to burn the evidence. That too.

Almost a year later, when Yoli called Ana for her to return the favour, she would no longer feel so relieved. She cursed herself for not having called earlier. The truth hurt, but it was definitive. A lie holds your hand forever. Ana would agree to see her. Ana would return the favour: she would take her to a town that didn't even have a name, she would watch her disappear into thick bushes.

The accounts would be settled. That's what they would tell each other.

In a much more distant future, Yoli would return to the night of the dog, adding strange details. She would eventually tell the interviewer that the animal was hot, that it was actually boiling. That the dead meat smelled of something very odd, something she'd never encountered before. Later it would no longer seem so strange to her: when she dragged bodies away, when she had to bury dismembered people or mutilate corpses to make them fit into the pits, pressed together. She would experience that same smell. And after a slow close-up into her callous-hard gaze, after a subtle battle between the prurient lens and her stoicism, the screen would fade to black without her looking away.

Ana sat next to Yoli. She couldn't see Lis inside the car. She must have been sleeping it off. She was angry with Lis for having recounted what had just happened as if she had the final and ultimate version of things; as if she were the protagonist, the main mourner, choking back tears between sentences. If the accident had been a story, a film sequence, Ana thought, it was obvious that she would be the protagonist and not Lis. But Lis spoke on behalf of both of them without having consulted her, she appropriated her story, manipulated her memory, attributed the wrong feelings to her, imbued everything with a vulgar dramatism.

Sandokan's body was slowly being consumed, but the only one who kept her eyes on the fire was Yoli. Salvador smoked. Lucho watched the edges of the wasteland in case someone appeared. Ana fixed her gaze on the earth and saw maggots, or earthworms. Maybe they were caterpillars fleeing the fire. They crawled along like chromosomes. It seemed to her that there were so many of them that they covered the whole patch of wasteland and overflowed onto the road.

*

When Ana returned to the car, Lis was curled up in the back seat. The car reeked of marihuana. She had several more urgent problems, but she thought she should take it to a car wash as soon as possible. If she let it sit, the smell would penetrate the upholstery. Yoli and the two guys were waiting for her to drive off. They were standing side by side, soldiers in formation. First Yoli, skinny and dark, with those pointy tits that Ana had envied ever since she saw them first sprout. Then Lucho, tall and solicitous: nothingness itself. Third was Salvador, solid as a totem pole: one of those men who, even in baggy clothes, look tight and sinewy.

Yoli insisted that they stay at the finca and leave in the morning.

Ana said she would rather go back. She didn't want to deal with Lis. She wanted to get her off her back, leave her at the door of her house, unconscious as she was, ring the doorbell and run away. Lis had suddenly become that itchy spot that you can't reach. She couldn't tolerate her. She wanted to erase Lis from her life. She wanted to erase that night from her life. She could do that. She could even erase her life and make herself a new one. That's what she thought as she closed the car door, waved to them and said to herself I am never coming back here, I am never seeing you all again.

'Thanks,' she said from inside the car, though she wasn't sure any of them could hear her.

'Have a good day,' said Lucho, though it was still night time.

Yoli was watching the smoking embers.

Salvador didn't open his mouth or make a gesture of any sort. Ana pulled away and continued watching him through the rear-view mirror: his face blackened with soot, his green eyes like encrusted emeralds. In his hand he was holding the machete he'd used to dismember the dog.

The way back seemed different to her. It had quietened down. She looked out the window at the trees: branches stretched skywards, looking for something to catch and devour. Night birds. Country folk always looked at the sky. And they spoke to it: they asked for things to happen (for it to rain) or for things not to happen (for it not to rain). They had faith in it. The sky was powerful, always there, a witness to everything.

For the first time she thought that the stars on the ground was a perverse idea. Perhaps a kind of escape. Better the stars on the tarmac than crushed guts, she reasoned. Everyone had a way to escape things over there. That's what she was used to. But only now did she realise that this escape could be consensual. Let's agree that this is not a boiling shithole but rather a tropical paradise with banana trees, ghosts and neon stars decorating the road.

In the back seat, Lis let out a weak moan.

Ana turned on the radio so as not to hear her. It was the time of ballads: *rain or shine, this love is yours and mine.*

She opened the window and the warm breeze entered. Her face was smeared with tears that were saltier than usual. Poor Sandokan. In the future she would think of the dog often. She would dream of the dull thud against the glass, his head cracked open and his skull exposed.

She entered the city, skirted the Bahía de Manga, parked at the mouth of a pier.

At that hour, with so little light, the opposite shore was a gap-toothed stretch of coast. It looked misty, jagged. It was about to dawn, but the moon lingered, watery and dilute. It floated on the horizon, like someone late at night and lost. That was her city and yet, sometimes, depending on the angle, depending on the mood, she felt like she didn't know it at all. To be able to know something, you need to get inside it and then get out again and look. Years later, she would try to tell this to her mother, who hadn't ever stepped away from her Vélez-branded brown leather diary.

'Getting out, ma, escaping from yourself and taking a look, that's what I'm talking about,' Ana would tell her with a majestic hand gesture, which would start at her chest and climb above her head: 'Doing that, doing that is knowledge.'

Her mother would look at her hesitantly, associating that gesture and that phrase with things that made her uneasy. She would think: Ana looks like a shaman, a witch, a woman who has been alone for too long. And then she would nod. Her mother was used to nodding. Her life was a constant affirmation of lies: the big lie, the substitute lie, the original lie. She moved like a fish in water between the different gradations of deception. Her brothers were male, they lived in a different dimension. They lived in another lie, in the great universal lie.

Ana closed the windows, put the air conditioning back on. The day was beginning to warm up and many confused thoughts floated about in her head. But they were feeble thoughts, not very dense, like those of an ill person who has slept too much and wakes up disoriented, with everything and nothing to do.

'Are we there yet?' It was Lis talking.

Ana didn't reply.

'Did you find out what it was?' she asked now.

The outline of the opposite shore began to take on definition: Castillogrande, a wealthy neighbourhood.

'Hey you.' Lis prodded her on the shoulder, twice. Not hard, but annoyingly.

'What's wrong?' said Ana, curtly.

'Tell me what it was.'

'Don't touch me.'

'Eh?'

'Don't talk to me.'

Confusion crossed Lis's face. Ana thought she looked older

than a few hours earlier. As if the years had come down on her. A rain of stones that dented her head.

A long time would pass before Ana and Lis found themselves alone together again. By then, Lis (who would now call herself Lisette) would indeed be older, as well as more pimped up: yellow hair, whitened teeth, huge tits and a small life in Coral Gables. It would be Lis who would tell Ana (who by then would call herself María) about the documentary in which Yoli had appeared (who by then would be 'alias Lorena') on a European TV channel. By that time that sort of documentary films would be two a penny on European TV channels. Initially Lis wouldn't be sure if it was her, but the detailed account of the night of the crash would seem proof enough.

'You never told me that we'd run over a dog.' Lisette's tone of voice would be reproachful. 'Take it easy,' María would say. 'It was twenty years ago.'

María wouldn't see the documentary until a few weeks later, back home with her husband, having set their only son up at a college in Florida. They would be in the huge master bedroom, she on the carpet, lying with her legs elevated on a chair to rest her waist. From there she would watch her husband pedalling on the cross-trainer with his buttocks raised like someone who expects – and desires – to be penetrated by surprise. Then she would press play and concentrate on the eighty-inch TV screen, on the huge face of Yoli ('aka Lorena') whom she would have no trouble recognising, because her face was identical to the one she remembered, only sadder and more lined. María would remark that the guy interviewing her was far too interested in gruesome details: What does a dead person smell like? Is it true that they burned people alive? Is it true that once your uterus came out while you were running? How many times were you raped? How many times did you have an abortion?

Her husband, without stopping his pedalling, would say: 'Maybe he should ask her about her hobbies?'

'Yoli was much more than a complex background,' María would settle the discussion, indicating the screen with her nose.

Her husband would realise she was wounded, gushing blood in a place somewhere out of sight. Her husband would think: María has hidden corners. He would say nothing to comfort her or to find out more or even to fill the air. He would look at her in confusion, trying to guess the reasons why she had never told him the story of the dog that had been run over, butchered and set on fire. What else might she not have told him? Did he want to know?

But it was years before Ana reached that day.

First there was an intense and complicated courtship in Bogotá, and a holiday romance in Cartagena, followed by an accidental pregnancy, a quick and discreet wedding, an affluent and hollow life. There was a penthouse in Castillogrande, a twentieth floor facing the bay, a panoramic balcony where Ana would adopt the name María – in the end (she would defend herself against the constant accusations) it was hers, she hadn't stolen it from anyone – and she would sit and watch the sunsets that lay in exhaustion on the horizon, like an anesthetised patient. There were also the hundreds of emails that she would exchange with her ex – Subject: endless list of all the ways you broke my heart – as well as her husband's jealousy, and her inordinate devotion to a son (blond and affectionate) who, as he grew up (blond and disdainful), would erase her from his life with one swipe.

'Please, tell me what it was we hit,' Lis begged from the back seat, her face swollen, her hair sticking to her skull, tormented and stinking.

The sky cracked open and a merciless sun appeared. An executioner revealing himself to his subjects, mocking them. Ana would keep the version of that night to herself. A secret version that no one would ever access. She would embellish it until it became a different version altogether. She would stack versions of that night on top of each other until it became a vague memory, a cloud.

She started the car and sighed.

'I'd better take you home.'

THE DRUMMER BOY

CAN XUE

tr. KAREN GERNANT
& CHEN ZEPING

FROM THE CHINESE

When I was young, maybe eight or nine years old, there was a young drummer whom I was enamoured of. The young drummer's face was snow-white, and his hair was black and glossy. When he walked at the head of the parade, beating his drum, I felt landslides and earthquakes in my chest. What was I then? I was like an earthworm that had bored my way out of the mud next to the road and gazed with my eyeless body at the threshing ground that the parade passed through. He was an angel, and I was nothing but a little boy who was just skin and bones.

Fifty years have passed, and I've become a mouldy dried vegetable, and the green countryside has become part of a big crowded city. Returning to my hometown from the distant capital, I remembered the young drummer right away. The hotel where I was staying was very hot, and it was hard to fall asleep at night. Later, I went to the roof where it was cooler and I could rest. In the city, one couldn't see the stars in the night sky, and even the moon was turbid. I sat at a stone table for a while and saw a shadow approach.

'Would you like something to drink, sir? I'm the server here.'

'No, thanks. I want to ask about someone. His name is Lu, and he was once a popular drummer boy in town.'

'Oh, you mean Lu Weichang!' the young man said, surprised. 'He isn't a drummer now. He formed a band that serves in funerals. I know him well. Do you want to see him?'

'Do a lot of people hire a band to play at funerals these days?' I asked, suppressing my excitement.

'Sure. Almost every family does. Otherwise, the dead would be so lonely. Just imagine that.'

The server was talking earnestly, but I had trouble reconciling what he said with the atmosphere of this city.

'He's well-known for his talent. There are several bands in this city, but the others can't hold a candle to his band! After work tomorrow, I'll take you to see him. He never married. He lives alone. Everyone imagines that he's rich, but he lives in a slum.'

The server Ian and I agreed on a time, and he went downstairs. I paced for a while, watching the moon turn a rusty red colour. An unpleasant smell was fluttering in the air. I couldn't guess what it was, but it dampened my mood. The young drummer of the past had always shown up for festive gatherings in the village. I would rush to those gatherings simply to see him. It was because of his good looks that the adults chose him.

After a while, I was sweating all over. My sweat smelled similar to the unpleasant odour in the air. This surprised me. I went back to my room and took a shower. After changing into clean clothes, I suddenly remembered: that was the odour you smelled in a home where someone had just passed away. I experienced that not long ago when my uncle died. So this was the smell of this city. But the city's name – 'Greentown' – didn't match.

I closed the window and door tight to keep the smell from seeping into the room. Sure enough, this was much better. Was the death rate here particularly high recently? Was an epidemic raging? I was apprehensive. I could see Ian's expression of concern for the dead – these customs of Greentown were truly unfathomable!

It was late at night, and I had nothing to do. I could only go to bed. There was no air conditioning in the room (how strange), but after I turned off the lights, I could feel a little cool air. Where was the breeze coming from? An indistinct voice on the ceiling said, 'This is Greentown. Understand?' The voice repeated this again and again, and I still didn't get it, but it helped me sleep. Everywhere in my dreams flowers were giving off an intoxicating fragrance. And besides, every now and then, that voice rang out in my dreams: 'This is Greentown.'

Despite my dreams, I slept well and woke up refreshed in the morning.

Many people were eating breakfast in the dining hall. They all looked unfamiliar. I even wondered if one of them was Lu Weichang.

I ate a pastry and drank some milk and fruit juice. I remembered the smell on the rooftop last night, and I was worried about it. Why hadn't I smelled it in the corridor and other places? The cook came over and asked how I liked the breakfast. I said it was wonderful. I thought a little and asked, 'Are some animals loose on the roof?'

'Animals? Yes, yes, some cats kill themselves by jumping

into the water tank... Cats are the hardest animals to understand. Don't you agree?'

All of a sudden, he exploded in a horrifying belly laugh. Then, evidently remembering something, he hurried off.

I continued sitting at the table, feeling feverish and confused.

After a long time, I stood up and headed outside.

I didn't find this city attractive; I didn't want to look around. After buying some food at a supermarket, I went straight back to the hotel.

Though I hadn't gotten another whiff of that unpleasant smell this morning, nonetheless I closed the window and door tight. Greentown left me with mixed impressions, and I was a little afraid to go out.

Someone knocked on the door: it was a chambermaid.

'You need to go out and walk around, sir.' Her gaze skated back and forth in the room. 'You'll come to like our city if you see more of it. Do you know why it's called Greentown? Because it can green your heart.'

'It's a pretty name,' I said mechanically.

'It's not only pretty, it also has tangible benefits. You'll see if you walk around.'

And so, this chambermaid persuaded me to go out, though I didn't know what she meant. Not until I reached the shabby, uninteresting main street did I wonder why she had urged me to go out. And why had I deferred to her?

I hadn't walked very far when I thought I'd like some tea, so I went into a teahouse.

No sooner had I taken a seat than I smelled that odour again. I frowned.

'There are too many animals here. Don't take offence. After a while, it'll be better,' the waitress whispered.

'I beg your pardon?' I pretended I hadn't heard her.

'I was talking about that smell... If your mind is quiet, it'll disappear,' she explained patiently.

I ordered a large pot of green tea, hot. I comforted myself: it's okay here, and the tea tastes fine. I hadn't come here for sightseeing; I had come to find the idol of my childhood, and everything was going smoothly. It was just as the chambermaid at the hotel had said: everything had tangible benefits... By the time I had almost finished the tea, I was starting to feel better.

There were some other patrons in the teahouse, all as quiet as cats. They slipped in, sat down, drank their tea quickly, and then slipped out, as though they were afraid of bothering others. In the capital where I lived, people didn't act this way. Is this what 'this city greens one's heart' means? Although I was a little sentimental, my heart stilled and I felt the pure air circulating all around me – the same feeling I'd had last night when I fell asleep. The waitress stood next to the counter smiling at me. I nodded to her...and all of a sudden, I was curious about this city.

It was overcast today, and the buildings next to the street looked even more out-of-date and monotonous, but I still wanted to walk around in the alleys. I entered a stone-paved alley with locust trees on either side. Plain white flowers were blossoming on the trees. The alley was clean and cool, and no vehicles were there.

'Liu Xiaojiang! Liu Xiaojiang!'

Wow – someone was calling me! Who could it be? A ghost from my hometown?

Gasping for breath, the person ran over to me. Ah, it was Ian, the server from the hotel.

His face was red. He said, 'You scared the life out of me, sir!'

'Huh?' I was astounded.

'I forgot to warn you yesterday. You can't wander around by yourself, and for sure, you cannot enter this kind of alley. Because you're a stranger!'

'What's wrong with strangers?' A faint anger rose in my heart.

'Nothing, but you aren't familiar with the customs here.'

'So what?' My tone was a little jeering.

'Nothing, nothing...' He said apologetically, 'I worry too much. Relax – enjoy yourself.' He turned and went back to the hotel.

This surprising incident made me nervous. I saw in my mind's eye the mysterious night scene of cats jumping into the water tank on the rooftop to commit suicide. I looked ahead, and in the distance I saw a greyish coloured mansion. On the third floor, someone opened a window with a bang, and then closed it again. Was that person looking at me through binoculars? I turned around, wanting to see the road that I had just taken, and again I heard someone slamming a door shut. Cold sweat ran down my back, but I continued walking. I wanted to walk to the end of this alley. Wouldn't it be just too funny if I went back at this point? It would be out of character for me. A small garden suddenly appeared next to me. It extended in from a narrow recess at the side of the road. I saw a stone table and stone benches, as well as reddish purple shrubs. I asked myself: Am I going to go inside? I'm an outsider here, but this is where my roots are. Would something go wrong because I don't know the customs here? Was I afraid something would go wrong? Who cares? I wouldn't die here in any case. And besides, hadn't the waitress said that I would receive tangible benefits?

I turned into the little garden and sat at the stone table. Aside from a dog growling at me under the tree, nothing happened.

For a while, noises came from the house in front of me. The back door opened. A worried-looking man stood there. He waved to me and then walked toward the stone table.

'Welcome, sir. Do you like my home?'

'Yes, very much. Your home gives inner peace to guests from afar,' I said.

'My father died three days ago. His funeral is today. I'm waiting for Mr. Lu Weichang. I'm afraid there's been a slip-up... My father had a hard life. Now, at the very end, I cannot let anything go wrong. This is such an ordeal. If I hadn't finally engaged Mr. Lu Weichang, I'd probably have had a breakdown. Do you know Mr. Lu Weichang?'

'We're from the same village and grew up together. He used to be a drummer boy... You can depend on him.'

'Oh my! No wonder you looked familiar. You have no idea what I've gone through these last few days. I've become quite world-weary. I've asked myself over and over: such a good father died, how can I still be alive? I think that only Mr. Lu Weichang can console me, and help me find reasons to go on living.'

Looking him in the eye, I said, 'Yes, that's precisely the kind of person he is.'

'Mr. Liu, you're exactly right! Thank you! I'm feeling so much better!'

'Huh? Do you know me?' I asked in surprise.

'Of course. This is a small place. News spreads like the wind. Now I have to go back to keep my father company. Ah, this is the last moment.'

On the way back to the hotel, I kept thinking of this incident. This had shaken me greatly. The drummer boy of the past, the Mr. Lu Weichang of the present: What did Greentown residents think of him? He could actually help people find reasons to go on living! Of course I knew it was true. I had seen the way he beat the drum when he was still a boy; it was extraordinarily powerful. And the way the locals treated their deceased relative also impressed me very much. They seemed to think the person was still alive, as if there were no difference between the living and the dead. Was it only because of Greentown's atmosphere that Lu Weichang became an idol among the common people? I really wanted to go and see the funeral band, but that person hadn't invited me. This was a private matter for his family...

While I was eating in the hotel dining room, Ian came over.

'Mr. Liu, I want to apologise for what happened this morning. It never occurred to me that you were an old hand – that you could get along on your own in Greentown. Sorry I acted like a snob.' He was looking down as he spoke.

I didn't understand what he was saying, and asked him to explain.

'I think you're already a senior resident of Greentown. The man whose family is having the funeral was very impressed with you.'

This was inconceivable. Were there eyes and ears everywhere in Greentown? Could no one keep anything secret?

Without saying a word, I concentrated on eating.

Ian still didn't leave. Leaning close to me, he said, 'I'll wait for you in the lobby at seven o'clock this evening.'

I nodded.

I didn't go out that afternoon; I sat in my room, lost in thought. Later on, I heard people arguing in the corridor, and I opened my door a little to take a look. But I just saw one person. It was the waitress who had urged me this morning to go out. When she saw me open the door, she bounced over and shouted:

'What do you think? Now you know more about the merits of Greentown, don't you? Are you moved by this? We are a real human world here, not only full of romance and love but also full of parting and death...'

She went on and on, but I couldn't keep up with what she was saying because she spoke too fast. She had been wiping the door. Now, because she was talking so excitedly, she even forgot to clean the door. Looking at me with wide eyes, she lowered her voice: 'Tonight, there will be a wonderful show on the rooftop. Are you going?'

I told her I was planning to see an old friend.

'That's all right. The person you're going to see is important.'

'How do you know?'

'Ian is always blabbing, so everyone knows.'

I slammed the door. Even though I didn't have a favourable impression of Ian, he was the only one who could take me to Lu Weichang's home.

After eating dinner at a small roadside café, I went to the hotel lobby ahead of schedule. Ian was already waiting.

'It's better to leave a little earlier. Something could go wrong if we have to hurry,' he said.

'How so?' I was puzzled.

'He isn't an ordinary person. Each time I go to see him, I'm ill at ease and confused. You surely know what kind of person he is.'

'No, I don't. I was a little kid when I last saw him.'

'You do know. Don't be so modest.'

I felt like slapping this guy's face. So I said no more.

Lu Weichang's home was a long way from the hotel, and for some reason it wasn't on a bus line. Ian and I rushed along the dusty sidewalk for a long time. I felt as if I were hurrying to a crematorium. Once in a while, Ian looked exceptionally solemn, as if we were going there to negotiate arrangements for a funeral. Damn it! Perhaps Lu Weichang had become the spiritual leader for the Greentown residents? An indescribable mood took hold of me, so I didn't even notice the city's nightscape. Yes, it was already night. All I remember is that we went through one street after another, and each street looked just like all the others. Suddenly, Ian turned in at a large compound.

The compound's shabbiness was shocking. The houses couldn't be called houses. They were just sheds constructed hurriedly with galvanised sheet iron: they didn't even have doors. Three old men were drinking tea on the cement area in the middle of the compound. As soon as they saw us, they stood up. Two of them went back to their own sheds.

'Uncle Lu, he's here,' Ian said to one old man.

By the light from the sheds, I could see that he had white hair, but I couldn't see his silhouette.

Lu Weichang invited us to sit down at the small square table and poured tea for us.

I heard my heart thumping. Why?

'You came from afar to see me. I'm truly moved. I have a hunch that we'll have a friendship that straddles the centuries. That's very rare, isn't it?' he said warmly.

I was excited. Just then, I noticed that Ian had disappeared, and so I was even more excited.

'Your band is very powerful, and... and dominating people. Right?' I was talking incoherently.

I immediately regretted saying that, but I couldn't take it back.

'Have some tea, please. Actually, this isn't the way it is. We have some music – the kind that can lead people back to happy times of the past. But we don't rely entirely on music. To be honest with you, we often don't even take musical instruments with us to a funeral. Not everyone needs to have instruments played. Serving at funerals is a subtle thing.'

As he was talking, he shifted his chair closer to me. His face was now in the shadows, and I still couldn't get a good look at him. Gradually, I imagined him as the boy from my childhood.

'If you don't take musical instruments with you, then how can you play music?'

'It is the pure silence of mourning. We sit with the family next to the departed elder. There is a natural air field in which everyone feels warm. Certainly, sometimes we do perform – playing the erhu or the flute. It's beautiful, whether we perform or not. Of course it's beautiful, because it's the final farewell.'

'What is the most important?' I asked, fascinated.

'Ah, that's the mutual trust. The group of people, including the deceased person, are entirely transformed into one person.'

'Miraculous,' I murmured.

'No, it isn't a miracle. We call this "internal affairs". The moment we take our seats, the bereaved family is at peace. They know everything will proceed smoothly. The elderly person embarking on his journey isn't cause for sorrow.' He smiled oddly.

'I see. You are the drummer boy; I know you.'

'Are you referring to the time I was the village drummer?'

'Yes. Back then, you were my idol.'

'Later, I killed a person.'

'Why?'

'No reason. Probably because I was greedy. After killing him, I thought about him every day, wondering about his inner thoughts. After I was released from jail, I organised this band. Why? I'll tell you: it was because I wanted to communicate with the man I killed. Friends and relatives thought I was possessed, and gradually drifted apart from me. I often tell my band members stories of my past. Others think that we're crazy. And so the first year that I went into business was rather difficult. We all pulled together, united as one, and things gradually got better. And it was also because my original aspirations were constantly being realised.'

While he was speaking, Lu Weichang was pacing around. He stopped in the middle of the light that was pouring from the building. All of a sudden, I got a good look at his face: it was scarred and pale, and absolutely expressionless, like an ugly mask. I was inwardly startled. I felt a multitude of emotions. Sensing my mood, he walked away from that shaft of light, and resumed hiding in the gloomy darkness. He asked me if he seemed a little like a ghost.

'No, brother. You are I myself. How could I forget myself – that drummer boy? You've been with me all along, and I've been looking for you all along. Today I found you, and I feel very lucky.'

'Thank you, Liu. I'm gratified.'

His tone revealed weariness; I thought I'd better take my leave. But where was Ian? Without him, I wouldn't be able to find my way back to the hotel.

'Ian is out in the back talking with my old brown dog. It's nearly reached the end of its life. It hates to leave us,' Lu said.

After I made my way around to the back, I saw Ian and the dog lying down together on a blue flagstone. 'I'm the one who is sending him off to cross the bridge,' Ian said. 'Recently whenever I have time, I come over here. Uncle Lu has a lot to do in the daytime and he's too busy to come over here. The dog understands everything I say.'

As Ian was speaking, the dog was panting; probably it couldn't make a sound. Petting it, Ian murmured, 'Dear Old Yellow, I have to go. I have a guest. Don't go off alone. I'll come to see you off. But if you're in too much pain, just let Uncle Lu see you off. Or you may go by yourself, like that person this morning. Anyhow, Uncle Lu and I will come to bid goodbye to you and see you off across the bridge. Don't worry.'

Ian and I reached the street again. His steps slowed, as though he were worrying about something.

'Ian, how did you get acquainted with your Uncle Lu?' I asked him.

'I ran into him by chance, and liked him. There's never a way to explain why one likes a person. He's terrific. In the last two days, you must have heard some rumours about him.'

'Yes, it's strange. I've heard a lot about him. He's the idol here, isn't he?'

'You could say that. This was all because of his supernatural powers. Most people have experienced the death of a relative. When a relative dies, we all have unusual cravings. Take me for example: I felt this way a few years ago when my father had just died. I was very much looking forward to communicating with my dad. Uncle Lu was able to help me fulfil this desire. I don't want to go into the details, but I can tell you: communication did indeed occur.'

As Ian talked, we walked into an alley without a streetlamp. We hadn't passed this alley when we came. In the dark, I sensed that he had disappeared; I couldn't even hear his footsteps. And I could only faintly distinguish the sky above. Nothing else.

'Ian, Ian...' I called in a low voice.

My voice had changed completely. It sounded exactly like my recently deceased uncle's voice. I covered my mouth and thought to myself: This is no good!

Because I was walking blindly in the dark, I was afraid I'd bump into something and get hurt. I stretched out my arms, thinking I'd feel my way ahead to the wall on the right side of the alley. After trying more than ten times, I finally touched it, but it was so bizarre: the alley which had looked narrow was actually so broad that it was like a plaza! I kept feeling my way along the wall, but I didn't know if I was going forward or walking in circles.

Because I was afraid and anxious, my clothes were soaked with perspiration. Just then, I saw a hole in the wall ahead; light was coming from inside it. When I approached, I found that someone was sitting on the other side of the hole with a large notebook on his knees. He was writing. Hearing my footsteps, he looked up. Ah, it was the man who lived in the house with the small garden.

'Oh, it's Mr. Liu! How are you doing? Do you like our Greentown?'

'Very much. I saw that your family's funeral went smoothly, and I was happy for you,' I said.

'Better than we expected! My father was fortunate to live at the same time as Mr. Lu Weichang. I'm not exaggerating. Mr. Lu Weichang is an era. Look, I was just talking with my father as I made notes. My life has become meaningful since my old man got in touch with me. Mr. Lu Weichang made this happen! Are you going back to the hotel? When you're free, please come to my place to visit. You may come anytime, and we'll talk about Mr. Lu Weichang.'

After I left this man, I found that I was near the hotel.

The moment I walked into the lobby, I saw Ian standing there. Maybe he'd been waiting for me.

'Ian, just now you left me behind. I was scared out of my wits. Still, it turned out all right,' I said.

'I didn't leave you behind, Mr. Liu. People who meet with Uncle Lu frequently have temporary amnesia and at such times they can't see their surroundings. Actually, I was beside you the whole time. It's hot and stuffy tonight. Would you like to go with me to the rooftop for a while?'

'Sure. Anyhow, I can't sleep now.'

Ian and I climbed up to the roof and sat at a table. We drank two bottles of beer that he had brought along. Everything that happened today had been stimulating, and I felt confused. I smelled that rotten odour again, but it was no longer terribly disgusting. I was curious, though. So I asked Ian, 'Cats kill themselves by jumping into the water tank, so are we drinking tainted water?'

'The cook's words were just a figure of speech. Cats are the cleanest little animals, so how could they pollute the water tank? Listen: this mother cat is about to give birth; it's meowing.'

I did indeed hear the weak meow that seemed to be floating in the dark.

'I congratulate you. In just two short days, you've become a qualified resident of Greentown,' he said quietly.

'There once was a young drummer boy. I was fascinated by him.'

I thought that I was telling a fable. But how could I tell a fable? And so I fell silent.

That night, I had unusually sweet dreams.

Early in the morning, Ian awakened me. He rushed in and asked me to go with him to help Lu Weichang, because Lu Weichang had run into difficulties. On the way, he told me what was happening: The wife of one of Uncle Lu's clients had died and hadn't yet been cremated. Unable to stand the grief, the man was waving a knife around, trying to kill himself. No one could talk him out of it.

But when we reached their apartment, everything was quiet. There was no sound in the apartment. We knocked on the door for a long time, but no one answered. We were nervous. Ian pushed the door gently and we entered the apartment, went through the living room, and saw Lu Weichang and his client playing Chinese chess in a side room. They were concentrating. Ian stopped me from going over there, and the two of us quietly stole out of the apartment and stood in the corridor.

'Out of danger now?' I whispered.

'It seems all right now. Uncle Lu is really a great master,' Ian sighed.

'Chinese chess can cure suffering?'

'He is talking with his wife.'

'Ah!'

'Only Uncle Lu can help people get in touch with the deceased. His method is unique. Only his beneficiaries can understand. Just now, I understood at a glance, but it would be difficult for me to explain how this communication occurs. It's miraculous. It reminds me of the extraordinary conversation I had back then with my deceased father – I knew that my father had passed away, but that wasn't a barrier to my conversing with him.'

His expression told me that he was far away in his memories.

I slipped into the apartment again, and saw that the two men were still concentrating on chess. When I slipped out, Ian's back was toward me; he was staring blankly out the window at the sky. He didn't hear my footsteps, nor did he hear me softly calling him.

And so I went downstairs and came to the main street outside.

'Hello, Mr. Liu!' someone shouted at me from behind.

I looked around: it was the man who lived in the house with the small garden.

'Mr. Lu asked for my help, and so I hurried over. On the way, I heard that the danger had passed. The situation had been extremely critical. However, there is nothing Mr. Lu can't handle. Don't you agree?'

'Absolutely.' I nodded my head, deeply moved.

'I think I'm very fortunate to live in this city. Can you understand that?'

'Absolutely. But how exactly does one communicate with the deceased? Can you describe it for me?'

'Regrettably, I can't. I'm so sorry. You can't understand it unless you join us in these activities.'

'It's really too bad. I won't have this kind of chance, for I have to leave tonight. But who knows? Someday, I might suddenly come back to Greentown and settle down here. This is my hometown, after all,' I said emotionally.

'I think, too, that you'll come back sooner or later. I heard Mr. Lu speak of your situation. Let me ask: Did you see those cats?' His eyes were twinkling.

'Cats? Yes. Although I didn't see them with my eyes, I smelled them. And I heard a mother cat moaning. She was giving birth. Oh God, it was so beautiful!' I sighed.

'They are spirits, always transmitting messages...'

As we talked, we walked into his small garden. He went inside to get breakfast for me, and we sat down and began eating. Everything was so natural. Pointing at the shrubbery, he said, 'The yellow cat is the one my father liked the best. It keeps many stories about my father in its mind. Whenever it was excited, it would look for him to talk.' But I never saw a trace of the yellow cat in the shrubs. Maybe my eyesight wasn't good enough. He asked me to listen closely, and once again I heard a weak voice. All at once, my eyes filled with tears. 'Everywhere, there is...' I was about to tell a fable again, but I stopped myself in time. What I did say was: 'I'll come back here soon.'

I stood up and said goodbye to him. He shook my hand vigorously, and a warm current rushed straight to my heart.

Ian was sitting in the hotel lobby. The moment he saw me, he walked over.

'I've asked for leave. Uncle Lu asked me to accompany you. He said he wants you to take beautiful memories with you.'

'All of you have already given me beautiful memories. This is simply my own memory. Now I can connect the image of the drummer boy with him – the two are one. That's right, isn't it?'

He laughed and made a face.

'I know you'll come back soon. A falling leaf returns to its roots. This root is our Uncle Lu.'

'That's so beautiful. I might cry. I'm sorry.'

'You may cry as much as you like. We're in Uncle Lu's city.'

Ian and I shook hands vigorously, and then I went back to the room.

That night, I lingered in an ocean of flowers.

DJINNS

SEYNABOU SONKO
tr. POLLY MACKINTOSH

FROM THE FRENCH

An excerpt from the novel,
2023

J't'abîme m'abîme, j'dois t'oublier
J'suis le djinn de mon djinn, j'suis bousillé.
PNL

HARD TRUTHS

The phone rang in the living room. I picked it up because my grandmother, Mami Pirate, had told me that if I wanted to be a good healer, I should start by answering the phone to arrange appointments, and say hello you've reached Mami Pirate's practice, what can I do for you, amongst other things. Except it wasn't a patient on the telephone at all. Not at all. It was a woman who introduced herself as a doctor at a permanent welfare centre near the Bonne-Nouvelle metro station, but who had not at all, no really, not at all, called with a *bonne nouvelle*. I didn't catch her name, but she said she was calling because she hadn't been able to get in contact with the mother of Jimmy, a slightly 'special' neighbour that Mami and I looked out for. He lived on the floor above us, the same door when coming out of the lift. In an area where everyone knows each other, a building where everyone knows each other, everybody was aware that Jimmy was a bit special, if not *jnounned*. From *jnoun*, the plural of *djinn*, in Arabic.

Then Madame the Shrink handed the phone to Jimmy, and it took forever for him to pick up the handset. It took so long that I had enough time to imagine how he might answer my questions. But he didn't say psychiatric hospital when I asked where he was; he didn't say yes when I asked him if he was ok; he didn't say no when I asked if it was serious. So I wrote down the address that Madame the Shrink whispered to him. Jimmy repeated it after her, twice, before I hung up.

They were expecting us there that very same day, Mami Pirate and me. We would've gone even if the shrink hadn't given us an appointment. I didn't really know how to explain to Mami what had happened without making her angry, given that she was already putting so much into finding the right cure for Jimmy. So I told my older sister, knowing she'd be better at telling Mami than me. And surprise, surprise, Shango told her everything. About the fight, the cops, and the police custody. Shango didn't stop there. She said it was our fault, Mami's and mine. According to her, what we were trying to do for Jimmy was basically magic and we'd just been wasting our time. She hung up on Mami and then sent a message apologising a minute later.

I would probably have blamed it on her djinn if she hadn't made a habit of snitching at every opportunity. That was classic Shango: flaring up and then apologising. When we were younger, she snitched on me many, many times, and my djinn and I really cannot stand snitches and assholes. Afterwards, when Mami was lecturing me, Shango would say sorry I didn't want Mami to tell you off but it's not fair; all you had to do was not eat all the Thiakry. Shango has stayed the same since she was a kid, even though she has a job, a flat, and a fiancé, as Mami says.

Shango said she'd come with Mami and me. As we came out of the metro, she gave us such a black look that it was clear what she thought, otherwise she wouldn't have tutted so loudly, twice in a row.

She wasn't totally wrong about Jimmy. Maybe he was, as she said, socially disadvantaged; maybe he had, as she said, had mental health problems ever since he was born, and Mami and I were in denial. But what good would a psychiatric hospital do him? I asked the question out loud when we arrived outside the building, and all Mami said was, you know Penda, shrinks are for white people, so let's get Jimmy out of there.

Later we found ourselves in Madame the Shrink's office, and she explained to us that after being held in custody, Jimmy had been transferred to this centre because his was a psychiatric case. Jimmy had obviously told her that Mami was a healer because the shrink was choosing her words very carefully. She was trying way too hard not to offend Mami. After a few moments of hesitation, Mami turned to me and said imagine Penda; if I had to explain my job to all the white people I met, I wouldn't get any work done; it just wouldn't be sustainable. There was a silence. Was I supposed to translate what she was saying, even though the person it was meant for knew exactly what Mami was getting at? Madame the Shrink placed her thumb and index finger on her chin, in 'that's interesting' mode. It was like she'd spent her whole career waiting for an opportunity like this to present itself: finding herself face to face with an old-fashioned healer. That's what her patronising look seemed to suggest. The awkwardness was too much for me. To fill the silence, I asked the first question that sprang to mind, and Madame the Shrink replied in a quavering voice. This was a GHU, a group of psychiatric and neuroscience university hospitals that included Sainte-Anne, Maison Blanche and Perray-Vaucluse. Jimmy was in Maison Blanche, which provided care and psychiatric aftercare for residents of north-east Paris, that being the eighth, ninth, tenth, eleventh, twelfth, seventeenth, eighteenth, nineteenth and twentieth arrondissements. We lived in the tenth.

What were our thoughts on the matter? Shango repeated the question Madame the Shrink had just asked, then said, irritated, that if we'd had any thoughts on it then we wouldn't be there. Personally, I can't exactly say what my thoughts were on the matter. Madame the Shrink tried again. She repositioned her glasses with the tip of her index finger, then said that she could understand our concern. For my part, it was mainly that I didn't understand, but since everybody looked as if they had an objective opinion on the matter, I kept a straight face. Madame the Shrink seemed to be hiding her djinn behind her white coat and her diagnosis. Shango motioned to Mami not to say anything else, and Mami didn't say anything else, or at least not before Madame the Shrink had given her white diagnosis.

She started by listing the symptoms: visual and auditory hallucinations, amnesia, incoherent speech, withdrawal, all of which suggested that Jimmy had schizophrenia. I gulped. Shango was struggling to hide her excitement; she was lapping up everything Madame the Shrink said. The doctor added that Jimmy's heavy cannabis use was only making his symptoms worse, the trips in particular. Mami told Madame the Shrink that the spirit she was calling schizophrenic was in fact a djinn who wasn't happy, wasn't happy at all, and that she'd been looking after Jimmy for ages and was going to use a foolproof method to drive away his djinn.

I felt like I was hearing two different languages, even though they were both speaking French, but Madame the Shrink's words, being scientific, made a much, much bigger impression on Shango, who had never really believed in djinns anyway. Rubbish, she'd sometimes say about them. When Mami mentioned the idea of using Iboga, Madame the Shrink, who thought she'd said Ibago, got her to repeat it and then started making notes in her notebook. Right-handed. No dyslexia to blame for mixing up the letters of a three-syllable word. Iboga, I don't know what that is, she said. Mami explained: it was a root that would wash out Jimmy's brain. Shango muttered her disapproval. Madame the Shrink repeated: wash out? She repositioned her glasses with the tip of her index finger once more, then said that it would be best if Jimmy didn't take anything apart from the medication he'd been prescribed on arrival, before adding that they'd be keeping him under observation for a few days anyway.

How many days? She couldn't say exactly, it would depend on his behaviour and test results.

Today, they were allowing family to visit the psychiatric hospital. The posters on the wall said so, but the problem was that Jimmy wasn't family. I insisted on seeing him all the same, just for 10 minutes, and to illustrate how tiny my request was I indicated the distance between my thumb and middle finger. Madame the Shrink said we could, if we gave her his mother's contact details. I was surprised when Shango shot back that we were his family, that Jimmy's mother was seriously ill and that she shouldn't play games with us. It was the first time she had shown any empathy for Jimmy in public.

Jimmy was in room 302. Madame the Shrink led us down a long corridor filled with wandering pale blue pyjamas. Over the course of the walk, which seemed to last forever, my eyes fell on the vegetables around us. Blue artichoke, blue carrot, blue fennel, and even a blue pepper gasping for air near a wall. None of the patients in this clinic were like Mami's patients. None of Mami's patients banged their heads against walls. None of Mami's patients dribbled. None of Mami's patients had blank stares. None of Mami Pirate's patients were locked up.

But Jimmy was. In room 302, right at the end of the corridor. When Mami, Shango and I went in, Jimmy was sitting on a chair next to a single bed, smoking a cigarette with his back to us. Madame the Shrink tried to assert her authority by pointing at the rules and regulations, which said that smoking in the rooms was strictly prohibited. There was a designated courtyard for that. Mami thought he was smoking a spliff and asked him to put out his thingy, then she went over to him and placed her hand on his forehead. He was sweating even though the room was a normal temperature. His nails were bitten to the quick, his dark pupils surrounded by bright red blood vessels. Shango and I stayed in the background. I didn't know what to do with my body. Jimmy stubbed out his cigarette on a bit of paper and came towards us, very, very slowly, so slowly that Madame the Shrink felt the need to explain why he was being so slow. It was because of the medication he'd taken at breakfast that morning, allowing him to temporarily leave his hallucinations at the bottom of a paper cup. Madame the Shrink pointed out that the medication seemed to be working on Jimmy, but it was still only provisional. It must have been working because we were there in the flesh, so much so that he took us into his arms.

I squeezed him so hard I could've broken his ribs; I never wanted to let him go, but I also wanted him to say something, anything, so I could hear his voice. He was desperate to speak; his lips were trembling, but nothing came out. The medication must have been super powerful to dull his mind that much.

How does a schizophrenic think? I wondered.

It was neither the time nor the place for the question. Madame the Shrink, who was already waiting for us at the door, gave all three of us her card. She would let us know when she had more information, and we shouldn't hesitate to call her if we heard from Jimmy's mother, or had any questions.

I had so many questions that on the way home, I gave up on getting any answers. But when I put my cold hands in my coat pockets, I knew that all of it had really happened. Jimmy had slipped me his keys without me realising. I could tell they were his because he had a mini bottle of gin on his keyring. He would usually hook it to the loop of his belt. All of it had really happened. The card in my hand was further proof. On the front it said GHU Paris Psychiatry & Neuroscience Maison Blanche, and on the back Lydia Duval / Psychiatric Doctor.

CIAO

The next day, my stomach was empty as I pulled on the jumper that served as my work uniform while Comma, the manager at Flammèche, berated me for my tardiness. Strategically positioned in a busy shopping area, the convenience store catered to the poor families in a neighbourhood where boutiques selling bikes, scented candles and organic cucumbers were springing up at every corner.

Alimatou and Inès, my two co-workers, were already at their tills when I started counting mine up. Comma's job consisted of breathing down our necks and having a go for no apparent reason. She was clutching a burning hot plastic cup, pretending to talk to a chatty customer who was a regular while keeping a trained eye on my float. Once I'd opened my till, I indicated that the impatient customers who'd been staring at me as I counted could come towards me. Cue five hours of non-stop beeps. The only thing I could enjoy over those long hours of mindless dreaming was the fact that my till, which was the one closest to the sliding doors, offered me a not insignificant view of the road. Between serving two customers, sometimes even between scanning a packet of crisps and a bottle of Coke, my gaze would vacantly linger on the many pigeons living their best lives right next to a drain.

Comma didn't dare tell me off for anything, apart from my lateness. But I had quickly worked out why I was spared her baseless fits of rage. Unlike Inès and Alimatou, Comma couldn't work out which box to put me in. She couldn't place me, and it made her uneasy. Alimatou, who had been hired two months before me, put up with the fallout of this on a regular basis, and she'd always say yes ma'am and bow her head. That's what happened on this particular day. Having put up a sign saying 'till closed' for the first time that day, Alimatou went off to change her tampon. I knew she was on her period because her skin was twice as greasy as it normally was, and she tapped her head twice as much to scratch her scalp, which was partially covered by a weave. While Alimatou was gone, Comma turned on her flashing lights, would you believe it, vape in hand. She asked me where she was, and I could already feel my blood boiling – 'she' had a name. Inès shot me a questioning look but ended up answering her. We both knew things were about to get nasty for Alimatou.

It's crazy how customers can be completely oblivious to anything going on beyond their shopping trolleys. I was still only a few centimetres away from them, but they didn't hear Comma's irritated sighs or her manicured fingernails nervously tapping on Alimatou's stool; instead, they were listening to the ad on the radio about the latest special offer. They didn't see the fear in Alimatou's eyes; instead, they were thinking about who could get to her newly reopened till first.

There were plenty of people in Flammèche, and I thought Comma was smart enough not to make a spectacle of herself in front of the customers. Wrong. She didn't give a damn about them. You no speak French, she said, reminding Alimatou that she must always ask her permission to leave her till. The fact that she brought up Alimatou's Soninke accent once again really pissed me off. She would never have done that to me; she found it harder; there was a discrepancy; I spoke a French that she thought comprehensible enough not to turn me into a linguistic target. So I couldn't stop myself from reminding her, bag of onions in my hand, that what she'd just said was unacceptable. The customers suddenly started paying attention, and Comma hadn't been expecting it. In a trembling voice, she shot back that I should mind my own business, raised a finger in warning, let out a Neanderthal gurgling noise and then yelled at me to get lost. I hesitated, then I carefully put down the bag of onions, stood up and extracted myself from my till. Alimatou hadn't sat back down at hers yet. She took me in her arms, tears in her eyes, more to say ciao than to thank me. She knew I'd have kept my big mouth shut if I'd wanted to keep my job. Instead of feeling sorry for Alimatou, my djinn had just one strange thing on his mind: making me feel guilty. Oh well done, he said, you've lost your job. I tried to concentrate on the strong smell of incense emanating from Alimatou's clothes rather than listen to the voice of the other person inside me. Inès rushed over to me to remind me of my rights. None of them mentioned dignity. At the end of the day, they were the brave ones, the ones who'd stayed and would collect Commas where they should put full stops. And the customers were super racist too. If we'd worn badges, they'd have said 'the little African', 'sweet mango' or even 'island flower' instead of our names, all the nicknames that the predominantly old and bald white men enthusiastically gave us. If Comma had been there on the Sundays when I insulted their mothers, the mother of their mothers, the mother of the mother of their mothers, I would've left as soon as I grew a thick skin.

What was I going to do now?

It was the first day of autumn I think, and my life was irrevocably no longer behind a till. It wasn't anywhere else either; I sensed that I needed to create it. Jimmy had been sectioned; Mami wouldn't be around forever. There was some urgency to things.

RED (HUNGER)

SENTHURAN VARATHARAJAH

tr. VIJAY KHURANA

FROM THE GERMAN

An excerpt from the novel,
2022

•

We cannot give ourselves a name; we can't give ourselves a name of our own. But we c
an wait for it to be taken from us. This is not a question of time.

10:12 AM.

An announcement over the loudspeaker.

A. – which is his provisional name, a name that won't say more than *this is not
a beginning*, than *we could always begin differently*, than *we consider each thing from the point of view
of a dream, slowed down and rotated by 90 degrees, i.e., as these things will appear, from the same end*
– waits. He stands beside the tracks, on the paved platform. The sky: grey as smoothed
cement, crossed out and held by black cables. A. stands here. He stands next to a pillar
and beneath the curving roof. His hands: in his pockets. In his left: a lighter. His car ke
y. In his right: five Marks. At the end of a long day   comes a day. It's raining.

Every form presupposes substance.

We will destroy the jaw, to reach the jaw.

In a trash bin: half a croissant. A crushed coffee cup. A copy of *Stern*. A group
of people stands behind the white line. A woman coughs. In the track bed: three pigeon
s. It's chilly, 8°C. A. takes his hands out of his pockets. He places them flat on his thighs.
He folds them. He lets them hang, as if they were incidental skin, peeled away and of n
o meaningful weight, after he said, *I'll be there*. After he said, *Patience*. His trousers: black.
His jacket: black. A red-checked scarf: around his neck, as agreed on. A. puts his hands
back into his pockets. B. – which is his provisional name, a name that won't say more t
han *there is no continuity in this alphabet*, than *a line is a line until it is broken*, than *where language
ends there will be no difference between a body and a verse* – will recognise him by his teeth.

He knows that.

10:14 AM. Platform 2.

The train arrives. The red line along the carriages is interrupted by people. A. s
ees it, he can see it: between them. Intercity Express 793, from Berlin to Munich, 2 hour
s and 33 minutes from Berlin Zoo station to Kassel-Wilhelmshöhe, via Spandau, Brauns
chweig, Hildesheim, Göttingen, from the right; later. And this will only have been a stor
y. The train is on time. The house: cleaned. A. leans against the pillar, his index finger
on the key of his Lancia, parked in the station car park. He presses the metal into his sk
in. He had wanted to wait for him somewhere else. He described it, precisely, yesterday
in his last email, as precisely as if he had already known that he wouldn't wait there. *In
the middle of the platform there's a wide ramp leading up to the station building. Walk up the ramp a
nd you'll see a dark blue figure of a person, about four meters tall. To the left of the figure is an informati
on booth, on the right will be a bistro. This figure is where we will meet. I'll be wearing black trousers
and a black jacket, with a red-checked scarf around my neck.* At the end of language

we will only be
another story.

We give what we don't have.
It goes without saying.

First verse: this summer has lasted, longer than expected. It's Tuesday. Ears of wheat have left white marks on his legs, on the outside of his thighs, on his calves, Septe mber; 1970. A. stands here, in the middle of this field in front of his parents' garden, se parated from it by a gravel track, after it has gotten warmer, even though it is warm. A rural road: to the right. The air doesn't move here. A. hears Simon's voice. A. hears him counting: with both hands in front of his face, and the bark on the other side; A. hears him at the tree, from ten to zero, A. can hear him, slowly. It's afternoon, after 1 PM.

A.: on the ground, between a sentence and the wheat. When a body kneels, a name will kneel as well; until soil, until small dry clumps will remain in his skin, and pieces of grave l when he stands up, as always. Wüstefeld: Rotenburg, on the Fulda River. One can wait 31 years for 9 hours and 45 minutes, or 39 years for a single day, and we will speak of *h unger* as if there was a hunger that meant only our mouth, and that no hands will carry. Behind the field, beside the house, which is not a house but a 36-room manor on nearly an acre of land, where the road enters the village: his father. A. sees him. A. sees him w alking to his car. A. hears his mother. A. hears the car door. A. runs. He runs

through wheat
through the field
over dry soil
and dust
across the white
line at the edge of
route 3336
on asphalt
A. runs
as his father
drives past
the sign
where the name
of this village which will
not become

his name
is crossed out A. runs

beside his father's
car as it drives
past
him behind his father's car as it
keeps on driving he runs.
He runs

until he doesn't run anymore.

As if language could only ascertain, i.e., say the least; as if nothing had happene d; as if no sentences had been broken, no legs. The platform is emptier. A conductor s peaks with a passenger. On the ground: other pigeons. For 32 days, A. and B. have spok en of this: of a number, to keep his teeth from forgetting. Zero is said to be the number of elements in an empty collection of objects, *the cardinality of the empty set*. It is represente d by a circle slashed with a line, or by curly brackets. The circle: is a mouth; a bracket: r emains a kiss. A. stands beside the pillar. B.: stands in front of him. Green Nike baseball cap, pale blue jeans, size 30/30, a white shirt. Grey-green summer jacket, dark blue snea kers, size 41; blue socks. Mark the first page of this book with a red marker. Because a wound is, in the beginning, visible; because a wound will have preceded each beginning.

We give what we don't have.

They shake hands.

•

The blood on the mattress is black; like a circle, a moist circle dried at the edge. This al
phabet begins with the second letter. Every sentence must be a last sentence. It's raining
again.

My flesh belongs to your teeth.

A trace leaves us behind.

Patience. It won't be long now. B. lies in the slaughter room. A. has heard him. A. h
eard him, soft, softer and almost without a voice, after two and a half hours through ba
throom tile, and through the thin wall, to the right, to the right of his room. A. heard hi
m, once. The water was moving. And the sound

stays gentle because

a rind might appear slowly like a second
in the middle of the wound

in our names. Until each word can pass through flesh, through veins and six inflections
nearly torn, through the reddened parts of B.'s skin, later. Out of the dark, into the nigh
t. A. held him. He helped him back to the second floor, with his left arm around B.'s hi
ps, and his right hand on B.'s left shoulder. Past the Floral Wreath room, up the stairs;
past the cage that A. had built for Jakob, according to his hunger and the imagination
that follows, i.e., according to the measurements of his body, and according to the sha
pe of a day that didn't come. The iron and light-coloured wood: disassembled in six
parts by the door, to the right of the slaughter room. It must have been 10:49 PM.
Somewhere, someone is singing a song, which B. can't hear anymore. The German verb
verschwinden has three meanings.

How you taste.

As if language could only ascertain.

When you're here with me. In this room, the radio is a red dot; as always. *One has*
to know when
to end and I
know it I know how

I want
to end I know
a piece of me will stay with you.
You'll see. This

is not a beginning. 3:27 AM. The room in which A.'s mother used to sleep: nameless ac
ross the hall. A. lies on his bed, on the white folded cover. To his left, against the wall:
a steering wheel following the direction of leather, which imitates another direction, and
on which a brown wooden rosary hangs, to the right of the badge of the First Company
of the 52nd Armoured Infantry Battalion of Rotenburg, next to two certificates and two

newspaper clippings behind glass, above a metal sign; *Mercedes parking only. All others will be towed*, on the beige wallpaper with concentric circles on it. *I waited.* A. continues readin g. *I have waited.* His right hand: flat on his chest. *I thought this*
would never end.

We divide a shadow.
The hours   don't count.
The white plastic bag is in the conservatory. For three days, B. said: *Eat*

slowly. For three days, he said:

You've got
such a beautiful
big mouth which
shows
your teeth
all the way to the sides. He could only say it to him. There was nobody else he could say th is to. Only to A. did he say: *You have to grind my bones.* Only to him did he say: *That depends on you. I want to watch you biting*   *chunks out of my chest.* For three days, he sai d: *chew first, don't*   *just swallow. Chew first*

chew through first. A. doesn't hear the rain. He had laid another cover over B. He left the door to the slaughter room open. We wait on our knees. We pray on our knees. We rea d on our knees; until there is nothing left for us to wait for. The wound has stopped ble eding. The mattresses still lie against the angled roof. On the floor: three wooden boards from a white closet. B.'s forehead: against the black wall; because there are things we ca n't even say in the dark, on this evening that won't be an evening but a— 33 days ago i t was Monday, once. 33 days ago it was always February. 33 days ago B. didn't know th ere could be an answer to his hunger. 33 days ago B. wrote in the Nullo forum: *I am offe ring myself. I am offering myself to be eaten alive. Whoever really wants to do it will need a—* there must be a language that shows and hides nothing; that turns, each phrase, that has aband oned every image; that bears what we can't bear anymore. That knows: a body is not a border; that understands how it submits; how it succumbs. The fields we touch, touch us back. It's Saturday. Our hunger doesn't belong to us.
March 10, 2001.
The third meaning of *verschwinden* is: to cease existing.

Third verse: a day is divided into two halves; like a year that is distant; like a yea
r placed into both hands, with months parcelled out by weight, left and right. Until thos
e hands no longer hold. December. 1998. In his desk, stacked in the third drawer: eleven
issues. *Gay Boy. Playgirl. Männer Model.* It's Wednesday, again; after 11 PM. A. sits in his
study. A. doesn't turn the page. On the left: a man fucking someone's mouth. On the ri
ght, in front of six palm trees and a smoothed sea: another man; the orange light from
the desk lamp is lying on the magazine like a circle. The paper reflects it, low like another
sun. A. cuts him: out, slowly and bent slightly forward, with the scissors in his left hand
beneath the calendar; along the thigh, his muscle; around the hanging arms, and his nec
k. A.'s mother is sleeping. A. knows that. *Get up. Clean. Do laundry. Feed mother. Into the cit*
y, to work. Call mother. Grocery shopping afterwards. Drive back. Change her diapers. Wash mother.
Bring her food. Take her wet bedsheets downstairs. Remake the bed. Lift mother into the bed. Turn o
n the computer. Open magazines. Cut. Dismember. Dissect. Sleep. At the end of a long day

comes a day. A. places the body on the black paper. A. puts the refrigerator grill on top.
A. takes a Polaroid. He looks at the picture against the light. A. pastes it into the blue f
older. He rests his forehead against the steel. We will have spoken about
the innermost things. But an evening reveals itself in seconds. And a night: replaces ano
ther.

3:31 AM. A. hears the fall one floor above. B.: on the ground; to the left of the
wooden boards, and the table. We read in a wrong direction. *There's no way back. No way*
but forward.

Between your teeth *and further on through.*
Through your mouth.

•

A verse is a plea; a verse is the thing that breaks, and the breaking itself; a broken second;
until our hand has become another hand, and late, on the back, on the reverse side of e
ach word, between their curvature and this night. A. puts the apron on. It's March, still.

In this room, it is quiet.

Here, in this house, there are three levels.

25 rooms were guest rooms. A.'s parents had furnished them: with a sink, with
a soap dispenser, with a grey towel; with a double bed and a dark double-doored closet,
for the guests who never came. A.'s mother worked as a cosmetics advisor for Avon, b
efore she went to Electrolux to sell vacuum cleaners, radios, televisions; his father was
a policeman. It's 4:18 A M, and the manor is falling apart. It was already falling apart wh
en they bought it at an auction, 37 years ago. A. and his mother knew hunger, which th
ey named *Hunger*, after his father had left; they have seen it, in the evening, between her
warm fingers made thinner by each passing month, so that every sound might be remov
ed more easily, easier than in his imagination. A. is standing here. The knives: on the be
d, in a row. The rubber mallet: to their left; beside the freezer bags and the meat grinder
to their left again, in front of the circle, dry, dark and wider than a curved back, after th
e remains another hour had collected, folds, two pillows, two sheets; the last traces of a
wound. In this area, B. is lying on the table. In this area, he breathes shallowly. Here, in
this area, under the slow light of the neon tubes above them, A. does not see his ribcage
moving. A verse is a plea.

A. takes the four-stranded rope.

He ties B.'s hands and feet.

He labels the second video tape with a black pen. He points the camera at his
upper body. He speaks to him. He waits. There are things we only say in the dark. There
are things we don't say in the dark. There are things we can only say in brackets; there
are things we will only have spoken into them; like a sentence held between two hands,
between the left and right hand, like a face before a kiss. A. sees the marks on B.'s right
thigh, low and almost, on the left side of his chest, on his right forearm. His upper and
lower jaw: there, on B.'s softened skin, cold from the water, like two red rinds or two h
alves of a zero, split in the middle. A bracket holds something together: this sentence,
which would break, which would collapse without it; a sentence, weak and alone, which
would fall apart without both of our hands placed on its cheeks. A.'s apron consists of
a transparent plastic mattress protector attached with eleven safety-pins to a white cloth
apron, and the army belt that holds it. A. turns the camera on again. He's standing to
B.'s left. He says his name. He kisses his mouth. *Cator, March 10, 2001. 2/3*. It is possible
to wait 43 years for 18 hours and one minute, or 38 years: for one day. Maybe this is ho
w to speak of the first hunger.

A. hears it.

A. can hear it.

Every form presupposes substance. A. doesn't see B.'s lips; he doesn't see them moving, barely, like a detail. A. waits. A. puts his index and middle fingers into the curve between B.'s neck muscle and his trachea. A. can't feel a pulse. He folds his hands. He prays, before letting them hang; as if they were incidental skin, torn off and of no meani
ngful weight, after he said: *Lord. Forgive him.* After he said: *Father. Father, please*

forgive me.
A. takes the knife from the mattress, from
the left of   the other
knives 16
centimetres of steel A. uses
his right hand to move
B.'s head
to the right A.
puts the knife beside his face.
A. waits.
A. prays.
A. applies   the blade once more high
on B.'s throat over   his larynx like
a gesture   passing through
verbs and out   the other side so that
A.   can see the knife again
and again through   his muscles A. sees
the narrow   region made of
tissue of fibres   and sinew like a second
bound up A. pulls the knife from the flesh A. pushes
again into the   most precise passage
from which no sentence will come slowly
A.   cuts B.'s throat with seven strokes; until each cut will— a ve
rse remains a plea. In German, the verb *verschwinden* has two meanings. A. opens B.'s ne
ck.

In this light, his blood is gentle.

The second meaning of *verschwinden* is: to dissolve, into nothing.

Fourth verse: it will always have been September. Atzelrode Cemetery, 1999. T
hey recorded the funeral on tape. A.'s older brother is a pastor. He gave the eulogy after
Bach had been played from the cassette recorder on the table, *My Bonds are Broken*. The
wind arranges the grass in one direction; here, on this hillside, in the shadow of those t
rees. A. stands to the right of his brother, in front of their mother's grave, in front of h
er gravestone, on which her name is written, like the dates beneath her picture, because
a face is only a face, even on white marble no sun divides. The photo is a circle. A. holds
the glue in his left hand, and the statue his brother bought in Cairo, Anubis, in his right.
The stone is bright, brighter than yesterday; 40 centimetres. And the branches: move.
The branches: are moving. A. knows: that you can touch a body. A. knows: that there i
s skin that will distinguish us from tomorrow. A. knows: *now   I am
alone. Now   everyone has left me.* His mother died 20 days ago. 20 days ag
o: A. was in Kassel, and his brother in Egypt. 20 days ago: her beige blanket with the p
eacock-eye pattern lay half on the floor. A.'s mother didn't want last rites. She was not
laid out. But the branches: still move. The branches: keep on moving. A. applies the glu
e to the flat top of the gravestone. He sees the light reflecting off the liquid. He places
Anubis in the centre. It must be after 2 PM. There are   so many songs
that do not sing about our arms. But this language: speaks of them.

*I felt anger, anger and happiness at the same time. I hated myself. Because I wanted to do it.
Because I was doing it. And I hated him, because he came to me, because it was me he had come to. M
y happiness was indescribable. Everything was exactly how he wanted, the way he wanted it to be.*

The camera is a red dot.

A. hears the spine.

DEMATERIALISATION

MUTT-LON

tr. RACHAEL MCGILL

FROM THE FRENCH

An excerpt from –
Ceux qui sortent dans la nuit,
2013

This is how I became the first male *ewusu* in our lineage for over a century.

Grandmother Mispa, devastated by the failure of her project, had agreed to my demand more readily than I'd expected. The fact that she'd *talked*, by sharing her story with me, was evidence that she expected nothing more from life. By talking, she'd violated the most fundamental rule of the shadowy world that had practically brought her up. Since my sister Dodo's disappearance, though, Mispa had lost interest in everything. Her depression had worked in my favour. Thinking back to the evening I'd sat in her kitchen, smouldering with suppressed fury, and grilled her for information, I still tremble to think what could have happened to me had Mispa been on her usual form. She would've dismissed my questions, I would've forced the issue, she would've acted to silence me. With more than 60 years of practice, she could have liberated her *ewusu* spirit just by concentrating for 10 seconds. I would no longer be of this world.

Fortunately for me, Mispa's low mood had the effect of bestowing on her a touch more humanity. Not only had she spared me, she'd revealed everything. I now knew *who* I was looking for. An unexpected vestige of family feeling had sensitised my grandmother to my plight and she'd also agreed to initiate me, with the aid of her nine concoctions, into the world of the *ewusus*. I now knew *how* to look for my target. Whether Mispa would have agreed to transmit her powers to me if she'd known what I wanted them for was a different question.

I wanted them for one thing only: to avenge Dodo's murder. My plan had been to first identify all those who had contributed to the elimination of my sister, then to find ways to punish them. After hearing Mispa's story, I no longer needed to search for the guilty parties: I knew every one of them personally, and most were within easy reach. Thanks to Mispa's confidences and my new initiated status, I also knew two important facts: firstly, that Dodo's executioners had not acted for personal reasons; and secondly, that the deacon and his acolytes in the village were protected by two years of immunity. As a condition of my initiation, I'd had to promise to take no action against them. Mispa had perhaps been more cunning than I'd at first thought: through this pact she'd succeeded, for the time being, in protecting our clan from internal conflict. But there was one person I was still free to target: the Yaoundé patriarch, Ada.

I remained in the village for another month, engaged in a sort of accelerated training programme. My first nocturnal outings were a revelation. My scientific and Christian education had taught me to be sceptical of the very possibility of human beings possessing capacities like those I was now discovering. Colonisation and evangelisation, we were constantly told, had wiped out our barbarous indigenous customs. I would still be sceptical today if I hadn't myself experienced passing through a closed window and jumping from treetop to treetop. It was agonising not to be able to share these discoveries with anyone else.

I felt more invulnerable with every night that passed. But whenever Mispa joined me at the top of a mango tree, just watching the way she moved brought my humility back. It was incredible to see an old woman, who in daylight was never without her cane, leaping over bushes, rocketing from place to place, levitating above rooftops. When she patrolled the village at night, Mispa seemed truly alive. The gulf between her proficiency and my own was so large that, despite my fierce determination, I had moments of doubt about the success of my project. If old Ada also recovered all the vigour of his youth the moment night fell, our confrontation would be explosive. I would certainly come off the worse. It was a discouraging thought, but there was no question of abandoning my plan. I hadn't become an *ewusu* just to gaze in envy on others.

In the daytimes I wandered around the village, looking at every inhabitant with new eyes. Some still cast hostile glances in my direction, but most had softened towards me since my display of raw emotion at Dodo's funeral. They began to invite me into their houses again. When I managed to get up early, it was Betehe who entreated me to drink palm wine with him. At midday, it was Ngo Bayi or Ngo Moussi who invited me to eat *ndolé* with them. Ngo Moussi was 22, with a beautiful face, breasts like pears and a behind that would fluster a monk. I knew every one of the village dignitaries entertained fantasies about her. When I saw the young men swarming around her, the huntsmen who claimed to have caught nothing in their traps sneaking off to leave a hedgehog in her kitchen, even the pastor begging her to join the choir, I could only pity them. Those poor idiots had no idea that Ngo Moussi was a fearless *ewusu*. When they crept out at night to knock at her window, she was watching them from the top of a coconut tree.

In the evenings, I ate my plantain ragout with mother Lydia, or visited old Lingom if he had a spare serving of adder. Old Lingom was considered by everyone in the village to be a sorcerer. He did have a goatee beard, deep-set eyes beneath bushy eyebrows, stubs for teeth and skin as wrinkled as a tortoise's, and he always went barefoot. I suppose he corresponded to the popular perception of what a sorcerer looks like. In fact, old Lingom was a kind soul with no evil in him at all, apart from the odd little (alleged) theft from other people's fields. After my initiation, I felt privileged to see the village and its inhabitants as they really were. When I went to church on Sundays, I looked at the stooped old deacon, who for nearly sixty years had stood at the church door before mass, taken the collection box down the aisles, held out the basket of communion wafers, and knew it was he who was the sorcerer. He was an *ewusu* with a long and active nocturnal career behind him. He'd murdered a young woman in cold blood. Whenever I met him, I greeted him courteously, while praying silently to God that he wouldn't die before his period of immunity was over, so I could have the pleasure of turning him to couscous myself. He had experience on his side, but I had motivation and the advantage of surprise. While I waited for that day, I had other things to be getting on with.

As I criss-crossed the village, greeting some, sharing food with others, I marvelled at how little I'd known about people I'd thought I was close to. Now it was no longer me who was ignorant of the truth, but those I talked to, who had no inkling of my real thoughts. Only a select few in our village knew that the town hall truck only remained in circulation because Dodo had rescued it, at the same time revealing ultra-confidential information. I'd joined the ranks of the few who had access to extra intelligence.

I was enjoying the peace of the countryside, but after a few too many sweltering nights, I decided it was time to return to Youndé. The annual leave I'd taken had run out 10 days before.

To extend it, I converted it into sick leave, with the help of an unblemished health insurance record and one of the many doctors in our health centres prepared to strike a deal. Without wasting another moment, I launched myself into my project. I'd estimated that two reconnaissance expeditions in the vicinity of Ada's house would be enough to give me an idea of his habits. This was made easier by the fact that Ada lived on Many Ewondo Street, just as I did. All I had to do was cross the road, walk down towards Ahmadou Ahidjo Square, and I was outside his door. The thought that, the night they'd murdered my sister, I'd been fast asleep a couple of blocks away, made my blood boil. Perhaps Dodo had even passed over my roof during her final night raid, on her way to see Ada, already surrounded by her executioners. I was prepared to understand the need for the *ewusus* to follow codes and rules, but I could not accept the elimination of Dodo. Someone had to pay, and until the time came when I could attack the deacon, that person was going to be Ada.

I'd examined the problem from every angle and reached the conclusion that my only chance of beating the man would be to attack his physical body. If I tried to engage him in a duel in a tree, he would crush me immediately. The easiest thing would be to wait for him to leave on an astral voyage, locate the physical body he'd left inert, in his room, and cover it from head to foot in pepper. Ada would then be trapped in the air, and would die after ten days of separation from his body. It was perhaps not the most chivalrous of battle tactics, but one cowardly act deserved another.

My stakeouts were extremely informative. On the first night, Ada left the house at 22:15 and went in the direction of Mfoundi. He met with three other *ewusus* beneath the railway bridge and they dived into the tunnel that passes under Ministry building No 1. Unwilling to risk following them into the tunnel, I went back to wait outside Ada's house. He returned at 23:08. On the second night, he didn't go out, so I was forced to repeat my surveillance the next day. This time, he left at 23:50 and went towards Kennedy Avenue. He entered the Shell building, where whole floors are disused. Five minutes later, he came back out, looking to left and right. I had to squint to recognise him: he'd retaken a human form, and he looked years younger. When he bought a cigarette and had someone light it for him, I was forced to accept the improbable truth: Ada was visible to normal people and capable of interaction with them. He continued on foot, with an easy, relaxed stride, towards the central market. He was whistling. He went into a trendy nightclub. It was a Saturday night, and there were so many young people queuing to enter the place you'd have thought it was a polling station. I waited on top of a hotel opposite. About half an hour later, Ada emerged holding the hand of a young woman who couldn't have been more than 20. She seemed completely enamoured of him, unless it was just the alcohol she'd consumed. When they'd had enough of embracing on the pavement, they jumped into a taxi. Instead of following them, I returned to wait outside Ada's house. It was two hours before he came home. He was alone and had retaken his *ewusu* form. It was 02:47.

My grandmother hadn't told me everything about the powers of the *ewusus*. She'd focussed on how one first became an *ewusu*, so I could better understand my sister's trajectory. On the subject of her own later experiences, she'd been much more oblique. Thanks to my observation of Ada, I now knew there were *ewusus* who could reincarnate themselves at some distance from their physical body, become younger, and mix with ordinary people. It sent shivers down my spine. I tried to imagine Mispa heading to Douala every night, disappearing down a cul-de-sac in the Angel Raphael district, regaining the striking appearance she'd had at 20 and going dancing in a club. She'd certainly be a hit with the students.

It was time for me to act. My stakeouts had established that Ada would be a challenging adversary, that I should definitely abandon any hope of equality in the balance of power between us. My first idea still seemed the best. I spent a whole day buying up large quantities of red pepper, which I crushed in a blender. Wearing gloves, I put the resulting paste into a plastic bottle. Before night fell, I stashed the bottle in a gutter near the home of my target. I lingered for a few moments at a newsstand, imagining the headlines in 11 days' time, every title announcing the death of Jean-Paul Ada, Ewondo patriarch, Captain of the Order of Merit, Professor of physical sciences and honorary member of three sporting federations. He would be eulogised by all. The *essani*, a warrior dance reserved for the most important members of his tribe, would be performed in his memory. The country's prominent citizens would scramble to express their condolences at his funeral. No one would imagine it was Alain Nsona, a nobody, who'd brought down the great man. In a matter of hours, Dodo would be avenged.

Night fell with encouraging swiftness. When I took my place at my habitual vantage point opposite Ada's house, Many Ewondo Street was still buzzing with the whole array of recreational activities for which it was so well known. Street traders selling whisky in sachets or pirate CDs weaved their way between women selling doughnuts or grilling fish and their throngs of customers. Even the children hawking kola nuts and roasted peanuts were still there with their trays, working the tables of the terrace bars, where hookers disguised as waitresses concentrated for the moment on serving drinks to their rowdy customers. Music poured from the speakers of innumerable bars and mingled into a cacophony of sound that was ignored by everyone.

From my hidden perch, I wondered whether Ada might not come out this evening, or not until very late. However this was not my greatest concern.

Of all men, polygamists are paradoxically the least likely to share their sleeping quarters with women. All seem to be agreed on the best arrangement: they give their spouses private rooms at opposite corners of the living space and choose a room at the centre for themselves. They then go alternately to join one or other of their wives: the cold, embittered one who was the first to arrive, the sex-crazed gossip who came next, the vain one who turned up after that and against whom the first two sometimes conspire, the affected one with the bleached skin who thought she was the last until the young illiterate appeared to incite the scorn of the whole of the rest of the harem. A serious polygamist obeys two important rules: he encourages rivalry, animosity even, between his spouses, and he always keeps a room for himself, which, to keeps things fair, none of the spouses is permitted to enter. It was this room I would need to locate as quickly as possible after Ada left the house: it was where his physical body was most likely to be. This would be no mean feat. Along with his wives, Ada still had three daughters living at home, one with her husband, and seven grandchildren.

Ada appeared at 23:35. There was a chill in the air and the pavements had emptied. On the terraces, the waitresses were turning their attention away from the drinks and towards the customers. Ada seemed more alert than ever. He went in the direction of the health centre, then, at the crossroads, took a darker, quieter road to the left. I tailed him for a while, keeping my distance. When he crossed Gros Bonnet Boulevard and headed towards Germaine Avenue, I decided it was time to beat my retreat. The coast was clear. I judged I had at least an hour in which to find Ada's room and embalm him.

I entered Ada's palatial abode as if I were entering a church, my bottle of pepper paste gripped beneath my armpit.

During my reconnaissance missions, I'd never observed any other *ewusu* activity, so I proceeded from the assumption that Ada was the only *ewusu* in the house. The place was dark apart from a light coming from the living room on the ground floor. Two boys of around 12, the only people still awake, were concentrating intently on a porn film that was playing on a cable channel with the sound muted. I left them to their studies and moved upstairs. Four bedrooms later, I still hadn't found the sleeping body of Ada, but had become acquainted with those of his daughters. A sudden intuition caused me to go back downstairs: a room on the ground floor would be more suitable for a man of Ada's advanced years. I hit on the room I was looking for at the end of the first corridor.

It was a very large room. I scanned it quickly. Beside the door was a table stacked with books and papers. A soft armchair and a side table were positioned in front of a large television with its red power light still illuminated. A heavy curtain had been drawn across the blinds of a window that seemed to look on to the wall opposite. A low table held a coffee machine, mineral water, two cups and the means to prepare various brews. A white mosquito net fell from the canopy of a large, old-fashioned four-poster bed. Through the fine mesh of the net, I saw him. He was lying on his back, his arms thrown out beside his body, his chin lifted, a severe expression on his face. He was within touching distance. All I had to do was put on my gloves, open my bottle and daub him with pepper. He would be mummified. As I reached out to pull the mosquito net aside, a shiver travelled down my spine. A ghostly voice spoke in my ear.

'I've been waiting for you.'

I jumped to one side, pulse racing. The bottle fell from my hands and rolled towards the entrance to the bathroom. For about 10 seconds, which seemed to stretch out endlessly, I felt a bizarre sort of bliss. Then the terror gripped me. Ada calmly collected my bottle of pepper. He brought it to his nose and sniffed it, then he turned and moved towards me. I prepared to take my final breath.

'Here, take your bottle and carry on with your work,' he said, almost jovial.

'But...'

'Don't mind me. Act as if I was in the bed. Go on, smear me with pepper.'

'Please, stop making fun of me, and – '

I didn't finish my sentence. With lightning speed, Ada grabbed me by the throat and hurled me against a wall.

'Who sent you? Speak!' he growled, jutting his chin towards me.

I was so terrified I didn't even feel pain as he compressed my carotid arteries with his iron grip. All I could manage by way of response was to cough in his face. He threw me to the ground. I found myself under the table with the pile of papers on top of me. Ada towered above me, his eyes glowing like fireflies. I scrambled to my feet.

'Who are you, young man?'

'...'

What could I say? I'd missed my target and was about to become the latest victim of the formidable Ada. I'd be discovered, lifeless, in my bed, the next morning, or later, with ants crawling out of my nostrils. No one would ever know what had happened. I thought of my two daughters. What a ridiculous way to die! My moment of introspection was brief.

'Give me one good reason I should let you live,' said Ada. He moved softly towards me.

'I want to live!' I exclaimed.

'That's not enough.'

'I'm Alain. Mispa's grandson.'

He jumped in shock. 'That's impossible!'

'I am! I'm Dodo's older brother. Mispa can confirm it.'

'So she's the one who sent you?'

'No. She doesn't know anything about it.'

'If you're here tonight, that can only mean one thing: Mispa *talked*.'

'Er...'

'Mispa talked,' he repeated gravely. After a few seconds of silence, he said, 'You're free.'

'What?'

'You're free to leave. Take your bottle of pepper and get out of my house.'

BAAL

ENRICO REMMERT
tr. ANTONELLA LETTIERI

FROM THE ITALIAN

The bar in the square, like the rest of the village, was dirty and shabby. We were sitting outside, where the owners had arranged a couple of sun umbrellas and half a dozen white plastic tables, as grimy as the chairs that surrounded them. A man and four women, all well over sixty, were sitting at the table next to ours. I studied the women: they were all wearing their Sunday best, long skirts and dark jackets of a cotton so threadbare that it sagged on their bodies. On their feet they had black shoes that looked soft, very similar to slippers, and flesh-coloured knee-highs that must have been torture in that heat. Nobody was talking.

Fabricino and I weren't talking either. We were each drinking from a bottle of Moretti. I was smoking Winstons slowly, the heat was making my head spin and I could feel drops of sweat slide from my forehead down my neck and then disappear, absorbed by the cotton of my t-shirt.

'Let me make it quite clear that I can't give you anything,' said Fabricino, staring at me.

He was a stocky man, roughly 50, his stubby hands clenched around the empty beer bottle. His nose was as thick as a bulb and his face round and flabby. His eyes, however, were beautiful, a bluish grey, intense and aloof at the same time.

'I'll give you room and board,' he continued. 'But nothing else. When you're bored, you can go.'

I just nodded.

'Understood?' he asked.

He reached his arm across the table and I shook his hand.

The breeding kennel was in the middle of a flat area. All around, fields as far as the eye could see, sun-scorched grass, flies and mugginess. Fabricino's pick-up left the motorway and took a dusty dirt road bordered by two dried-up ditches. The air was hot as in a desert, at the edge of the road some poppies lit up the weeds with red. And yet, despite everything giving off a sense of desolation, I felt it was the perfect place for me to play at my jigsaw of lost pieces, to disappear until the dust settled. I'd go back to the city at the end of winter: even if it was less than an hour away on the train, it felt like being on another planet.

Fabricino's place was an old two-storey cottage with

a roof of curved tiles that was sagging worryingly on one side. There were two entrances, on the left and on the right, and a small balcony with aluminium railings that looked relatively new. In front of the house there was a huge fenced rectangle of grass enclosed on the right by a long and squat hut that in the past might have been a pigsty or a chicken coop. At one end of the hut, there was a pen within the pen and a huge pit bull, the colour of a cigar, thrashed about inside it. Two more pit bulls were inside the large pen, lying down like sphinxes, their tongues lolling because of the heat. When we got out of the pickup, they stood up and came towards us right up to the wire net. They were barking and I was pretty scared – I still knew nothing about dogs then – but they looked happy to see us. Fabricino put his right hand through a small opening cut in the wire net and the pit bulls stood on their hind legs to be stroked. The dog in the inner pen, on the other hand, was growling, he had huge jaws and was so big and sinewy that he looked like he was of a different breed from the others, more perfect and meaner.

I followed Fabricino along the edge of the lot and we ended up behind the pigsty. There were six more pens side by side, long and narrow, that were half covered by the roof of the building and half outside. The smell of dog was very strong, I had to stop myself from retching. 'You'll get used to it,' said Fabricino.

We walked past the first two pens, which were empty, and in each of the other four we found a pit bull barking joyfully. I'd always been under the impression that pit bulls were a very aggressive breed and so I was surprised by how friendly they were.

Fabricino dispensed some hasty pats, then led the way towards the house. He unlocked the reinforced door on the right by turning the key four times and we went in. There was a nauseating smell, the floor was covered in grass and soil and there was dust everywhere.

'You'll stay upstairs,' he said.

We went up the stone stairs and it was even dirtier upstairs than it was below. There was a calendar stuck at December 2009 hanging on the wall.

Fabricino flung open the door to the bathroom, which was

big and covered in cobwebs, then showed me the room opposite: inside, there was only a wooden double bed, in a reasonable state, and a French window that led to the small balcony. I opened it fully and a wave of humid heat came into the room. Fabricino ran a finger along the headboard and showed me the fingertip grey with dust.

'The rules are simple. You're up here. You have your room and your bathroom. I'm downstairs and you mustn't set foot there. Downstairs you're only allowed into the kitchen, when we're eating. You'll find everything you need to clean under the sinks.'

'Got it,' I said, putting my rucksack down on the mattress.

Fabricino shook his head: 'I'm no chatterbox, but you, son, you're basically mute.'

I smiled, out of embarrassment.

'Thanks,' I said. 'I don't know how to thank you.'

He stared at me: 'I do. Get to work.'

I went down to the kitchen and opened the cupboard under the sink. I took some rags, disinfectant, cleaner. The detergent bottle said FOR ALL SURFACES. As I wiped away months or perhaps years of neglect, I couldn't stop thinking about the situation I was getting myself into. Two hours later, I was so tired and exhausted by the heat I couldn't think about anything, I wasn't sad or scared, I realised I wanted to see how things would turn out, and so I needn't do anything else but wait. A tenuous but lukewarm trickle confirmed that the shower worked, but just as I had decided to get in I heard Fabricino shout from below.

I ran downstairs, breathless, as if I were late for something.

'Come with me,' he said.

First of all, he made me fill two huge watering cans at the outside tap. Then he walked towards the gate of the main pen, which was locked with a padlock as big as a cigarette packet. He fumbled for a bit, then opened it with a key that he kept around his neck, hanging from one of those lanyards with a clip that people wear at trade shows or concerts.

'Get in, quick,' he ordered.

The two pit bulls stood there in front of us, barking, but I didn't want to show that I was scared, so I went in. He closed the gate behind me and stayed outside. When I realised, my heart skipped a beat. I put down the two watering cans to protect my legs, the dogs were jumping around me, they were standing on their hind legs and putting their muzzles and tongues on my trousers and on my t-shirt, I froze. Fabricino slipped inside, shouting the names of the dogs – Sid! Ala! – and they calmed down as if it was a magic trick. Suddenly the huge pit bull, the one in the inner pen, started growling furiously. He shoved his muzzle and teeth against the wire net and looked like he could tear through it with one bite. Fabricino didn't so much as look at him.

There were some metal bowls in the shade, in front of the hut, they looked like small flying saucers ready to take off into the sky. We filled them with water and the two dogs started drinking noisily. I'd been in there only for a few minutes and I was already done with it.

We went to the back of the pigsty and repeated the procedure. I learned the names of the other dogs. All three-letter names.

'What's the large pit bull called?' I asked.

Fabricino was finishing emptying his funnel into the last bowl. He shrugged: 'That's not a pit bull. That's Baal.'

Later, while we were sharing half a kilo of spaghetti for dinner, Fabricino started talking about Baal. More than just telling me about him, he warned me.

'All my dogs have excellent bloodlines, apart from Baal. He's a mix between a pit bull and a Neapolitan mastiff, a bandog.'

I stared at my fork coiling up the spaghetti as if it was guided by the hand of a stranger.

'You see, pit bulls are nasty towards one another and other dogs, they don't accept submission. You need to keep them away from children, of course, especially the younger ones, those who don't smell yet of human. But it's rare for them to attack an adult: they *live* for people.'

I waited for him to continue, but he didn't.

'Whereas Baal?' I asked.

'He's a killer,' he said, faking indifference but making a poor job of it.

'Son,' he continued pensively, 'anything you've ever heard about dogs, it doesn't apply to him, so just forget about it. Baal is an unhinged dog. Even among so-called normal people, every now and again there's a homicidal maniac. Baal is the dog version of that. I built the inner pen last November: I needed to keep him completely isolated from the others. When I put him in the large pen with a female pit bull, he killed her right away, I didn't even have time to do anything. He was wrecking everything, snapping his chains off...'

I stared at him.

'He's ruthless with other dogs, just like all pit bulls,' he continued, 'but he's also ruthless with people, just like all mastiffs. You must never go anywhere near him. If you go into his pen, he'll tear you to pieces. If you try to feed him, he'll tear you to pieces. That dog respects only me.'

'Why don't you give him away?' I asked, wiping my mouth with a paper napkin of such poor quality it was barely there.

Fabricino shook his head.

We threw the plastic plates in the bin and I washed the pots and the cutlery. Then I joined Fabricino outside. He was sitting on a wicker chair, smoking, I couldn't see any other chairs around so I took one from the kitchen. I went back outside and put it down one metre from his. I lit a cigarette.

'You need to defrost the meat for tomorrow,' said Fabricino after a while.

I wasn't happy to be treated like this in my thirties, as if I was a shopboy, but I had no choice. Something in my expression must have betrayed that thought as Fabricino's tone became gentler: 'There's a freezer in the storage room by the kitchen. Take three or four pieces of meat, the big ones, and put them in the fridge: there's a shelf for them, empty.'

I went into the kitchen and then into the storage room. I turned on the light. A dim bulb, hanging directly from the wire, dangled from the ceiling, feebly casting light on the concrete corridor. On the walls, there were dozens of rusty nails holding up tools of every kind: shears, pliers, jigsaws. On the right, there was an old chest freezer, just like the ones used for ice cream. I slowly slid one of the panels open, reached inside the coldness and pulled out the first thing that came to hand. At first

I didn't understand: it was oddly shaped, it looked like a whole rabbit, frozen, with fur and everything. I lifted it towards the bulb: it was a pit bull puppy. There were four more in the freezer.

I put the puppy back exactly where I'd found it and took a deep breath. Then I slid the other panel open: I found the meat, packed in thick vacuum bags. I took four packs and went to put them in the fridge in the kitchen. There was indeed a shelf for them, empty.

During the following weeks, I didn't mention the frozen puppies to Fabricino. I just did what he asked me to do. I'd go to the discount store with him to buy fresh meat and huge sacks of rice, as well as dry food and tins of every possible kind. I'd load everything onto the back of the pickup, it looked like it'd last for months, but it was all gone within a week. Three times a day I'd fill the water bowls and twice a day I'd prepare the food for the dogs, clear away their shit, check they didn't have fleas and, if I found any, I'd pull them off one by one, twisting them delicately with a cotton bud, then I'd put them into a paper tissue and set them on fire with my lighter and every flea would go poof, like a small, dull explosion.

Every day I'd let the pit bulls into the large pen for a couple of hours each, in turns, making sure to never put two males together. Over time, the dogs had grown used to me and, when I'd get one of them from behind the pigsty to take it to stretch its legs in the large pen, it'd always welcome me joyfully, pushing its front legs and its muzzle everywhere. Fabricino had taught me to listen to dogs – 'A dog howls to call, barks to converse, growls to warn and whimpers to complain' – and I was starting to be able to tell their voices apart.

At night, I'd lock the six pit bulls in their individual pens, behind the pigsty, and then I'd go and sit in front of the house and smoke a few cigarettes while I enjoyed the cool breeze, in spite of the relentless mosquitoes.

At that time, Fabricino would let Baal into the large pen. It was a fascinating and terrifying sight. Baal, who was more compact and sinewy than any other dog I'd ever seen before, gave off a supernatural energy. As soon as Fabricino let him loose, Baal would break into a frenzied run towards me, as if he'd been waiting for nothing else all day, and in a matter of seconds he'd reach the wire net. Then he'd stare at me through the mesh, growling, his eyes small and sunken, his huge jaws wide open revealing his blood-red gums and sharp white teeth, with four jutting canines like a tiger.

He'd stay there until Fabricino called him back. Then he'd run again headlong towards the old pigsty and start growling at the dogs locked inside, who would answer with feeble wails, as if they were even more scared than me.

Fabricino would leave Baal free to roam in the large pen all night, and he spent his time there convulsing from one end to the other, pissing everywhere to mark his territory and raising hell to show everyone who was boss.

I'd sleep with the French window open, but some nights the heat was relentless and I'd often get up and go out onto the small balcony to smoke. Every time I did, whether standing under the moonlight or in the light cast by the lamppost in front of the house, I was welcomed by the same scene: Baal, staring at me from the edge of the pen.

Fabricino introduced them as the Serbian 'twins' but they didn't look like twins at all to me. Sure, there was a strong resemblance, but it was clear that there was at least a couple of years between them. The younger brother was called Dejan, he was about a hundred and eighty-five centimetres tall and must have weighed at least one hundred kilos. The older brother was taller and had biceps as thick as my thighs. He introduced himself as Slobodan, but both his brother and Fabricino called him Slobo. The two brothers had the same army haircut, almost a buzz cut, and two anonymous faces lit up by small, piercing eyes, constantly searching for weaknesses.

They too bred dogs, Fabricino told me, so they did business together from time to time.

As a matter of fact, they'd come around often to check on Ala, one of Fabricino's female pit bulls, as she was pregnant by one of their champions and they'd agreed to share the litter. When they came, Fabricino would take Ala out of her pen and they'd start checking on her, stroking her skilfully, although she was wary and over the last few weeks Fabricino had ordered me to keep her isolated even when she was in the large pen. The two Serbs were very pleased, while Fabricino often sounded dejected: 'You never know until they're born. Ala's first litter was a disaster.' The two Serbs would touch wood to ward off the jinx and then leave.

Over dinner one night, Fabricino explained that, in a litter, it's quite normal to lose some of the puppies: 'Maybe she'll have seven or eight and two or three will die, but, worst case scenario, it could even be five, as happened to Ala.'

This was one of the many facts I'd learned about dogs. I'd become so involved with the dogs that, at night, I'd forget to call the city to find out if anything had changed, to the point that, over time, I'd even stopped carrying my phone around with me and would often leave it uncharged, somewhere in my room.

Those months of physical exercise got me in the habit of carrying out my tasks quicker and quicker, and, during the long intervals of free time between looking after the pit bulls, I started taking on as many chores as possible. I convinced Fabricino to buy some paint, took down all the shutters from the windows, rubbed them down one by one with sandpaper, and gave them all a coat of primer and two of gloss. When I was done with them, the glassy finish of the wood shone and the façade started to look less dilapidated. I'd mow the grass, trim the hedges, spend my time sweeping the flagstones in front of the house with the meticulousness of a soldier. Once all the rooms in the house, including the kitchen, looked spick and span, I whitewashed the façade. I was slim, nimble, sinewy and tanned. I didn't drink except for a couple of beers on Friday nights, when Fabricino would take me to the village to have a margherita pizza in the bar on the square, where Fabricino never talked to anyone and no one ever talked to him. At night, I'd collapse in bed exhausted by the hard work and the heat and, in the few lulls when I'd allow my head to think, I'd tell myself that I'd ended up in limbo, a sort of parallel dimension where only Fabricino and the dogs existed. And I was trying to disappear into that limbo, to make the loneliness and the sadness go away by forgetting everything, knowing that this was the only present possible now.

'You're definitely weird,' Fabricino said to me one night over dinner. 'No one ever comes to see you, no one ever calls. Don't you have any friends, a girlfriend?'

I stared at my plate.

'When your uncle asked me if I could take you on, I thought you'd be a different kind of guy.'

'What kind?' I asked, looking up.

The question caught him off guard. He slowly studied his nails, which were as thick as shells, and eventually shook his head: 'I don't know. Someone... Someone normal.'

We stared at each other for a bit. I remained locked inside my silence, I felt comfortable in my silence, I was getting used to it.

'I used to know your folks, you know,' he said, getting up.

He went outside and sat down in his usual wicker chair.

'Do you want to know my story, why I'm here?' I asked. Fabricino stared at me for a bit, then shook his head.

'No,' he said.

I did the washing up, then went to my room for the night. I turned my phone on, I didn't have a single missed call, a confirmation of sorts that Fabricino was right, that I was all alone in the world. But I knew that wasn't the case. Over the weeks, I'd realised that my sadness was losing its edges, fraying away. My loneliness was so perfect that it had stopped tensing my nerves and was now relaxing them instead. Sweating the day away was good for me and I felt there was something noble in all the loneliness, a set route, a sort of purification process of what I'd been.

While cleaning the basement, I found two crates of books, including dozens of novels by Agatha Christie, and at night I got used to falling asleep reading. That too was a way to remain suspended, to not think about anything, like a hermit trying to put as much distance as possible between himself and reality by condensing his life into small tasks.

There was only one moment, the briefest of moments between being awake and falling asleep, when the edges of what I'd done, the faces of the people I'd deceived and who were probably looking for me, would come to the surface of my mind. They'd never find me here, of that I was certain, and soon they'd lose all hope and give up.

At the end of summer, Ala had her puppies: there were eight of them and only one was stillborn. The others were all gorgeous: small, strong and soft all at the same time. I was very keen to keep by her side and help her out, but Fabricino told me to leave her alone, that she knew very well what needed doing.

The following evening, at dinner time, I found the four frozen puppies laid on the steel draining board by the sink. Fabricino was thawing them. I didn't feel like asking questions, especially since I was starting to guess what his plan was, and so we played cards for a bit and then I went to bed to read.

The next morning, Fabricino went into Ala's pen and put the four best-looking puppies in a cardboard box, which he then hid in the storage room. In their place in the litter he put the dead puppies, which by then had thawed. Though bewildered from the exhaustion of nursing the puppies, Ala didn't want them anywhere near her, kicked to keep them away from herself and the healthy puppies.

The 'twins' showed up less than three hours after Fabricino called them, driving an old Mercedes. As I opened the gate, Dejan, the younger of the two, noticed the tattoo on my left forearm and grabbed my wrist.

'I know where they make tattoos like this,' he said. 'I know where you was.'

It was a rudimentary tattoo with thick, blurry edges, the kind of tattoo you'd get in prison. That wasn't where I'd got it but I let him believe it was: I nodded as if we were sharing a secret. He let go of my wrist, unable to wipe off his face a smile of superiority and smugness.

That smile was stifled soon after, when he stood in front of the litter. The two brothers talked to each other in Serbian, handling the dead puppies, stroking them, dumbfounded. No one said anything for several minutes, Fabricino and I stood in a corner, completely still.

'You know the story of King Solomon?' asked Dejan after a while.

Fabricino looked at him suspiciously.

'So we have deal,' the Serb continued. 'I gave you my best dog and you gave me your best bitch. Same deal as always: up to five puppies, I choose the first and you keep others. More than five, I keep two puppies, first and third choice. But here there's three left. How do we share, Mr Fabrizio? I think we share like Solomon, with the sword.'

Fabricino was unfazed. 'Nonsense. You keep two puppies, I take the other one,' he said.

The two giants stared at him.

'Next time, though, you get one less puppy,' said Fabricino.

The two were kneeling next to the dead dogs. They stood up and came up to Fabricino, slapping him hard on the back approvingly and shaking his hand.

'This choice we like,' said Slobo. 'You choose your puppy,' he encouraged Fabricino.

Fabricino feigned hesitation but then chose the one that seemed to be more beautiful and stronger and left the two frailer ones for the Serbs. They made a deal: Fabricino would look after the puppies at least until they were weaned and the Serbs would come by from time to time to see how they were doing. Dejan and Slobo shook hands with him once more and slapped him, and me, hard on the back, then said they needed to be on their way. When the four of us were back in front of the house, Baal started growling from his pen even more furiously than usual. Slobo gave him the finger and jeered at him, while Dejan stared intently. Then they got in their car.

That night, Fabricino told me that dog fighting was allowed and very popular in the former Yugoslavia.

'There were plenty of fighting pits in Belgrade and sometimes they even had pit bulls fight in stadiums,' he said. 'At some point, they banned it all but that didn't change a thing.'

'When was this?'

'In '95.'

'At the end of the war?'

He looked up, astonished.

'You don't know about Sarajevo? Srebrenica?' I asked.

'It's their business,' he said curtly.

He went back to talking about dog fighting, but I had him figured out already: all the stories were just a diversion to avoid talking about what he'd done, how he'd conned Dejan and Slobo. Fabricino dismissed my disappointment with a shrug. 'Life can be cruel,' he said. 'In fact, nobody makes it out alive.'

A few weeks later, as agreed, the Serbs came to pick up the two puppies: even though they'd been weaned by the book, they were still frail and kind of ugly compared with the five puppies Fabricino had kept. He'd sold them a few days earlier to a dealer, pocketing three thousand five hundred euros.

And then it was autumn, the days were getting shorter, the air was chilly, I'd read all the whodunnits in the house and Poirot had become the person I exchanged thoughts with the most. I was increasingly glad not to be in touch with anyone but the dogs and Fabricino, and with him I only exchanged a few words over dinner and played cards. While it was true that probably no one was missing me, it was even truer that I missed no one.

I'd got very quick at taking care of all my chores and there was nothing left to repair or paint, so in my free time I'd taken to walking around the area, crossing fields and woods with Sid, my favourite pit bull, and more and more often I'd go as far as the village. After the business with the puppies, Fabricino had rewarded me with two hundred euros, which I'd added to the savings I had when I arrived. I only spent the bare minimum, I'd gone from smoking Winstons to loose tobacco, and my only other luxury was splurging every now and again on a Moretti at the bar in the square.

I'd sit there drinking for half an hour and then walk back to the kennels, almost a forty-minute stroll. I was not an outgoing kind of guy and nobody ever tried to strike up a conversation with me, only some old men from the village who would offer, from time to time, perfunctory comments about how beautiful my dog was, to which I replied both kindly and concisely.

The Serbs showed up very early one morning, it must have been half past seven. I was on the grass when I saw the front of the Mercedes stop in front of the gate and heard honking several times.

I went to let them in with a certain sense of embarrassment, but they'd not come by because of the con. They'd come for Baal.

They asked for Fabricino but as I was doing all the work now, he'd got into the habit of getting up late, even as late as 10, after being up until two or three in the morning watching sport. I explained this to them and asked them to come back later, but it didn't wash. The two Serbs sat in their car and waited for Fabricino to wake up.

When Fabricino came out of the house, they jumped out of the car, slapped him hard on the back and shook his hand, and he invited them both inside and asked me to make some coffee.

They sat around the table where we ate dinner every night. After a while, Dejan motioned something to his older brother, who opened his jacket and pulled from an inside pocket a wad of fifty euro notes, all crumpled. He put it down on the table and pushed it in front of Fabricino with the back of his hand.

'We're buying Baal,' said Dejan.

Fabricino shook his head. He took the wad and started counting the notes, but so half-heartedly that he threw them back onto the table half-way through.

'Four thousand,' said Slobo.

Fabricino shook his head again.

'What do you need him for?'

Slobo was about to answer but Dejan stopped him with a gesture of his hand: 'Baal's born for fight. We take him to fight. And we bet.'

Fabricino stood up abruptly. 'Finish your coffee and then go,' he said, leaving the room.

I found Fabricino in the inner pen. He'd shaved, which made his cheeks look saggier and waxier than usual, and he was playing with Baal, giving him commands, stroking him.

'Why won't you sell him?' I shouted from behind the wire net. Fabricino turned around to look at me but didn't answer.

'Four thousand,' I carried on. 'I'd sell him right away.'

Fabricino bent down to pick something up from the grass. He threw it at me with incredible precision, had the fence not been there it would've hit me right in the face: a bone.

At sunset one Friday night, when we were sitting in the bar on the square eating our pizzas as usual, something unusual happened: someone spoke to Fabricino.

An old man took a chair, pulled it up to our table and sat

down without saying a word. He was wearing an elegant suit, he had watery eyes and the skin on his nose was so taut it was white on the bridge.

'Good evening, professor,' Fabricino greeted him without warmth.

'Good evening to you, Fabrizio,' replied the other. Then he introduced himself to me and we shook hands.

The waitress, usually extremely slow, rushed to the professor to take his order, a coffee with sambuca.

The old man took half a Toscano cigar from his pocket, cupped his hands around a match and lit it, sucking in large puffs.

'It's six months now,' he said.

Looking more contemptuous than embarrassed, Fabricino said: 'I'll settle up in one go, professor, rest assured.'

The coffee with sambuca was delivered. The old man downed it in three consecutive gulps, then went back to his cigar.

'When?' he asked, standing up and tucking in his chair.

'By the end of the month,' replied Fabricino.

'Who was that man?' I asked Fabricino later.

Fabricino said that the man owned the house and that he was six months behind with the rent. I didn't ask any more questions.

When we got back to the kennels we realised there was something wrong. Instead of welcoming us back by barking furiously as usual, Baal was standing still by the gate in the fence. The headlights of the pick-up shone on him: behind him, in the middle of the grass, there was a huge white spot. We couldn't understand what it was, it looked like a big pillow had been ripped open.

We hurried out of the car and Fabricino checked the padlock, which was still secure in its place. He went inside the house to get the keys. I stood there, studying the ground in front of the fence: the headlights showed dozens of footprints and what looked like track marks. I couldn't figure out what had happened. The air was icy and piercing.

Fabricino came back with the keys and a black torch that

was longer than his forearm. He opened the gate and went in on his own, then led an unusually docile Baal into the inner pen. As usual, I stayed well away and only went in when the dog was locked up. At that point, Fabricino turned his torch on and headed towards the white spot in the middle of the grass, where I caught up with him.

A huge Maremma sheepdog, almost twice Baal's size, lay in the middle of a pool of blood.

I had to stop myself from retching. Fabricino pulled me away and I showed him the footprints in front of the gate. He shone his torch on them, then told me to go and park the pick-up.

I found him sitting at the kitchen table with a bottle of grappa and two glasses. We filled our glasses and started drinking, in silence.

'I really don't understand,' I said eventually.

Fabricino filled our glasses again, took a long sip, then shrugged: 'Bets.'

I still wasn't following.

'They know we leave the kennels unattended on Friday nights. They've been keeping an eye on us. So they came here with the sheepdog and took bets.'

'But who's they?'

Fabricino shrugged.

'And how did they manage to get the sheepdog in the pen? The padlock was untouched, wasn't it? Why didn't they cut it open?'

Fabricino moved his hand as if waving away a fly: 'As soon as they'd cut it, Baal would've torn them to pieces. Too dangerous, they couldn't do that.'

'So? Did they cut the fence somewhere?'

Fabricino shook his head: 'Impossible, for the same reason. As soon as they'd cut it, Baal would have got out and that would have been that.'

I was toying with the empty glass in my hands: 'So, how did they do it?'

'Did you see the track marks?' asked Fabricino.

'Yes.'

He lit a cigarette, it was the first time I saw him smoke in the house. 'I guess they must have come here with one of those tiny cranes, the kind they use for roadworks. They harnessed the dog, then lowered it beyond the fence. That's how the show started. Clearly it was worth their while.'

'There were plenty of them. And they took bets,' I said.

'Exactly.'

We had one more look around outside before heading off to bed. We checked the wire net: it was untouched. Then we shone the torch on the track marks again. Everything seemed to confirm Fabricino's theory.

'Who do you think did it?' I asked as we headed back inside.

'I thought you were smarter,' he said.

From that day, we never left the dogs unattended. When we needed to go shopping, only one of us would go, and the same went for every other errand or task. Of course we had to give up our little pizza ritual on Friday nights.

Life at the kennels resumed as before, the only difference being that the cold winter air made all tasks harder, so we did the bare minimum. The intervals when I had nothing to do grew longer and I spent my time in my room reading. Soon I'd been through all the books in the boxes, so I had to go back to those I'd initially discarded, some boring guides on Alpine herbs and also a manual on meditation, which I started reading warily and then couldn't put down.

It wasn't long until the Serbs showed up again.

It was a cooler morning than usual and a hazy mist made everything seem ethereal by blurring edges and distances. The sun was hiding behind the grey dome of the sky like a soap bar left in a tub full of dirty water. I was smoking on the balcony when I saw the Mercedes: on the right-hand side, it had a dent at least a metre wide that I hadn't noticed before. I ran downstairs to let them in.

I told them that Fabricino was still asleep, as usual, and that they'd be better off coming back in a couple of hours. The customary scene ensued: the two got back in their car, sat there with the engine and the heating running. Fabricino had become a very light sleeper, and after a few minutes he appeared at the door, wrapped up as if it was the Arctic, and invited everyone in.

After coffee, Dejan pulled out of his pocket a wad of notes

much larger than the previous one. He laid it on the table in front of Fabricino, there was no need to explain what they were after.

'Eight thousand,' said Slobo.

Fabricino scratched his head for a bit. I'd never have imagined it possible, but he looked like he was wavering. Then, as if fighting a battle against himself, he said: 'Baal is not for sale.'

The two brothers exchanged knowing smiles. Then Dejan pulled out of his pocket a piece of paper folded in four: he unfolded it on the table and handed it to Fabricino. It was handwritten, dated and signed.

'The professor sold us your debt,' said Dejan, pleased with himself. Fabricino's face was ashen. The notes were still in the middle of the table, like a deck of cards ready for a game. A few seconds went by before Fabricino lowered his eyes to the piece of paper and read it.

Then he pulled out of his inside pocket a large wallet of worn leather I'd never seen before. He opened the zip and took out a wad of fifty-euro notes. He counted them slowly in his hands once, then laid them on the table, next to the others, and counted them again in front of the brothers.

He wrote PAID on the piece of paper, then handed the pen to Dejan to countersign and Dejan, despite his disappointment, could not object.

In December, my tasks were reduced to the bare minimum. Throughout the day, I'd spend no more than two hours looking after the dogs and it was a special time. I'd grown fond of all the pit bulls, and Sid was my favourite by far. I'd even asked Fabricino if the dog could sleep in my room, a request he declined categorically, explaining that I should by no means grow attached to the dogs, though I was already well beyond attachment. I walked around the fields and the woods with Sid by my side, and I felt him close. He was special in his affection, fondness, and devotion, so much so that I'd even begun to think that heaven might even be real, but that it was a place where dogs, not people, deserved to go.

There was nothing left to do in the house: over the last few weeks, I'd carried out any improvement I could think of. I'd climbed on the roof several times to inspect it and, having realised that I didn't have the skills to repair it, I'd reinforced the beams in the attic by nailing boards and wedges in the spots that I thought looked dodgiest. The sagging in the tiles on one side of the roof was still the same, but I'd made sure that the water could run neatly towards the gutter so that we wouldn't get any leaks. I couldn't tell whether Fabricino was happy with my endless bustling about: if he was, he certainly hid it well.

At night, since I could not keep Sid by my side, I practiced meditation. Sometimes I'd imagine my body as the wick of a candle and my mind as a flame flooding the room with light: I'd see myself float cross-legged in the sky, rise towards the stratosphere with slow spiralling movements, while the house remained down below, just some fluorescent lines far away, until it disappeared altogether.

Every morning I'd chop some firewood for the three stoves in the house, which we'd feed regularly, only for a few hours a day, in the morning and at night. As the days went by, I grew more and more pleased with myself: I felt I was in peak physical condition, but above all I felt I was in a mental state that I'd never experienced before. I was no longer suffering from loneliness, I'd stopped asking myself questions about the future, I was completely calm and at peace with the way things were going. I felt ready to go back to the city and face the music without any fear, but at the same time I also wanted to stay. Living in close contact with the dogs, walking in the woods, breathing in air that was so different from the air of the city: I felt I was being flung upwards by the will to live.

A few days before Christmas, as forecast by the radio, we had heavy snowfall.

It started in the afternoon, with a uniform dome of grey where the sky should have been and tiny snowflakes that melted before reaching the ground. Then the flakes became bigger and thicker, it looked like a feather factory had exploded, and by 9 p.m. from the balcony I could barely see the lamppost in front of the house, which had become nothing but a blurred glow surrounded by the storm. I filled my lungs with clean air and went to sleep.

It snowed without any breaks throughout the following day and night. On the morning of the third day, I opened the French window and the view from the balcony was spellbinding: a white blanket, forty centimetres deep, covered everything. The sun was shining in a clear blue sky and everything was enveloped in silence. The dogs were calm in the shelter of the hut: they'd peek with curiosity at their rectangle of grass all covered with snow and, through the wire nets, they looked as surprised and fascinated as I was.

I shovelled snow all day long, freeing a big chunk of the large pen and even some of the space reserved for Baal. It was my first time in there. Of course, before letting me in, Fabricino had locked the bandog away in his box and, for as long as I was working in there, Baal wouldn't stop growling and barking at me with a brutal fury. I had to draw on all my inner strength to keep calm, but more than once a crack would appear in my armour: during those moments, I'd turn towards the dog, clearly sensing his blind hatred, his desire to tear anyone apart, as if violence was his innate role in the order of things. There was no explanation for Baal in my new, luminous love for nature, and, although I realise it's hard to believe, more than once I had the impression that he understood as much. More than once I had the impression that he perceived that my world view had no place for him: his small, mean eyes would stare at me as if to say that he did exist, though, and that I needed to find an answer for his existence, that I had to find a square for him on the chessboard, a space that he was ready to fill with blood at the first move.

The next day the dirt road, which had been cleared by a passing snowplough, was one long slab that looked like a frozen river.

Fabricino didn't hide his anxiety: we didn't have snow chains for the pick-up, and, unless we came up with a solution, going to the discount store the next day to replenish our supplies for the dogs would prove to be very difficult.

We only had a twenty-kilo sack of salt and a couple of shovels. Fabricino pulled out two colanders and we started spreading the salt meticulously, trying not to waste a single grain. We had split the dirt road into sections, and every so often I'd turn around to look at him, spreading salt from his colander like some kind of sprite sowing magic dust.

This task took us the entire morning, while we spent the afternoon shovelling as much as we could. Eventually we fed the dogs without ever letting them out of their pens, and Fabricino decided to put Baal in the large pen since the snow seemed to make him even more highly strung than usual.

At 7 p.m., the Serbs' Mercedes stopped in front of the house. They said they weren't there for Baal: they wanted to celebrate with us because they'd sold some dogs, including Ala's two puppies, for a great price.

Fabricino was suspicious, but they pulled a case of red wine out of the boot and he let go of any hesitation: he let them in the house and started cooking one of his usual pasta dishes. We drank, we ate, then we drank some more. Later, we played cards in pairs and kept on drinking. It had been at least an hour since I'd had any semblance of lucidity, though I'd noticed something strange: the brothers hadn't been drinking from the last bottle. The last thing I remember is my eyes closing on Fabricino, who was in the same state. Then there was darkness.

When I opened my eyes I saw a line of empty bottles on the table. Fabricino was sleeping opposite me, his head leaning on his right forearm. I had a terrible headache and was feeling nauseous. I stood up and went to the kitchen sink, opened the cold tap and washed my face several times, trying to shake off the stupor. I dried my face with a sauce-stained rag, and when I opened my eyes again they were drawn to something in the window frame.

The gate in the pen stood wide open by the back door of a white van I'd never seen before. I rubbed my eyes trying to recover some lucidity and shook Fabricino, who mumbled something incoherent. I filled a glass with ice-cold water and threw it at his face. He gave a start and stared at me, and closed his eyes again and leaned his head back on his forearm. I filled the glass once more and repeated the process. This time he started cursing, stood up and put his head under the tap.

'I fell asleep here,' he said, disoriented. Then his gaze drifted towards the window. A few moments later we were outside.

Our eyes didn't know what to focus on. Snow. Blood. More snow. More blood.

Dejan was lying on the whiteness, next to the back door of the van, his throat torn to pieces. A metre from him there was a female pit bull that wasn't ours, mauled. Slobo was by the door, lying on his face in another pool of blood. Everything was so appalling that it looked fake, a horror film staged with an excess of brutality.

Fabricino knelt next to the bitch and felt her, then felt for a pulse on Slobo and Dejan. They were all dead.

He stood back up with a deep sigh, then looked around, trying to take in as much of the snowy expanse as his gaze could encompass. There was no sign of Baal.

'What the hell happened?' I asked.

Fabricino pointed at the bitch. 'They'd thought about everything,' he said. 'They put us to sleep, then went to get the van. They had a bitch in heat in the back and counted on the fact that Baal would leap on her. They just needed to close the doors behind him and that would be it. The dog would be trapped.'

He kicked Dejan's side lightly a couple of times, with no malice. 'But things didn't go to plan,' he said. 'When they broke the padlock, Baal leapt on the bitch, yes, but to kill her. Then he sprung on them too. Maybe they were too slow. Maybe they expected him to be too busy with her.'

I could picture the scene as he spoke. I thought about their cries for help and us sleeping, all drugged up. I looked around, shaking with fear rather than from the cold.

'What do we do now? Do we call the police?'

Fabricino made a sharp motion with his hand: 'By law, the owner is responsible for their dog. And there are two bodies here.'

'So?'

He pointed at the house.

I followed him inside. 'Pack your stuff,' he ordered.

'Can I keep Sid?' I asked.

'Don't be ridiculous.'

'What will you do with the dogs?'

He shrugged: 'Forget about it. We must disappear. And quickly too.'

And disappear we did.

Over the years, I've happened to think back to this story many times. 'From a certain point on, there is no more turning back. That is the point that must be reached,' wrote one of the authors I love the most. I only understood what it really meant at Fabricino's kennels.

I often think of those months of isolation, the purity of those places, the love I felt for Sid, the meaningful silences between Fabricino and me, the card games, the clean air when I went out on the balcony at dawn, the meditation, the hard work, the Serbs.

I see them laughing and shaking my hand in a loop, slapping me on the back, joking around. Then I see them in the bloody snow.

For many months I followed every piece of news online about the case of the two mauled Serbs, even the tiniest reference, the shortest of articles. They were looking for the owner of the breeding kennel, but he was nowhere to be found.

On Baal, not even a word, ever. I never heard a single thing about him. He's out there among you.

Quoted aphorism taken from The Zürau Aphorisms *by Franz Kafka, translated by Michael Hofmann (Harvill Secker, 2006)*

SCHATTENFROH

MICHAEL LENTZ

tr. MAX LAWTON

FROM THE GERMAN

An excerpt from the novel,
2018

We went the wrong way, I say to Father. He hears not. This is the wrong way, I say. Father continues on, undeterred. According to the map, we should have kept to the left instead. There is no instead, Father says, it's a question of either/or. It also wouldn't suit him to admit to an error. I stay there, Father walks onwards, he no longer reacts to my calls. Perhaps he has changed the route and is unwilling to inform me of this. He goes on. He has always been at peace within himself. When I once asked him why he likes going on walks, he said: to disappear into the landscape. Man has the ability to become part of the landscape, he says, then the bereaved remember you as a landscape, the most beautiful would be the notion that they would travel through this landscape, then you would be omnipresent to them. They would look around the landscape and say, that is Father. I feel the same way about Grandpa in Prüm, Father said, each street, each brick, each hillock, each tree is Grandpa. There he goes, I soon lose sight of him. Nothing compels me to follow him.

Many years ago, when I was about fourteen, Father lost his bearings during a hike. Tomorrow, we'll climb Traunstein, he said. We'll approach the mountain from behind, that's the safest way. Father had estimated seven to eight hours for the hike, including a two-hour break. Coming from Gmunden, we drove down the Traunsee-Uferstrasse, the paths were signposted, the cardinal directions they were heading in too, the steep 'Mairalmsteig' was the easternmost ascent, that was the one we had to take, this had been told to us the night before, but Father felt such an attraction to the 'Naturfreundesteig' signpost that, in the sure assumption it'd always only been the Naturfreundesteig that'd been spoken of, he parked the car in view of the 'Traunstein Victim Memorial Stone' sign above the yellow trail indicators. At about 6 a.m., we hiked through two Mairalm forest road-tunnels and were soon confronted with the steep entrance of the Naturfreundesteig that Father, who didn't wish to let his astonishment show, as his son might have been able to take this as an opportunity to declare the hike to be already at an end, immediately resolved to master by obdurately leading the way, initially, no path at all could be seen, indeed, nothing at all could really be seen except for steel cables fastened to the rock a bit later on the left-hand side, we were climbing into Traunstein in the fog, fog was to be our constant companion, in certain places, we couldn't even see our legs, but this didn't worry us much more than the fact that the width of the trail was just as difficult to recognise as the proximity of the abyss, the latter a direct function of the former, at around 7 a.m., Father expressed his surprise that we could see Traunsee from the mountain, even if it was only through clouds of fog, he paused briefly, as if he were considering turning back, a thought experiment he ought to have abandoned immediately, not least because I then would have had to walk in front, after all, Father was so clairvoyant that he didn't consider the dangerous option of slipping in the context of possibly walking past one another, thus did he continue on his way, in shorts like me, with his father's mountaineering boots, while I wore his mountaineering boots, which were much too big for me. Going up, I had no sense of stride-distance, the toe of the boot was rather inanimate, later, going down, my feet gathered up in the toe of the boots while the heels were abandoned. The steel cable gave way to step-supports, foot pegs, then, later, a long aluminium ladder and a staircase hewn into the rock, whose slants, Father suspected aloud, hadn't been installed properly or they'd been wantonly destroyed, in any case, he preferred not to climb it, he went down a path to the left below that staircase, from that point on, we were as free as the chamois upon the mountain, coming back to the village, cantering lightly, their gait will be heavy ahead of your corpse, sooner, perhaps, perhaps, than we have passed that gate in the rock that I see now flashing up above. The climbing trail of the Naturfreundesteig, which we managed by way of all sorts of hand- and footholds, afforded us a kind of certainty that we'd not strayed from the right path, but had simply taken the wrong one, which Father saw as a sign from God, a challenge to master in his name, thus does Father's hike around the mountain, which proceeds in a northerly direction so as to avoid the sloping staircase, a path he feels to be justified, nay, unavoidable, turns into a test from the moment when, after about an hour of walking parallel to the Traunsee-Uferstrasse, having resumed the ascent through the northern plunges of Traunstein, all strength leaves me and, free-floating against the wall and incessantly calling out that no more climbing would be possible for me, I cause Father to hand over to me the whole of our provisions, which I then exhaust within a few minutes, without this measure influencing my condition at all positively, I'll wait a bit more, I say to Father, soon, it will be better, even after fifteen minutes, it hasn't gotten better, I initially observe the falling boulders and fragments of stone with fascination until the sight of them fills me with fear, heat penetrates the fog, it nails me to the rock face, black salamanders, also known as Wegnarr, Wegmandl, or Hölldeixl in Austria and Bavaria, one ought not be surprised to find them in the Alps, crawl over my shoes, which I haven't shifted from their spot for minutes now, they leave a trail of slime behind on the leather, perhaps it's also the dampness of the ground that they wipe off on my shoes. Father urges me to keep going, I can't even imagine turning back once more in the direction of the path, I say, the fog clears to reveal flowers along the edge of the path, which I recognise as Stemless Enzian, Lady's slipper, and wild orchid, Father shakes his head, there's no Stemless Enzian here, he sees no broad-leaved marsh orchid, no Lady's slipper either, and oh wouldn't a lady's slipper suit you perfectly, but it's much too unspecific as far as names go, I'm fairly certain that there's Stemless Enzian here, I repeat, and thus do we go back and forth like this for a while, Father takes a huge stride toward me, he's standing right behind me, I am on fire and everywhere I turn is fire, plague, and death, I manage to turn left by using my right foot, however, I immediately lose my nerve once more, and now do I stand with my belly to the wall, behind me, Father is pushing past, not without whispering an imprecation into my ear, so close that I can feel his genitals, we are completely without via ferrata equipment, without safety ropes and without helmets, I say to the wall, which causes my voice to be perceived as very close to me, as if it were reaching behind my ears, enclosing my head, and simultaneously sounding out from the front and from the back, and I say that a sign points out the elevated risk of slipping and that, when it's damp out, one should avoid this mostly pathless, unmarked stone, which leads along the most difficult rock ledge, at all costs, what beautiful words, I had thought as I read the sign, they immediately imprinted themselves upon my memory, they are my only foothold here, Father has vanished, he simply kept on walking, I briefly consider whether I ought to turn around instead of following him to the left, but the thought that it is the left foot that is nearest to the rock face compels me to follow Father, the actual width of the path can't be made out even now, water runs down the wall, I hold my lips very close to the rock, the water runs down my bosom and into my pants, the refreshing effect immediately turns into the fear of a bad chill, the rock is entirely mossed-over, little insects clamber over the moss, shimmering-green and black, I feel them upon my lips, they tumble down my throat, the water flows down the narrow path and into the depths, it shall prevent a sure footing if I wish to turn and catch up with Father once more, I'm completely in love with my own voice, the way the rock catches it and gives it back to me, I grow cold, my voice is drawing figures upon the moss, a certain Schattenfroh is there and wants me to turn left and follow Father, right through his name, I can now see my father, he speaks, but I hear him not, he seems to be furious, the veins upon his temples protrude, I now see his right hand pointing in the direction he disappeared in, the image trembles, fades, the word 'Schattenfroh' becomes legible once more, before my very eyes, it transforms to 'Storchenhaft' (Stork-like), then 'Hattenschorf' (Hadscab), then to 'Schattenfroh' once more, when the last 'h' vanishes from the word, I read 'Schattenfro' and I lose interest in this trickery and am about to turn left when a voice says to me, 'Behold,' I behold and see that the letters are changing places incessantly, as if they were inscriptions upon Father's face, which fades into the background and seems to be slowly coming forward, inscribed with mutating words: 'Ortschaft' (Locality), 'Nachtfrost' (Nightfrost), 'Schafott' (Scaffold), 'ernsthaft' (genuinely), 'Toter' (Dead man), 'Echo,' I read, the words write themselves onto Father's head, as if they were program-triggering passwords, thus is Father somebody who runs programs, but is he still 'somebody' at all, is he still a person, isn't he actually a machine, only there to be of service? I know that Father is Doctor Mabuse and I shall be Doctor Mabuse, Father shall have snow-white hair and I shall have snow-white hair, Father-in-Moss looks at me intently, eyes, nose, mouth, and ears are formed from the letters of the word 'Schattenfroh,' insects crawl forth from his letter-mouth, they clean themselves, then scurry on their way, following the little flowers that are flourishing so wonderfully through the water, my testicles hurt from the cold, I manage to turn to the left, following Father's outstretched right arm, I stand with both feet on the path for a little while longer, then set myself into motion, Father must have fled and cannot be caught, this thought surfaces and I immediately seek to superimpose it with other thoughts, it is only by thinking that one can do away with thinking, 'Überraschung' is written on a sign right next to a hole in the fissured rock face rising up to the left of the path and that means 'astonishment,' stones likely broke off of Traunstein, then bored into the ground not far from it, like a window, the hole affords a view onto the lake and its environs, wind and weather gnaw at this Schauinsland-fragment, it has a protective aspect, there's a completely windless corner here that Father must have already visited, on the ground is a scrap of paper weighted down with stones, I recognise Father's script, which always gives the impression of a command, 'Here, I waited for my son for a long time, he did not have the decency to rejoin me. Therefore, I set off in the direction of the Gmundner Hütte on my own.' I fold up the note and put it in my trouser-pocket. When I'm on the verge of continuing, I pull out the scrap once more, when folding it up, I had the sensation that something was also written on its backside, and, to be sure, there, one reads: 'Chains, via ferrata, rope-secured paths, rock gate, from the southwest via the Naturfreundesteig, Gmundner Hütte, Traunkirchner Hütte, summit cross of the war veterans on the Pyramidenkogel, a large difference in altitude of 1250m, a certain level of fitness required, ascent-gully, Zierlersteig too difficult, the Dechant (the Dean) and Schattenfroh call off the hike, Father and Son not mountain-tested,' the longer I stare at the scrap, the more text appears there, the script below the scrap has now been entirely freed, it continues to write itself through the air, I read: 'Even Naturfreundesteig too difficult, don't get lost on the Zierlersteig!, then A L L will be lost.' So, we're on the Zierlersteig. And before I can begin to despair about this, I read: 'Quit reading, follow the line of my script,' and I see a line snaking out of the tail of the 't', it runs before me at waist-height , a blue thread, a worm that adapts to my speed, but shall not condone my stopping, it passes through me silently, it flies a metre up ahead, it dissolves some two metres behind me. If I walk too slowly, it forms words like 'Come on' or 'Faster' or 'Don't just hang around there,' a formulation that causes me to see hanged people everywhere, if I go too quickly, I read words like 'Caution!' or 'Don't slip!', and once even, 'Slow and steady wins the race', the six words in tight succession in such a way that the reading focus, which doesn't wish to let a single letter escape, throttles the speed of my strides, I've just overtaken the blue threadworm, then it gives me an entirely different and distorted word to read or it's simply my view that is distorted, 'Schattenfroh,' 'Father' and 'Death' are so intertwined that they crawl toward me as a many-legged insect, DeathFather, it has a black-shining carapace and shimmers green on the belly, the little beast seems to be battling itself with its legs and arms, it laughs at me while knives or wings protrude from beneath its carapace, I stop, then, from a certain distance, I read 'That's what happens.' Likely one of Father's amusing disciplinary measures, for which the world begins with language, then ends with language later on, and if Father hasn't yet signed the world with his script, it is on that day that it shall be annulled. I reach for the word 'happens', the thread of which dissolves as a sewing needle describing a pattern dissolves the part of the sweater into which it wasn't worked neatly enough when one pulls at it, I can effectively hold tight to the word-thread, somebody seems to be pulling at its other end, as all I have to do is lean back and I'm already being pulled in the most pleasant way, I unfold, flow, I myself become gliding script, which follows the trail of the pre-scription, the path that I follow in this way is made up of words, with all the detours that I need to gird the letters, I am script's slow dancer and I even dance errors, the correction of which the thread I hang from hinders by way of its guidance, with time, I come to notice that an error is imminent, I then seek to go in the opposite direction, but I can only manage to do this within an insufficient radius, so I go, fully cognisant that I am adding an error to the name of Jesus of Nazareth, and should my father be guiding the thread, of which I have no doubt, he will accuse me of having made the mistake on purpose, as a provocation of Church and Fatherhood, and, once again, he shall point out to me that only he is able to guide me onto the right path. The punishment follows right on its heels, the punishment is called 666, which I have to go through, for *that's what happens*, I've already completed the second 6, I made it to the third just as I did from the first to the second, by walking up half the belly in order to find the path from the belly of the one 6, through a straight line, then into the neck of the next 6, but the belly of the third 6 no longer lets me free, walking in a circle with no way out, as if I needed an invitation to stride forth from the circle, the endless thread wraps round me, my shoes are laced so tight that I can only turn around my own axis with the most halting of steps, my calves are wrapped tight, involuntarily, I lay my hands onto the trouser-seam, the thread encloses the hips, stills the arms, I breathe in deep, the turning around my own axis ceases, it waits, I breathe out, the thread continues its work, it works its way up to the throat, it is gentle, it treats even the lips with decorum, it doesn't strangulate nose and eyes, enough air to breathe shall remain, however, I cannot open my eyes, I rotate some more, I rotate, then I stand still, and the innkeeper of the Gmundner Hütte – who introduced himself to my father as Schattenfroh and to whom Father initially kept silent about my absence, until his disquiet brought him to the brink of tears, as the innkeeper later told me, but I could hardly believe it, after all, I had never seen Father weep, brought to the brink, that doesn't mean actually crying, so said the innkeeper, who, up until that moment, had assumed that my father had ascended Traunstein solo until Father urgently begged him to do something, anything – said that this standing-still is what allowed him, as he expressed it to Father, to grab hold of the loose end of the thread, which, fortunately, stood out clearly from the back of my head at a great distance and was not worked into a much-too-long sentence, then, as the several-kilometre-long thread was unwound, its other end having been bound to my bosom with an unsolvable sailor's knot, which surprised me, the thread had woven round me from the feet up as described, to get me safely from the summit to the lodges, a measure that, for the notorious alpine lifesaver he was, caused him approximately as much trouble as spreading butter onto bread. Until my rescue, the innkeeper maintained an almost unsympathetic calm, as he called it, but then, from the very moment I arrived at the lodge, the whole of my body trembling, but otherwise safe and sound, he showered Father with reproaches of the worst sort.

Father will later claim that it was a species of high-altitude fever that put me out of action for hours at the Gmundner Hütte, that the dizziness tangled up my imagination for the whole of the ascent, even though it was Father who, a year before our Traunstein climb, had almost been hurled to Traunstein's rocky foot by Menière's Disease when we wanted to use the car to scout out whether the mountain that descended deep toward Traunsee could be bypassed by way of the Miesweg, he'd never heard something so stupid come out of my mouth, with this, he merely wished to parry the reproaches of the innkeeper, he did, Father did, we were told of the presumptuousness inherent to climbing Traunstein without any kind of prior experience, not to mention the decision to do so in such critical weather, from the choice of footwear to the apparent disorientation that finally led us to the almost completely unmarked and very steep Zierlersteig, which offered our shoes almost no support when damp, indeed, this trail claimed a certain number of lives each year, he had done everything wrong, and it was a miracle that we weren't to be numbered amongst the dead, and, as it was a miracle, we ought to kneel down before the cross, Father shall say that he sees no cross, up there, in the corner, it hangs just below the ceiling, the innkeeper shall retort, the cross is plain, without corpus, one does not kneel before a cross without a corpus. If one stares at the cross for long enough, the innkeeper shall say, the corpus appears, namely, Christ's battered body from during the Crucifixion, the innkeeper shall grin at these words, his crooked mouth shall reveal a row of rotten teeth, I shall sit in a chair and drink pink Skiwasser, Father shall stare at the cross for some five minutes without budging, the innkeeper shall bring me salted and smoked meat and he shall also offer Father some of the salted and smoked meat, which he, however, shall brusquely refuse, he wishes not to be disturbed in his benevolent attempt to bestow belief upon the innkeeper, the innkeeper shall reply that it isn't him who should be believed, but Christ, which Father shall seek to do for a further five minutes, then he shall sit down in the chair opposite me, eating the meat in silence, he shall cover a slice of freshly cut bread with fine horseradish shavings, take the horseradish off of the bread once more, lay the smoked meat onto the bread, pile it high with horseradish, take the meat and the horseradish off of the bread once more, spread the bread with butter, lift the horseradish-bedecked meat back onto the bread, and thereupon gobble this down with evident appetite, only to then prepare a second slice of bread in the same fashion, this time without any detours, and to also gobble down the second slice, thus fortified, Father shall say, a cross must have a corpus if one wishes to visualise the sufferings of Christ, after all, the Son of God is not formless, with his father, it is a question of faith, whereas some find the notion of God the Father having a form, which is to say a physical body, ridiculous, a ridiculousness that culminates in talk of the 'Word of God,' as if God had a speaking human mouth, others acknowledge the necessity, the inevitability even, of visualising God in manifold forms, after all, thinking of God evokes images of his appearance that can only come from the realm of perception and the combinations derived therefrom, up to and including the monstrous, one would thus do violence to oneself to think of God as an empty space, however, empty space would progress to eventually becoming the appearance of God if this association with God and his appearance were made just often enough. I am in favour of the ban on images, the innkeeper shall say, it is enough for him to have an image of how Father and I climbed Traunstein in the most threatening of situations, though, fortunately, we knew nothing of this danger, in town, the rumour shall later be passed around that, after the innkeeper said that Germans were the stupidest of mountain-hikers and he'd never seen any stupider than us, Father took the cross out of the corner and threatened to beat the innkeeper to death with it, whereupon the innkeeper countered cross with meat-knife , a story that, over the years, would be told in the most colourful, the bloodiest even, of shades, depending on the occasion, Father himself circulated different versions of the Traunstein-ascent incident in the closest of friend and family circles, we didn't even set out, for example, as the fog prevented it, another time, he claimed that we lost our bearings after just a few metres due to the fog, then climbed

Traunstein without any climbing equipment by the most direct route possible, a rock ledge would have been just as incapable of keeping us from our goal of the Gmundner Hütte as rock-fall, rain, or exposed climbing areas with the associated risk of falling, we mastered the ascent with great bravura, then the inn-keeper congratulated us effusively and took a photo of us, which can still be seen today in the lodges, nowadays, in a third version, there is no talk of a masterly ascent, instead, I, the utterly inexperienced boy, was overtaken by a fever on the way and it is out of this fever that all of these phantasmagorias, together with the fable of Father's differing Traunstein Versions, arose, sometimes, the fever overtook me on the way, at other times, it only did so once we'd reached the lodges, the question of the descent was never made issue of by Father, but I know that the innkeeper shouldered him with the remark that the containers full of groceries he was used to carrying up the mountain were heavier and more unwieldy than the burden of Father he now had to carry and he only let him back down once Father was able to recite the route to him seven times in a row with no errors, he was going to have to cover this route with me, who would be following both of them at a distance of some two metres, at least until the valley had been reached, the descent was no longer dangerous from that point on.

For years, Father shall say this sentence to me: 'You are an empty cross,' and neither of us shall know what exactly he means by it, but both of us shall indulge in the memory of the cross hanging in the corner at the Gmundner Hütte, hanging there like some slumbering bat.

Do you remember how we got lost on Traunstein once, I ask Father. The abyss was on our left, Father says. Was it not *too* dangerous, I ask him. It was tantalisingly dangerous, Father says, for a man came from behind us, he pushed his way past, even though there was no space beside us, he walked quite quickly and we clung to him. I don't remember that bit, I say. He slowed his pace so that we might follow him, it was the inn-keeper, up top, by the lodges, he scolded me, how could I have dared to walk such a difficult trail, and with a child at that, one who didn't even know how to put one foot in front of the other. I don't remember that bit, I say.

I only remember that Father led me from the Gmundner Hütte to the summit-cross on the Pyramidenkogel, with its bolted cladding of grey metal plates and the four iron cables meant to secure the cross against storms, it is characterised by a certain ugliness, which seems to suggest tanks dismantled and rearranged into the shape of the cross more than it does God. It is 10 metres tall and dedicated to the fallen of both world wars, it was inaugurated on August 20th, 1950, after the 4,000 parts that had been transported up the mountain by 520 men and 80 women over the course of 2 days had been assembled in a short time, says the plaque attached to the cross. 3,000 people were able to fit onto the summit plateau during the consecration.

Father made the sign of the Cross from a position that allowed him a full view of the cross and the thought came to me that one can only make the sign of the Cross before a cross, but not a crucifix, for, while the one already bears a body that is Christ, oneself is the very one who takes up the empty space of the cross with one's own crossing oneself. Perhaps, that's what Father meant when he told the innkeeper not to kneel before a cross because he would thus be kneeling before himself. Then Father demanded that I do the same as he had, but I refused. Then Father took me by the hand and went with me to the very edge of the stone, behold, all of this can be yours, he said, you must simply venture far enough, but Father, I said, there's nothing there, I can see nothing, a couple more steps, Father said, and I took a couple more steps until, in the depths, I saw three horse-drawn barrows upon which men and women were bundled up right next to one another, they were awaiting the continuation of their journey. Who are they?, I asked Father. They are being taken out of history, they have been waiting for you, Father said, then shoved me into the depths. As I fell, I saw their red, white and rose-coloured robes, the heads already partially without flesh, their bare legs covered over with boils.

Even now, there must be a thread, an invisible one, at play. I see Father upon a hillock, he's sitting on a bench and looking off into the distance, perhaps, he's also looking into himself, in the deeper distance. Oddly enough, he seems to have our provisions, which I transported in a rucksack, he devours one slice of apple after another, he also eats the smoked-and-salted-meat sandwiches with great aplomb, now, he opens the thermos flask with the coffee, pours himself one, shuts the flask once more, then sticks it into the rucksack, out of which he also takes a plastic bottle of water, which he unscrews and puts to his mouth. I never gave him the rucksack. It must have been the thread that transferred the provisions over to him. The more he consumes, the younger he looks, if, by the time I get to him, he has exhausted all of our provisions, I shall be the father and he shall be the son. Then I could scold him, I could think up a nice punishment, harass him, but not without showing him that I love him.

Edited by Matthias Friedrich.

FLYING IN THE RAIN

HEUIJUNG HUR

tr. PAIGE ANIYAH MORRIS

FROM THE KOREAN

An excerpt from –
Failed Summer Vacation
2020

There were always spare flowerpots in the greenhouse.

It had taken a while to realise the building was called a greenhouse. Granted, it had taken just as long to learn that the things crammed inside the greenhouse were called flowerpots, and that their whole purpose was to serve as receptacles for growing plants. *Greenhouse. Flowerpot.* Such strange words. There weren't many people left who knew these words.

– Why do people grow plants anyway?

– Well, all sorts of reasons. You can use them for food, plus they're nice to look at. Though maybe the most important reason is because they produce oxygen.

– Oxygen? You mean O_2?

– Yeah. Back then, people breathed oxygen.

Q explains this as he trims the overgrown shoots from a plant. The thick glass walls of the greenhouse block out all the outside noise, and the artificial lights overhead are so bright it's impossible to look at them straight on. The protective gloves Q is wearing are thick and encumber his hands. He keeps clipping the gloves with his scissors but the metal-ceramic casing is sturdy enough that the rusted blades don't leave a scratch. Still, G can't stop staring at the backs of Q's hands. Snipped-off stems fall to the ground, green on endless green. Q lets go of the plant he had been holding to keep it still. It sways from side to side before settling into place. Its leaves rustle, the lights catching on the fine hairs that stand along their edges.

G watches for a moment before he turns to go. Water rolls down the glass face of the greenhouse in little beads. The rain today is a quiet, steady rain – not like the downpour that fell the previous night. G walks away, leaving the greenhouse behind.

*

These were the sort of scenes G remembered every time he closed his eyes. His memories were like a well-designed algorithm. When he input the action (closing his eyes), the program would generate certain scenes to play on an endless loop. The more of them he watched, unable to stop or intervene, the lower his chances were of being able to fall asleep.

Passengers were advised to sleep while travelling through

space. While this measure was no longer mandatory as it had been put in place a century ago, many travellers still heeded the recommendation. Many passengers on return flights to the Union especially made the trip back in a sleep state, the whole spaceship submerged in silence. Sleeping was the easiest way to escape the unpleasant thoughts that wormed their way into the limited space but unlimited time on the ship, which is why G was among the passengers who had opted to sleep. But nearly all of his attempts so far had been unsuccessful.

G was one of the survivors of the final expedition. He was also a key witness in the case of Q's disappearance. The survivors of that mission, including G, were now required to undergo counselling. But the counsellor, who had existed for the last several years in name only, never seemed to know what to ask or even what he was getting at with his own questions. It was awful. G tried to spend his time outside of counselling sessions in his sleep capsule. But it was no use. Thanks to that unerring algorithm, the time he spent with his eyes closed was overrun with memories of Q. Like an orchard blooming even with no one tending to it.

*

Q took meticulous care of the plants. He probably would have said chloroplasts were the only things worthy of his affection. Of course, the only living things in the part of Earth they were exploring were the crew members themselves and a mass of impossibly overgrown plants. Q spent most of the long, entropic expedition in the greenhouse. He watered the plants, checked the condition of the soil, provided them with adequate organic matter, observed and recorded the shapes of the leaves and the appearance of the stems. As if to repay him for his devotion, the greenhouse plants flourished more and more by the day.

It was the same for the plants outside the greenhouse, too. He even started to think the plants outside were thriving more than the ones inside. But of course that's only natural. The plants in the greenhouse had once grown in the wild, after all. Ever since he first started cultivating the plants, I'd wanted to know: what was his end goal? What was he trying to do?

G swallowed. The moment he opened his mouth again to speak, the chime bell sounded. His session was over. G pursed his lips, stood up, and pushed in his chair. The next person would be coming in soon. He thought back to that conversation he'd had with Q about his intentions, to the story he hadn't been able to finish telling. He remembered how Q had feigned ignorance then, like he hadn't understood what G was asking.

G didn't like plants. He thought they were a menace, a grotesque alien life form. Trees and grasses grew everywhere with abandon, shooting up in dense, leafy clusters without tending, readily seizing new territory. These were the simple conditions of their survival. G was terrified of that simplicity, though, which made it that much harder for him to understand Q's attachment to the greenhouse. At the same time, he once took a strange kind of pleasure in watching the plant domestication process. G would never admit it, but there were times he went with Q on his visits to the greenhouse not only because of the rule that they always had to travel in twos but because it meant he got to watch Q care for the plants.

All activities on Earth had to be done in pairs – this was one of the main rules of the expedition. It was to prevent anyone from being left behind. You had to keep a close eye on your partner at all times, and if you noticed anything even the slightest bit suspicious, you had to report it. The measure was meant to protect the crew members as they toured the Earth, the landscape of which had been altered in unknown ways in the aftermath of the catastrophe. If someone were to be deserted there, they would die a painful death, starving and suffocating on the unbreathable air. It wouldn't be long before their body became yet another means by which the living things that had taken hold of the planet multiplied.

G didn't want that. What he wanted was to be a successful engineer, to have the financially secure and stable life that came with the position, to grow old and happy with the people he loved. As soon as he graduated from the institute, he found a job at the Interplanetary Union's research centre. He thought this was the best career decision he could have made.

The centre studied the survival and adaptation of Union constituents throughout space. If the humans who had left

Earth in the wake of the disaster had been able to adapt to even one planet without issue, there may not have been a need for the research centre to remain in operation. But for all manner of unavoidable reasons, humans had been forced to live scattered on a host of other planets – all with extremely different features. Thus, the research centre became committed to a single goal: the continued survival of humankind.

It wasn't as though private institutions with a similar mission hadn't been established before then. But none of them compared to the research centre, which possessed massive amounts of data and advanced technologies, as well as the government backing that came with the Interplanetary Union affiliation. The planets in the Union spared no expense when it came to investments and support. Working for the research centre meant that G would have ample opportunity to achieve his ambitions as an engineer while also having the chance to interact with the greatest scholars of his generation. He never once doubted that until he was assigned to the Return to Earth project.

*

In vivo experimentation.

No one in the conference room dared to utter those words. G instinctively recalled the phrase and felt goose bumps surface on his skin at the mere thought. Like *greenhouse* and *flowerpot*, *in vivo experimentation* was a phrase that had died out long ago. Living organisms, including humans, had not been used as the subjects of special-purpose experiments since the previous century. But what Q was suggesting now seemed no different at its core than an in vivo experiment, one with live human subjects. Only an extremist Returnee could have put forth such an idea.

G couldn't agree with him on this. The rest of the crew felt the same way. Yes, they had uncovered a problem with their equipment and were having trouble communicating with the research centre, but G didn't think the situation was so dire. As soon as he shared his honest thoughts, however, he was met with opposition from Q. The situation may not be that extreme as of now, he said. But we can't rely only on our existing resources when we don't know when or how it will be resolved.

No one else responded. G couldn't tell whether this meant they agreed with him or not.

As soon as G returned to his quarters, he took off his helmet. The air was familiar. His breathing felt intuitive. He had the sudden urge to wander around the basecamp like that. But as an employee of the Union research centre, he had to keep his respirator equipped at all times. Each member of the expedition team had to comply with this instruction – a vain attempt to avoid sowing any seeds of discord among the crew. Yet to G, it felt as if the discord had already flared and spread enough to saturate the atmosphere inside that conference room.

Q believed that until communications with the Union were restored and the expedition crew was able to notify them that a part of the research vessel had been destroyed, they could prolong their survival via the active cultivation, harvesting, and consumption of plants. More people agreed with him than G had initially thought. They insisted: wasn't this an inevitable step of the process if their end goal was indeed to return to Earth? They explained: this was a rational conclusion derived from reason. But G couldn't accept their words. To him, this was a delusion, the product of irrationality and naivete.

Most of the people who agreed with Q in the beginning came from similar regions as him. The descendants of those who had just barely managed to adapt to life on a barren planet. Their infant survival rate was low, and their average life expectancy was short compared to other planets in the Union. There were still regions where people suffered from syndromes and complications that had emerged in the process of adapting to space. They couldn't help but hold onto a certain fantasy about Earth. But G could never have imagined the return they insisted on would be so absurd and backward. In a way, the very idea of returning seemed to contradict their positions as members of the Union. G lay in bed, staring at the ceiling. Old prejudices he had carefully tried to stow away seemed to come out of hiding with every exhale.

*

Most people didn't believe the return project would actually be carried out. G was among the sceptics. Of course, the Returnees were always trotting out the same claims and talking points, so over time he grew accustomed to their views. The conditions of each planet varied tremendously, and even after several centuries, humans still hadn't been able to adapt perfectly to any of them. The problems each environment posed were always specific, individual, and existential. Returnees believed the only way to resolve these problems was to return to Earth.

It made no sense. The Union research centre had been established a long time ago to solve the problems humans were facing. Of course, the centre's role was not to address every problem on every planet with equal attention, and the reality was, with issues being sorted by priority, there were some that were more urgent and others that had been left unattended. Still, the number of concerns the research centre had resolved or improved was not insignificant. Yet the Returnees hardly gave them credit. They didn't even seem to recognise how it was that they had come to breathe so naturally, with such ease.

It wasn't that they didn't have the technology needed to return to Earth. What they lacked was a central point around which to gather funds, as well as enough intel. They knew astonishingly little about how Earth's environment had changed after the humans who were able to leave the planet had left. Even so, all the Returnees insisted that a return was the solution to their problems without any basis for that claim. Furthermore, the research centre dealt with the affairs of all the planets within the Union, and there were still scores of unresolved issues from other planets piled up. In other words, there was no real incentive to find out more about Earth and the changes it had undergone. As such, people had no choice but to consider the Returnees' claims to be baseless, and at times, even the Returnees themselves seemed to agree.

Literature about Earth did exist. But most of the literature focused on the planet before the catastrophe. The planet and the stories surrounding it had been taken apart and reassembled over and over again, generation after generation, century after century. In the process, Earth had been transformed into a universal homeland, strange and beautiful and serene, and the cowardly decision to abandon the homeland, as well as the names of the people behind the decision and of those who were the first to be abandoned in the process, were wiped clean from the records.

None of that really mattered anymore. It was all so far in the past. What was important was the state of Earth's landscape now, several centuries after the disaster. After the Interplanetary Union elected a new leader, there was a sudden surge of unprecedented interest in the idea of a return. The leader announced that while he was in office, he would draw up plans for an expedition related to the return project and set those plans into motion.

Scholars began drafting hypotheses, running simulations, presenting papers. Their claims were all based on secondhand data. Unmanned probes began making regular trips to and from Earth, but they never touched the surface. All sorts of reasons were given for this – the shifts Earth's surface had undergone, concerns about the damage those changes might do to the machines, the cost of recovery in the event of any problems – but the general feeling underlying each of the reasons was the same. Fear – that what they imagined might be at odds with reality. That every belief they had held onto all this time might be shattered.

*

The flight was long. When travelling between planets, the ship could fly with relative ease and stability. But the moment the vessel entered Earth's atmosphere, the crew was confronted with an entirely different environment. There seemed to be no major issues crossing from the thermosphere into the stratosphere, but once they entered the troposphere, the alarm began to sound.

Droplets of some unknown liquid were beating down on the exterior of the ship. It was impossible to estimate the mass, density, or makeup of the substance, or even the impact it would have on the vessel. All they knew for sure was that the falling droplets were having some effect on the spacecraft's flight. To make matters worse, the Earth's atmosphere itself seemed to be in an unstable condition. They hadn't foreseen an encounter with these external factors, and they would need to run more calculations to get closer to their planned landing site.

The probe ended up docking away from the scheduled spot. It was technically a crash landing. Fortunately, the vessel wasn't destroyed in the process. But even after checking that they had managed to land the ship safely, the expedition team couldn't bring themselves to disembark. The idea of unexplored land, a mission with no manual, sent emotions of all different colours and textures coursing through them. Soon, they would be taking their first steps on the very earth that no other human of their generation had walked.

*

The hatch door opened, and as the unit touched the ground, our internal displays lit up green. I'm not exaggerating when I tell you everything we saw was covered in the colour. Not only the ground, but the remains of what were clearly man-made structures were covered in clumps of green, too. I'd never seen anything like it.

Honestly, I had thought the crash landing was what caused the problem with the display. I only realised that wasn't the case when crew members in all the other units complained of the same thing. I tried modulating the screen's brightness, but no matter what I did, all I saw was green.

After a while, once my eyes had adjusted to the surroundings, I realised there wasn't just one kind of these clumps out there. Some were long and outstretched, and others were wide and flat. Some were small and soft-looking, others big and easy to see, all of them slightly different shades of green. It felt uncanny looking at them. I could see glimpses of ruined buildings through the gaps. You've probably seen something like this in photos. It was – how can I put it? Overwhelming.

I found out what those green things were called from the operator who remained on the main ship.

– They're plants.

I heard him through the speakers that had been installed near the cockpit. A lot of noise was cutting in, and I remember thinking the sound quality was awful. An eerie feeling took over me.

Upon closer inspection, I could see that the plants were swaying a little. The bigger ones weren't, but the littler offshoots and even smaller sprouts on those offshoots were trembling slightly. Only then did I remember that droplets of liquid were falling from the sky. The droplets were made from a compound formed from oxygen and hydrogen as well as traces of mineral. I could hear a rustling sound that didn't seem to end. It felt like I was listening to white noise. Yes, exactly – it was raining.

*

The first expedition was successful by its own measure. It seemed that Earth's environment was shifting and becoming more welcoming of living things. The greatest evidence of this was the fact that plants had started growing again. These weren't just isolated incidents, rather a phenomenon that could be observed across the entire planet. Of course, a long time had passed and no one could rule out the possibility that the plants had mutated, but this was hopeful evidence nonetheless that pointed toward the fact that the Earth's ecosystem was in the process of being restored.

What actually ended up being a problem was the weather. For the duration of the trip, which lasted roughly 90 Earth days, there wasn't a single day without rain. It was inconsistent, too. There were days of thin, misty rain that fell quietly and for a long time, then there were also days where the rain came in torrents, in sheets. Some days a heavy downpour would start without warning only to subside just as suddenly as it had begun, and other days strong winds accompanied a seemingly endless shower of rain.

So the Earth's surface was always sopping wet. Every time someone on the crew took a step forward, they recoiled at the feeling of squishy, muddy ground underfoot. The ground was covered in decomposing matter. On top of the rot sat less rotted matter, and on top of the less rotted matter sat matter that would rot soon. Any time you tried to move, mud spattered and congealed clumps of wet leaves clung to you. Flecks of mud dried and caked into the narrow crevices of the safety equipment and caused minor malfunctions, while the rush of rain and clinging leaves obscured the crew members' sight. It became essential that they make overall improvements to the equipment and refine plans to account for the weather.

These were the main findings contained in the report drafted by the first expedition crew. They had no doubt that their report would be a tremendous help to future expeditions. It seemed there really would come a day when humans might be able to return to Earth. Not a single member of the crew could have imagined the report would be rejected and sent back.

There wasn't much to glean from the Interplanetary Union's response. For some reason, their captain didn't seem to want to tell his expedition team what he knew. Opinions were divided among the crew members. It might have been that public opposition to the return project itself was growing. Even so, the expedition team couldn't accept this request to amend the contents of the report so easily. They asked for more information, but the captain's response was the same. He said communications with the Union had not been smooth.

As such, dissenting opinions began to commingle in the air, from those who wanted the project itself to be cancelled and those who instead wished the current situation were different. But no matter how often they discussed the matter, none of them had any real choice. They spent the remainder of their flight revising the report. Rewriting conclusive sentences to be less conclusive, explicit references to be less explicit, and assertive sentences into ones that weighed possibilities. Instead of working on the report, G often found his partner zoning out, looking worn to the bone.

*

I thought he was one of the standard-issue Returnees. One of those people who lived their lives clinging to these vague, groundless beliefs. What else was I supposed to think? Everyone else on the expedition team had the same reaction when they heard the report had been sent back – they all looked a bit down, a little glum. But he seemed to be taking it especially hard. Now and then at mealtimes, the crew would discuss the future direction of the project, but he never once took part in the conversation. He would finish his rationed meal, then head back to his quarters without saying a word. You're right – he seemed depressed. But even then, I never thought of him as dangerous.

I think he was the one who needed counselling, not me. But as I'm sure you know, the return project ran into a lot of trouble, starting from the process of allocating the funds. No one had put together a proper budget for it. It was hard to believe the centre was the main organising force behind it. That's right – we had never been assigned counsellors. For a long time, there was nothing but a nameplate on the desk you're sitting at right now. I know. It was a violation of the rules. But back then, rules were bent as often as meals were eaten. There was no one to file a complaint to. If there had been, maybe I would have spoken up more. Because I was his partner. But I was stressed out and nervous, too. Just like everyone else on the team must have been. Right – right. I guess what I'm trying to say is there was nothing I could have done.

I'll be honest with you – I didn't think he was a good fit for what the expedition entailed. Sure, when you're at a desk, being stubborn and determined might come in handy. I'm sure it's helped countless scientists who spent decades grappling with complex problems. But now, as you know, most of the previous century's so-called dilemmas have been resolved.

Now, what matters are the tasks directly ahead of us. How we can increase the survival rates of our children, whether it's possible to develop a respirator that can be used on all planets across the Union, how we will settle the conflict between the pro-Union and anti-Union factions, how to ease the difficulties migrants are facing in adapting to their planets – those sorts of things. He had a tendency to approach every problem from a radical standpoint, which is why we often disagreed. But I want to make it a hundred percent clear that any conflicts we had were due to nothing more than a difference in perspective.

Either way, I imagine that to the other crew members, it must have looked like we really didn't get along. Outwardly, we almost never talked to each other about anything personal, and when it came to work, our opinions were on such opposite ends of the spectrum that I often ended up raising my voice at him – yelling. But I don't think you can say I must have done something to harm him just because that's how things looked from the outside.

*

It took a while before the expedition could continue. The problem was the oxygen. The plants that had overtaken the Earth's surface were endlessly emitting it. Because of that, the composition of the Earth's atmosphere was not only different from what it was in the past, but also quite unlike the air the humans who had migrated to other planets were now used to. The bodies of humans who had been living in space had been slowly evolving to no longer be able to breathe oxygen. Meaning, the Earth's current environment could prove dangerous for people.

Doubts were raised constantly about whether it was appropriate to go ahead with a manned expedition in that sort of environment. Everyone in the Union had their own opinions about the project and didn't hesitate to make them known. The Union government and the research centre entered long negotiations, and G heard from the people who were present at these talks that there was a mix of concern and contempt regarding the future vision for the project. But because the report drafted by the first expedition team had not been released to the public, it wasn't clear who opposed what. G figured the project would be called off soon. Or maybe it was truer to say he hoped. It was obvious no matter what they discovered on Earth, the findings would only be downplayed and disparaged. G didn't want to wear himself out over it.

In the end, the expedition was resumed – this time, with a drastically reduced budget and scale. The on-the-ground crew now mostly consisted of new researchers with little career experience. G was, of course, included among them. And Q, who had been his partner during the first expedition, was also on the new roster. Just like the other times they had taken part in research centre projects, they had to sign an agreement stating that they accepted all the risks that came with the expedition.

The sentences in the agreement read a bit differently to them now than they had before.

Landing on rainy ground was no easy feat. It meant the crew had to get used to the incessant wail of alarms signalling that they were in danger of crashing from the moment they entered the planet's atmosphere, until the moment they touched down on the surface. It also meant they needed to be able to make out their colleagues' voices above all the other noise. Since they couldn't suddenly change the coordinates and the predetermined route at will, they had to numb themselves to the fact that they would essentially be landing without a plan. And while they were all responsible for figuring out what was and wasn't possible, not one person actively stepped up to take ownership over their part in that task.

The expedition team's discovery of the abandoned greenhouse was as much a part of the process of deciding on a spot to land as it was a coincidence. At first, no one could even recognise the thing as a greenhouse. Beneath the coat of hardened grime that had built up on the outside were walls the crew presumed were made of something like glass, and a rusted steel frame was holding the whole thing up. The fact that stones had been stacked inside of it to create distinct sections, with narrow areas that seemed to have been left clear as paths, made this structure clearly different from other buildings the crew had seen. Yet the purpose of the building was not their main concern. It was a mere remnant of the people who'd left Earth long ago – something they hadn't been able to take with them.

But their expedition could be a means to explore such remnants, too. Most of their process entailed comparing and verifying the present conditions on Earth to records from the pre-disaster era. The crew had long discussions, gathered measurements and observations, documentation, conclusions. The sights that greeted them each time they landed didn't vary much. Plants shooting up in clusters through the downpour, stones rounded and hollowed out by the endless fall of rain, statues with vanished faces, columns with weatherworn reliefs. Before they made any meaningful discoveries about the possibility of life on Earth, they first discovered more traces of the people who had once lived there, and even more often, they came across the plants that had swallowed up those traces.

But keeping track of what they had uncovered and the details they had confirmed was tricky. The expedition team worried over what would be kept in and what would be redacted, what would be accepted and what would be thrown out. What would become an achievement of theirs? What would be remembered as a gaffe? No one could be sure. They knew from experience that things can easily be erased. It was why most expedition documents were left blank.

*

He was the first to take an interest in the greenhouse. There were a lot of them in disuse or in ruins in that area. This one had probably been a botanical garden. Q collected seeds from the different species of wild plants growing around the greenhouse and started planting them inside.

At first, everyone thought it was a kind of game, something fun to do. That's right – none of us thought it would turn into an experiment. I don't think he saw what he was doing as an experiment, either. The crew members tried to help him out, each of us in our own ways. It wasn't easy removing the grime from the greenhouse exterior. But repairing the artificial lights inside, getting the thermostat up and running again, inspecting the internal electrical wiring, and crafting a ventilator – these tasks were simple enough for anyone on the crew to manage.

While the others experienced some failed attempts at the very start, once they managed to cultivate the right environment, the plants started growing with abandon. Everyone was so happy to see that. The team had grown listless, feeling like we'd been demoted. The crew members got a small sense of accomplishment from their contributions to the cultivation of those plants. Soon enough, they all started treating it like a competition to see whether they could make them grow even better, even more.

No. I never took part in any of it. Even without my help, the plants were thriving. I couldn't see the whole thing as anything more than a form of escapism. Whenever we ran into each other, I asked my colleagues how the cultivation was going, but I did that for the sake of friendliness, nothing more, nothing less.

But their cultivation efforts never yielded any results. They never saw a single flower or any fruit that could be consumed as food. Because even though the expedition seemed long to us, it lasted only a little more than half a year in Earth time. It wasn't a good idea to stay on the planet during its dry season. Humans tired more easily and the machines quickly overheated. The expedition team often argued about the need to explore during the dry season, but they were routinely dismissed. In the end, the trips always ended up happening during the rainy seasons. Though we landed in a slightly different location on each trip, the team never failed to pay a visit to the greenhouse.

Q was always the first one to go and check on the plants. When he went, no one followed him. No one could forget what had happened the first time we had returned to see the condition of the greenhouse and its plants. They couldn't stomach what they knew they would find: rotted-black leaves, sagging branches, desiccated grass and the stench of decay. No matter what measures they took, it was always the same. The dry air and the heat from the artificial lights, the extremely high concentration of oxygen. These were completely different conditions than the ones the wild plants were growing in. Maybe this is a poor choice of words, but it looked like the plants had suffocated.

Q cleaned up the greenhouse alone. He uprooted the dead plants, evened out the soil, inspected the lighting and thermostat settings, and made plans to start anew. He planted all the seeds again in the cleaned-up greenhouse, and he tended them with all his heart. As though nothing had happened. Once the plants had grown back to a certain point, the rest of the crew started visiting the greenhouse again. And on each subsequent expedition, it was the same process over and over. To my eyes, it looked like he was saving them to kill them and killing them to save them all again.

*

When the rescue team finally arrived, the crew was in better shape than had been reported. They had rationed their remaining food and been mindful about allocating resources. Everyone was mentally drained and fairly hungry, but no one appeared to be suffering from any major health issues.

The crew members soon found themselves aboard a space shuttle headed back to the Union. The return flight was smoother than any other flight they had ever been on. The most surprising thing was getting real-time news from the Union. During the first meal on the flight back, they learned that the Interplanetary Union was in the process of changing its position on the return project. Apparently, the results from the first expedition had been heavily truncated. This was a decision made by research centre executives. It was decided that humans returning to Earth was against their interests. The crew was also informed that a full-scale investigation was being launched into the return project itself.

On nights when he couldn't sleep, G went out to the empty lounge and watched the Union's press video again and again on a loop. He knew it almost by heart. In order to breathe in outer space, you needed an air tank attuned to the atmospheric conditions of your particular planet. G couldn't breathe the same air as other members of the expedition team, and the same would have been true for Q. The air inside the tank G had been given had a similar composition to the air on Earth.

G thought of the plants Q had killed. There were always spare flowerpots in the greenhouse. Each time on his way out after inspecting the greenhouse, G secretly took off his helmet. Cool air kissed his skin. He felt as if his bones were being realigned. Rain fell and beaded on the tip of his nose, then rolled off. The endless sound of white noise and the fishy smell of grass. It was a scent he could pick up even with his underdeveloped sense of smell. Whenever he caught a whiff of it, G seemed to know exactly where he was.

He reached up and felt around where he knew his face would be. His fingers touched damp skin. The feeling was new. He started to feel a little breathless. Soon he would begin to hyperventilate, making it harder for him to catch his breath. G began to pant. *You all right?* Someone was talking to him. G quickly slipped his helmet back on. But there was already somebody behind him. G didn't see the way their face, hidden behind the respirator, crumpled.

*

Is he really dead? No one ever found his body. All we know is that he fell behind, and that he still hasn't turned up. He might even be living on Earth. He believed so badly that humans could make the return. I know the two of us fought constantly, but he was a capable scientist and a talented engineer. Knowing him, he'd probably find a way to adapt to life on Earth again.

*

Not long after leaving Earth, the crew received word that a search team was departing to locate someone who had been left behind. A commercial space airline had even provided the search shuttle. Rescue efforts centred on the greenhouse, the last place he had been seen. The plants he had tended and raised glowed a lush green, having been given water and nutrients and adequate light, and that image of them was transmitted to every corner of every city in the Interplanetary Union. A thorough search of the area including the greenhouse and the basecamp was carried out, but turned up nothing aside from smashed flowerpots. The edges of their shards suggested they had been destroyed in a powerful collision with an external object.

All the while, the plants were spewing out endless streams of oxygen, and it was deadly.

LITTLE ANIMALS

ANTONIO DÍAZ OLIVA

tr. CHARLOTTE COOMBE

FROM THE SPANISH

For once, it wasn't the parents. I started investigating the case for a Colombian; I'll call him 'the man'. He had been Ana Reitman's Spanish professor while working on his doctorate for seven years at Columbia; the same university I'd left almost a decade earlier. The man hired me, and I arranged to meet him at the movie theatre on 9th and Prince. I wanted to hear his reasons. To understand them. I wanted him to fill me in. He was still in love with Ana and was tormented by not knowing about her final days. He swore to me that in all his years teaching as a doctoral student, he'd followed the Ivy League morality to the letter: he never responded to the advances of any of his students; he never drank at 1020 (*bad things happen in that dive* he once told me, talking about the bar where the Columbia professors mingle with students); and he always kept the door open during office hours.

But then, in his final semester, Ana came into the picture.

He wasn't even interested in academia. The man had decided not to pursue a teaching career in the United States. He knew, he told me, from the moment he started at Columbia and felt alienated from everything: his colleagues, his classes and particularly his professors. He finished the second semester and requested a leave of absence. He returned to Medellín, desperate to intellectually cleanse himself after reading all that Butler, Laclau and Kristeva; he wanted to hang out with his people and perhaps try to build a life there. But other than a couple of casual freelance assignments for low circulation magazines, he couldn't find any work in Colombia and went back to New York a soldier of the perpetual war; resigned, dedicated, head held high. I get it: at some point the man realised that academia offered him the perfect opportunity to write the great novel that would eventually position him at the vanguard of young Latin American writers. And what could go wrong? Five years of being paid to study, plus the chance to live in New York instead of some backwater gringo college town. However, once he was back in the city after his time in Medellín, the man stumbled into that area so vocationally problematic for any Latin American writer involved in academia, and experienced the push-and-pull of American comfort versus Latin American instability; being paid to read, versus the lack of freedom with which one approaches that reading; and finally, between dating a student versus that student, one summer night in Brooklyn, winding up dead.

*

The same route as always. The same faces, the same avenues, the same neon lights; the smell of pizza, halal, or tacos de carnitas from the Mexican food trucks. I meandered along the streets like I had my whole life ahead of me. Walking around New York was therapy for me; it was my therapy and one of my hobbies. After almost five years, getting lost in the city still comforted me. It brought me relief.

I paid for my ticket and went into the darkened room of the movie theatre.

It took a while for my eyes to adjust. I was feeling unresponsive, mentally and physically, a state which only came over me when I was in a movie theatre or when I smoked animalitos. The man was staring at the screen. He wore a navy-blue jacket, white polo shirt and light brown chinos. His beard was neatly trimmed.

He was an emotional wreck, but he still retained his Colombian Paisa elegance. Wait, he whispered, looking all round him, did you come alone?

I always come alone, I told him. What's up?

He didn't answer.

Still paranoid? I asked.

Again, he said nothing.

The man reckoned he was being followed. Shortly before Ana's death, he started to feel unsafe.

I calculated that there were less than ten people at the screening, three of them hobos eating fried chicken out of Styrofoam trays. The trailers finished and the movie started. I'd seen it before. It was about an astronaut stranded on the moon with no chance of returning to earth, listening to David Bowie as he waits for his oxygen to run out. His only company is the spaceship's central computer, which constantly asks him what it feels like to be human and what it means to be alive. The astronaut would rather endure the tedium of space, gradually dying while talking to a machine, than commit suicide.

Well? The man asked.

Now it was my turn not to answer. That evening in the movie theatre, I found it hard to detach myself from the darkness. I felt trapped in my unresponsive state for longer than usual. I thought about the scene in the Brooklyn apartment. When she was found dead. Weeks earlier. Ana Reitman asleep, not caring that she had classes that morning, the alarm clock by her head (showing 11:15 a.m.) Someone – a neighbour – bangs on the door to complain about the noise. It's a Puerto Rican who had barely slept a wink the night before. The fuckin' music, he shouts, and the noise! Think about the decent people who have to go to work! More banging. I'll be talking to the landlord about this! Fuckin' yuppies! In the room where Ana Reitman is sleeping, there are signs of a guy's presence. There must be, I think. And that guy is the one who did it.

Well? The man asked again.

I couldn't speak. I could hardly breathe.

I had the sensation of being smothered by a plastic bag. It happened when I got too involved in a case I was investigating. Or when I smoked animalitos, too many of those little animals crumbled and rolled into a joint, the smoke dispersing into my mouth, lungs and brain, leaving me in a state similar to...

Pardon? The man said. I didn't quite catch that.

I pulled myself together.

Come closer, he whispered.

I'm fine, I replied. I'm okay.

Speak up then, he said.

I took a few deep breaths (one... two... three...) and then I spoke.

Her female friends, I told him, didn't attend classes all week. But the group of Latinos still met, at the place they always went to, that noodle restaurant where she liked to eat lunch alone on Tuesdays: Yasha Ramen. After that...

Did they talk about her? The man cut in.

I said nothing.

What did Ana's friends say?

Honestly, I replied, not much. At one point they talked about a game they remembered when Ana scored a goal, but that's about it.

The man shifted in his seat.

After that, I went on, the three of them, Cara, Tess and Gabriela, walked a few blocks and met up with two older guys. They had beers at 1020. They played pool. Later on, the men accompanied them to another apartment, Tess's, and they carried on drinking there. Vodka. More beers. I think someone made a comment, albeit briefly, I told him, about how many pills Ana took.

The man gave a concerned sigh.

At 2:15 a.m. or a little after, I went on, the guy said goodbye and walked to Koronet. He ordered a pepperoni slice which he promptly devoured. Then he took the 2 train to Brooklyn.

Did you follow him?

No, I replied. It was getting late.

The man fell silent. I could guess what he was going to say. Too suspicious, I told him. I want to keep a low profile. But Sunday... (I paused and lowered my voice), there's a game in Riverside on Sunday. I'll trail him.

I stopped talking. On the screen, the astronaut was explaining to the computer that the only difference between a human and a robot was crying. The computer could not comprehend.

Crying? But... isn't crying a sign of weakness?

The astronaut nodded.

Seriously – is that what it means to be human? The computer asked. Showing how weak you are?

I left the movie theatre before the astronaut could answer.

*

The university with the most cases was Cornell, in Ithaca, NY, where the students were known as 'ithakids'. Rupert was the second ithakid that winter and my first job, or assignment. I took it seriously, so seriously that I didn't allow myself to sleep until I'd finished drafting the narrative. Rupert hurled himself off a bridge the day they announced a fresh snowstorm coming in. I talked to his friends and professors and even visited his dorm. I also sat in on one of his courses thanks to my Columbia doctoral student card (even though it had expired over a decade ago). Two weeks later, back in New York, I mailed his parents an envelope containing Rupert's narrative. His whole life in just twenty little pages that had kept me up every night, reading and proofreading. I had even recorded myself reading it aloud. The mother wrote me an email thanking me. She said that the money would be in my account that afternoon.

And it was.

More often than not, it's the parents, although it can also be the grandparents, aunts, uncles and siblings. They all want the same thing from me. They want to know more about, or even get to know, their dead relative. What was their life like before they died? What did they get up to? What kind of things did they like? I travel to universities on the East Coast: Brown, Yale, Amherst, Princeton, Georgetown. It could be parental pressure, or a partner, or bad grades, or the economic crisis, or that inner void that comes with being young. Who knows why, but not a semester went by without at least one case. It was like a series of suicides, a narrative of deaths, that the universities downplayed when it came to the official press releases. And I was in charge of putting into words, narrating, and even humanising the story, then sending it to the parents, who had relinquished control over their children's lives the day they waved them off to start their university experience. That was my job: to narrate those final years. To do so, I talked to classmates and friends, I visited significant places in their university lives and even hacked into their Facebook, Twitter, Instagram, Grindr, Snapchat, Reddit and email accounts. I would back those files up to my computer, although the agreement was that I would delete any case information once the life narrative was handed over to the parents or relatives. I did, however, keep their photos on my computer. And a folder for each one, with their names, documents, profiles, likes and dislikes.

*

Why would she do it? She was happy. You could tell Ana Reitman was happy. She was studying Political Sciences and Spanish; she planned to spend a year as an exchange student in Buenos Aires; and every Friday she played soccer in Riverside Park with other undergrads from Columbia and Barnard.

That Sunday I put on a pair of shorts, a white T-shirt with yellowish sweat stains at the armpits and a Nike hoodie, rode the Yellow Line and jogged my way up to Riverside. I took in the view of the Hudson; Jersey City in the distance, so far away and yet so close, those buildings in the middle of that blue sky, so full of those little fluffy clouds shaped like the animalitos I smoked to ease my depression. As I jogged, I wondered why years back, holed up in Astoria, never leaving the house, I got bogged down. I got stuck. How did I get into that state? Was that other person really me? It happens sometimes: you think about the person you used to be, you even try to understand them, but the only thing your memory unearths are fragments and vague recollections of someone unknown. The outline of a stranger. A blurry face in the crowd.

I kept on running, thinking about my life. About my life story.

After quitting my doctorate, after resigning from that world of professors and theoreticians willing to sell their souls in exchange for an academic post, I went into one of those phases where I knew I had to wipe the slate clean and start over. But I was also unclear about exactly what I should do. Or rather, of all the things I had done with my life, what I should erase and what I should keep. I decided to give myself a few months and reflect. I had some savings. I started smoking weed and going on walks; I walked to cure my infinite melancholy, to take a deep dive into my existential petty bourgeois dilemmas; and I smoked to escape them.

Just as it does now, the city seemed infinite to me back then; on every corner there was someone in a worse state than me, some lonesome soul who helped put my problems into perspective. During those walks, I wondered what to do with all that time I'd invested in that thing called academia. How to use some of that theory and lofty knowledge in the real world. Of course, my long walks were as circular as my conclusions. They went nowhere and at some point, they just came back to the beginning.

Eventually I started to feel as useless and evanescent as the torrential, drenching rains which, sometime that year, announced the passage of another hurricane that might leave

New York underwater and in total darkness.

Strange times, now that I think about it.

For me and for the rest of the city.

The day before the hurricane hit, in a Puerto Rican deli where they had run out of everything except bar mitzvah candles and canned food, I met a Colombian literary agent. Andrea wasn't from Medellín, she wasn't some small-town Paisa like the man. She was refined, educated and polite. She'd had a pampered upbringing in Paris and obtained a degree from the Sorbonne. In the checkout line she overheard me speaking Spanish with one of the deli owners, and a few minutes into the conversation – in which I summed up my escape from academia and told her that my Spanish was good because my parents were diplomats (I didn't say CIA, of course) in Latin America – she told me that if I needed extra money, I should get in touch. So, I did. Andrea gave me a job as a ghostwriter. I started with the apocryphal biography of a Colombian rocker eager to break into the gringo market. Next, I penned the memoirs of a Puerto Rican judge unsure of her Spanish and determined to win the Spanish-speaking immigrant vote. And then I wrote the testimony of a distinguished Cuban university professor who, despite being accused of sexual harassment, was honoured by Obama at the White House. Andrea asked me to make the language cushier, to take those manuscripts and fill them with the Spanglish so common in certain areas of New York (*parqueando* the car, *aplicando* for a license, *lonchando* at a sidewalk cafe, *forgeteando* everything).

It was ideal: I could write from home, carry on smoking, and in my free time continue with my personal quest which, at that point, seemed more like an excuse to not leave the house, to carry on smoking and avoid thinking about anything at all.

Then the hurricane hit.

It was like a huge blur. I had to hole up in my room. And so, I sank back into that swampy melancholy as the hurricane swept through, flooding and destroying parts of the city. Something happened to me. Every time Andrea paid me for a job, every time without fail, I smoked all the money I received. I would roll a joint with weed and other unmentionable substances which left me spinning out. I stopped taking my walks around the city;

at best I managed to watch something on Netflix. I didn't eat either. I just smoked joints. Until, in the wake of the hurricane, the supply of weed and other drugs dried up and dealers were only pushing the latest high called 'animalitos'. I had nothing else to smoke, so one day I made a joint with the little animals. And then another. And another. Every time I bought and unwrapped them onto a rolling paper, I was reminded of when we were living in Chile (one of my parent's many postings), and I'd take those Safari cookies to school as a snack; the sugary cookies shaped like little elephants and giraffes and monkeys.

*

How idiotically happy I felt, jogging around Riverside and thinking about such existential bullshit. I was finally doing okay, I told myself. Seeing as I'd quit my doctorate, I didn't have any responsibilities anymore. Plus, I no longer depended on anyone. Now I could wander around and get lost in the streets of this giant fucking city until I died.

So, as I ran, I thought back to those days of indecision and depression. It was like a postcard of what I once was and will never be again. Then, to stave off the low mood even more, I imagined Ana playing soccer. That's what I did. As I breathed in fresh air along the Hudson, I imagined her happy. Ana was happy. There she is, a few months ago, playing soccer with her teammates; competitive, yes, sometimes too competitive, though she never broke the rules. Slightly anxious. Hence the pills that in the end killed her. Ana was short, just over five foot tall, with stocky arms and legs. Her brown hair was straight, and her teeth were a little crooked, although only the lower part of her smile. That's what she looked like in the photos she and her friends uploaded to an album dedicated to the soccer league.

I stopped running.

Walked for a while.

Took some deep breaths (one, two, three).

I pulled the hood of my sweatshirt up. After drinking from one of the water fountains, I walked to the soccer fields and sat down on a nearby bench. Ana's team was playing another group of undergrads; it was the first game since her death.

They joined hands and stood in silence for a few seconds. Cara said a few words and then recited a prayer. Tess and Gabriela couldn't take it, they started crying and hugged each other. I noticed the referee: it was him, yes, the guy from the night before. I'd been checking his Facebook profile and logging into his Gmail account for some time now. I won't reveal his identity in these pages; I will only say that he was a grad student and Ana's ex-boyfriend. Or, rather, they dated, because it was never actually official. The guy was studying for an MFA in Creative Writing at Columbia and was known for two things. One: Richard Ford kicked him out of his workshop when he found out that he took a gun to class. And two: the following semester Jamaica Kincaid told him that she had never read such phallocentric texts, ridiculed him in front of the whole class, and then failed him without further explanation. The guy had been there less than a year and was already the main eccentric in a program full of eccentrics. A member of the NRA with tattoos of Batman and the communist symbol all over his arms.

It didn't help that he never wore anything but a tracksuit and sneakers, and that almost every night he sat at the bar in 1020 and made conversation with whoever would put up with him.

The soccer game was boring as hell. Ana's team turned out to be a thousand times better than the other team. I witnessed so many goals that I wondered if they were in fact playing some gringo variant of soccer. Next to me, three hobos were laughing at the players, which got me a little riled up. It wasn't the first time I'd seen them in the park. They hung out there every Sunday and watched the women's league games. They drank beers wrapped in paper bags and munched on sunflower seeds. I felt that they were attacking Ana and that Ana deserved to be defended, even if she was dead.

But I said nothing.

At the end, each of the undergrads said goodbye to the referee. He picked up his backpack and walked to the subway. I followed him.

*

He lived in East Flatbush, Brooklyn. He went into his apartment, and I hung around nearby, walking around the block. At a deli, I bought a watery coffee with cream and sat down to wait for him. Then he came out of the building. He was still in his tracksuit and sneakers. He looked like he had showered but put the same clothes back on. He went down the steps of the subway, in the direction of Manhattan.

I headed towards his building.

I had no problems getting inside. The lobby door was open. I walked up the stairs. I reached his apartment and slipped in my Columbia card. I forced the door open with a gentle thump. It was small. It was a mess. It was worse than my apartment during my low months. I could detect the smell of incense and leftover pastrami sandwiches. There was a stack of DVDs on the coffee table, and I knew that one of those was Ana's. I took my time going through them. One by one. But it was gone. He probably had it with him. Next to the pile of discs, a camera on a tripod was pointed at the window.

Ha, I thought, so he was one of those creeps who films the neighbours? On the dining room table, I spotted a notebook; it was a diary with a transcript of what he'd filmed; a raw narrative, without much in the way of writing, just descriptions of people fucking or fighting, or a combination of both. So that was where he got stories for his MFA workshops.

I went through his drawers, searched his kitchen and bathroom. Nothing. Nothing in the rest of the living room either. I went back to the kitchen and inside the oven, among the trays, pots and pans, I found it. I tore off a piece of paper towel so as not to leave fingerprints on it and put it into a Ziploc bag. A gun. I imagined it in Ana's mouth.

My heart was racing, minutes later, as I walked down the stairs of the building and saw him coming in. I hadn't felt like that since the last time I smoked animalitos. Hi, he said, perhaps thinking I lived in the building. I laughed. I didn't return his greeting and hurried down the stairs, not looking back, waiting until I heard his door close. Only then did I make my way back up to his apartment. I stood outside for several minutes and heard him pacing back and forth. I waited until it grew quiet. This time, I opened the door using my bank card, quietly, carefully. I peeked in through the crack. Focused on his neighbours, the guy was filming and jotting down phrases in his notebook. He was wearing headphones, chuckling and muttering to himself. It felt good: he was watching people without permission, and I was doing the same to him.

*

The next day, in the afternoon, I called the man. I asked him what time he could meet at the movie theatre, and he replied that he could meet right now; in fact, he couldn't be at home anymore, the paranoia was back. The man was convinced someone was following him. He hadn't been out for two days. I told him to calm down, we could talk about it at the movie theatre.

I saw him sitting in the usual place, right in the middle row.

This time, my unresponsive state took a while to kick in. I was pumped with adrenaline. I sat down and waited for the man to speak. I wanted to hear his distinctive Paisa accent. The movie was about halfway through. Once again, there was the lone astronaut listening to Bowie, wondering if there is indeed life on Mars, the computer with the existentialist questions, and the moment when the astronaut, about to die from lack of oxygen, takes off his space helmet. And he realises that his lungs can withstand it. He will survive. But now he faces a new mode of existence.

The man was asleep. All I remember about his face is that he looked exhausted. And that later, when I dragged him out of the movie theatre, I saw that he was not dressed in his usual formal attire, but in ripped jeans, a red hooded sweatshirt and muddy black Converse.

I sat down next to him. What happened to you? I asked.

He said nothing.

I looked around and thought that there were too many people in the room. Or maybe not: it may have just been the darkness; I was pretty disoriented by it and was struggling to make out the human silhouettes between the seats. Are you okay? I whispered once more to the man. He shifted. Well, I said, I trailed him. That guy, Ana's ex. All the way to Brooklyn. I held my breath, still flustered. I carried on talking: I went into his apartment and... I sensed that the man wasn't listening to me. Are you okay? I repeated. I nudged him with one arm. I touched his shoulder and sensed there was something under his armpit. Like a stain. I moved him again, this time more forcefully, and when I brushed the stain, it was wet to the touch. Just then, the movie ended, and the lights came up. I was stunned, blinded by the lights. Slightly dizzy. I barely had the strength to move him. When I looked down at my hand, I saw it was red. Nobody was talking in there; the whole audience was made up of hobos, most of them asleep, a few eating fast food. I wiped my bloody hand on my trousers and went outside to get help.

*

Later that evening I went back to Brooklyn. This time it was quick. I knocked on the door, he opened it and looked at me. Tracksuit, but no sneakers: the guy was walking around in kids' slippers shaped like soccer balls. He smiled. He knew what was about to happen. I think he even predicted my punches; his eyes were already slightly watery. Yeah, asshole, I wanted to say, I'm gonna beat the shit out of you. But it all happened in silence. He stood there and took it. I even noticed a faint smile on his lips. Your friend, he said when he was on the floor, in between spitting out gobs of blood, I paid him a visit at the movies.

I resisted one final blow, choosing not to knock him unconscious. Once again, before leaving the apartment, I checked through the stack of DVDs. Nothing. I kicked the tripod over and the camera slammed against the wall. It was only then that I noticed the backpack slung over a chair. I emptied it onto the floor and scattered the contents with my foot. There it was. It was the video. A black USB flash drive with a red lid.

*

Later, in my apartment, I inserted the flash drive into my laptop.

It went like this: Ana, in front of the camera, between hiccups and giggles, confesses to stealing the bike. The guy – the referee – is behind the camera, recording and asking her questions. It's Brooklyn, somewhere in Fort Green, and it's nighttime. They are coming out of a bar, half-cut and laughing. They are happy. Ana pedals slowly down the empty street and at some point, she mentions the Colombian. She doesn't say the man's name, only 'my Spanish professor.' But that doesn't matter. What matters is that the camera falls to the ground and screams are heard. You can't see anything, but you can imagine the situation from the audio. A lovers' quarrel in the middle of the street: her crying, him angry; him crying, her explaining; the two of them getting closer and closer, then embracing; the two of them kissing and forgiving each other; the two of them looking for a place to spend the night. That happens. The video cuts to Ana, in a living room. It belongs to a friend who's away, he says. Oh yeah? Ana asks. She goes to the kitchen and comes back with two glasses of water. She puts them down on a table which she then sits on. Another cut. Ana slips two fingers between her legs, touches herself, her tongue glides wetly over her lips. He flips the camera around and records himself. He is also naked, masturbating, he moans with pleasure and at one point drops the camera.

The recording ended there.

*

I ground up a couple of animalitos, rolled them into a joint and smoked it out of the open window. I felt the city lights growing and fading. Expanding and contracting. Like my breath. I took a walk around Astoria to bring me down from my euphoric state. I have no idea how long I roamed the streets. Back at my apartment, I ordered Chinese. I ate a plate of broccoli with garlic chicken and three spring rolls with mustard. That night I pieced together her narrative. It was like starting a story when you already know the ending, and you have no way of reversing the tragic outcome. Always narrating in the past tense. There is no other tense when it comes to suicidal kids; those lost young souls, now dead. I typed: *Ana Reitman, aged six, learned to ride a bicycle. It was her first bike. Thirteen years later, she got on another bike, her last one.*

*

Ana can't sleep. She gets up and pads into the living room. The guy is still asleep in bed. It happens during that hazy, mercurial time of the early morning. It could be 3 a.m. or 6 a.m. Ana hunts around for her jeans and takes some pills out of the pocket. She swallows two, then goes to the kitchen and drinks water. She returns to the living room. Then she spies something in the guy's jeans, an odd-shaped bulge in one of the pockets. Ana reaches into the pocket and pulls out a gun. It's an old .45, the kind of thing you can pick up at a flea market. She starts playing with it. She points it out the window; she points it at a hideous, extremely Mark Rothko-esque painting; she points it at a full-length mirror and that's when she does it: she sticks the gun in her mouth. She shudders. Pulls it out. She laughs uneasily and then looks in the mirror again. She sneers: You talkin' to me? and lets out a nervous laugh. Then she says, more serious now: There's no one else here... you talkin' to me? It seems like she feels a little silly holding the gun. She's being watched but she doesn't realise it yet. What the hell are you doing? The guy – angry, worried – tells her to give it to him. Startled, Ana stretches out her arm and as she does so, the gun falls and goes off by itself. It gives them both a scare, but they are fine. It's alright, he says. Calm down, nothing's wrong. Sorry, she says, I was just messing around. She goes over and tries to hug him, but this makes him angrier. Then there's a fight, a slamming of the door, an 'I hate you'. The guy doesn't take off though, his plan being to walk to the corner deli for coffee and bagels, then to go back to the apartment and tell her that he's in love with her. That they should move in together. Or whatever.

When he returns, Ana Reitman is dead.

*

I woke up sometime after 2 p.m. I showered, dressed and walked to the subway. I read over Ana's file one last time.

Her life narrative was ready. I logged on to the Bank of America website from my phone. The money was in my account, the man had kept his word, although I was aware of a heaviness inside me, a guilt. I wondered why. Sometimes I didn't understand myself: what was wrong with me? He had hired me, so he had to pay me. It was my job. But something felt off. I imagined Ana's grieving parents, Mr. and Mrs. Reitman. Ana, their only daughter, learned to ride a bike at the age of six and, thirteen years later, she rode another bike, her last one, down an almost deserted street in Brooklyn. There she goes: pedalling hand in hand with an ex-boyfriend they never met and who, days later, would confess to following the Colombian to a movie theatre where he beat him bloody and barely conscious.

*

In Union Square I bought a falafel that I nibbled on all the way to the post office. I strolled along calmly; I felt content, naive, slightly dazed. New York seemed like more than a city: it was a possibility, a thousand possibilities, a constant churning of desire. I knew that my depression was a fog that would descend on me again. Although I also knew how to control it now. Without wiping the grease from my hands, I wrote down the address of Ana's parents, in Wisconsin, on the outside of the envelope. I wrote 'Mr. and Mrs. Reitman' and added a fake return address. It would take a week to arrive. Ana had overdosed on pills, perhaps because she could not stand being torn between two men. Both of them older, troubled, and insecure too. Or who knows, maybe she killed herself for a totally different reason. If there was one thing I realised every time I was tasked with reconstructing lives, it was that you never really know people. Not even the ones closest to you.

On the subway, on my way to meet my dealer, I imagined a white Midwestern couple in their pyjamas making coffee. It is the early hours of the morning. The grieving continues. It has been a difficult few days. They still can't face going into their daughter's room. At some point in the morning, they will hear the mail drop through the slot in the door. And there, among the catalogues and bills, will be a fat brown envelope with their names on it. Mrs. Reitman will pick it up and carry it into the kitchen. She'll take a pair of scissors out of the drawer and cut it open in front of Mr. Reitman. The two of them, eager, apprehensive, will find a file inside with their daughter's name on. And a USB flash drive.

*

I got a call. Someone hired me to write up the life of a U Penn senior. Gino Leviatan had slit his wrists while his roommates played beer pong in the yard. It was early on a Sunday, the last week of classes before winter break. All I could find on the U Penn website was a cursory news item about his death. Gino had attended all his courses and had one semester left until graduation. He was described as introverted, caring, sensible and so on. *Gino was a shy boy*, one of his professors said. *An overachiever. A kind and empathetic member of our community.* This was followed by the bureaucratic message so typical of universities: rather than expressing regret over the death, they made a point of reminding students that there was therapy available for anyone concerned about their mental health.

I created a new folder.

Someday I would do something with all those files on my computer, I promised myself.

I would create something.

A work of fiction based on all my dead young souls.

A requiem for a generation.

EXILS

GILBERT AHNEE
tr. ARIEL SARAMANDI

FROM THE FRENCH

An excerpt from the novel,
1989

At mass. This was the first time I'd come of my own volition. Just to see people, feel the crowd, forget that it was Sunday. I'd returned three weeks ago, and each Sunday had appeared like an absurd, ill-placed comma, an insignificant caesura in an agitated week filled with the illusion of living. Only weekdays held some charms.

I had returned on a Friday. Two days later, on Sunday, I let myself traipse to the beach with a group of friends. It made them so happy. I felt like they were consoling themselves in the best way they could, they were prisoners of the island and they'd come to love their jailer. I hated the sea when it was imposed on me like this, I could feel it creating a rift within me, a distance from memories I held too close, memories and their throbbing wake. The waves came from too far away, from places I thought I'd never see, or else they came from that elsewhere that I'd known too intimately.

Six of us were stuffed in an obliging taxi to get to the beach in Pereybere. Lindsay took some of the others in his old Austin; Clency and his wife came by scooter.

The beer was warm. The whole excursion had been organised for me, to celebrate my return to the prodigal country. They wanted me to say that I'd missed the pilao in the three years I'd been away, that there were no beaches like those of Pereybere, over there. That I'd soon be a teacher. I would have been sad, without a doubt, if something had happened to any one of them. But I felt that true apathy of not being able to share in their pleasures. I was indifferent to the sea. The sea and its transient vehemence, always the same. Two days since my return, and I was already measuring the extent of my solitude. What had happened in the three years of my absence? Had the distance really changed me, or had it only exposed the complacency that I used to demonstrate in the simulacra of happiness? On the beach, only a few tourists were able to taste the silent pleasures of the sun. We were too dark for that, my friends stayed under the shade of a filao tree.

Time for the inevitable guitar. I was still sensitive to the torrid beats of séga, the coloured strength of the Creole image. I suppose that the unaltered rhythm sent me back to the days of my adolescence, my hopes of being invited to sway in a first dance.

The repertoire was exhausted quickly, but the guitar had a few more strums to give. I feared *Jeux Interdits* would be up next.

The next Sunday I hoped to sleep in, what was the pagan rite of my Sundays as a student in Paris. But the heat, the first rays of sun, the church bell deprived me of that. I thought I'd make the most out of my early start.

The butter that melts in the still-warm pain maison, the sounds of Plaisance suddenly so familiar, the unchanged indicator of the radio station – I felt a vivid sense of belonging to this place. I'd sought this feeling so dearly – this conviction that I would be betraying something had I not returned.

They were all at church. I was alone. I decided not to go out, to spend my time writing a few letters instead, attempt to read. I wasn't worried yet about the difficulties I faced here when it came to reading; I thought, naively enough, that my laziness was due to the agitation of my return, to the trouble of measuring possibilities. It took me time to understand that I was worried by too many things to also find pleasure in my battles with the written word.

Oriane had offered me a novel as a parting gift. She had been so enthused by it, she'd recommended that I not be put off by the first 50 pages. It was a medieval history; it didn't hold much attraction for me. But I'd promised her. This Sunday would be conducive to a prolonged sense of loyalty, perhaps.

The book employed a clever artifice, a coquetry which I found amusing: the author recounted the discovery of an old text and claimed that his novel was the text's translation. I wasn't able to keep reading; my mother, coming back from church, reminded me that it was too late for the eight o'clock service but I could still get ready for the one at nine o'clock.

Would I admit that I didn't go to church anymore, or worse, that I believed in no God nor Devil? My brother returned a few minutes after the women. He'd bought two Sunday weeklies for me. I tried to appear enthralled by the newspapers and missed the nine o'clock mass. Now, it was eleven o'clock: the vivid smell of curry struck the time. Seated, I made as if I were stunned to know that there was no longer a service at five o'clock that afternoon.

My sisters had discreetly suggested it: my mother had

been devastated that I'd gone to the sea that past Sunday. I had deprived her of the festive supper that she'd planned to mark my return. For the Creole workers of my mother's generation, only Sunday lunch could mark a celebration. She waited, then, for the following Sunday, before killing the fat chicken for her son who'd returned.

Rice, chicken curry, tomato chatini. In my childhood, this princely meal seemed a miracle that only occurred at Christmas, Easter and Assumption. Since then, chicken had become a lot more affordable, a little more banal. But for nothing in the world would my mother change her festive offerings. She believed, perhaps, in the permanence of symbols.

The chicken curry was pungent. Just how Papa liked it, said my mother. My sisters dared to tell her that she may have added too much chilli. Rosemay and Marie-Ange were sweating, lit by the spice. Hedley, who had been observing me timidly since my return, ate without lifting his head from his plate. Like father like son, perhaps – I also loved those strong, burning flavours. I scraped a few preserved chillies from the Coca-Cola bottle that was used as a jar, placed them on the rim of my plate. Carried away by this epicurean masochism – Creoles, it seemed to me, had truly nailed the particular, subtle voluptuousness of the fruit – I bit into the chillies with every other forkful of food. My mother repeated how much I was like my father. I had to say that I appreciated her words, since in them lay her happiness as widow and mother.

Convinced that such a meal was possible only in the tropics, my mother asked me how I was able to survive such deprivation in all the years I spent over there. I served myself more chilli. I would have disappointed her too much, dispossessed her of her island pride if I had admitted that, by la Tour Montparnasse, in the exotic aisles of a Parisian supermarket, you could find mangoes all year-round and Antillean chillies that were even stronger than our Rodriguan variety. For her, my return only made sense when it was measured against the cold, the watery food, an imagined exile. I fought against the feeling that my exile had in fact only just begun. I served myself more chilli.

I felt a light headache coming on after the meal. Perhaps I'd drunk too much Bordofin, the South African grape juice that was made into wine in Mauritius, and whose proud label appeared more and more on the tables of Creole households. The television was turned on after the meal, a necessary imposition. Our house was small and there was no place in which I could isolate myself from the noise. It was impossible to read. At the time where I usually consulted *Pariscope*, the weekly bible of the Parisian cinephile, in order to pick my Sunday afternoon film, I was taking off my shoes in front of the television. My sisters were stunned that I didn't know the rules of the game elaborated by Jacques Martin.

The next Sunday I decided to go to church. The week hadn't been too bad; I'd gotten a job, I was to start in the new school term in September. I wasn't sure of the pleasure I was supposed to feel when I'd share the news at the dominical family agora. When I left the church I told my friends that I would soon become a teacher, just like they'd said. They wanted to organise a party, celebrate the news at the beach. I excused myself, invented a family lunch at my aunt Agnès. Solitude and company were both sides of insular ennui.

MARTA MARTA

LORANNE VELLA
tr. KAT STORACE

FROM THE MALTESE

An excerpt from the novel,
2022

Perched on a stool, rapt in puncturing the tightly woven cloth laid out in front of her with a fat sewing needle – upwards and downwards, downwards and upwards – Dolores was passing the time doing what she liked best: embroidering. Every now and then, and every few red stitches, she would pick up the magnifying glass from the nearby table and inspect her work to see if she had done the stitches correctly. Dolores was beginning to lose her sight, but she wanted nothing more to do with the eye doctor, for fear he would bring up cataracts again like he did the last time he came to visit. She had reproached him, declaring that no illness should be mentioned under her roof unless she herself had permitted it. And the doctor had simply shrugged his shoulders and smiled, because it was clear that dear Madre Dolorosa was the one in charge here.

The moment she heard the first deep-toned note of the bell, she lowered the square tray with the embroidered cloth onto the table and went over to the windows to let in the joyous peal of the Sunday morning bells. She rested her arms in her lap, closed her eyes and let the chimes ignite a fervour in her heart, a shudder throughout her body. None of the other girls had mastered the art of ringing those bells the way Marija Assunta had learned to, thought Dolores. Finally, she had found the one girl who knew how to transport her back to her childhood with her knelling, to a time when the ancient Sor Pawlina would ring the bells in the convent of San Ġuzepp. And to a time even before that, to the day she had heard the solemn tolls of the mourning bells for her father's soul, and understood that when death knocks, you must let her in. Thoughts of her father brought to mind the words of the saint Tereża, which had become so much her own that she knew them off by heart. 'So great was my father's love for me, and so great was my deception of him, that he could never believe that I was so wicked, and this way, I never fell out of favour in his eyes.' Words that immediately conjured up another memory, of the final warning her father had muttered into her ear on his deathbed. She would always say that the erratic words that had rattled out of her father's mouth before he took his final breath – words that wandered only a few paces from his shrivelled lips to Dolores's ear who, at 14, was still a child and had never before that day had the privilege of witnessing, with her own eyes, a person wrestle between life and death and lose – had stirred up something within her and made her blush. She would say that, in the embarrassment that ensued immediately after she had understood the meaning of her father's words, she had barely noticed his head droop slowly downwards and his chin come to rest on his breast bone, despite, according to her aunts, the audible click-clack of bone on bone heard by all those at his bedside. She had been standing nearest to him and she was the only one who had not heard it. She swears that she could still hear him clattering away when someone close by had bent over to shut his eyes. There was no doubt in her mind that his chest had still been radiating warmth when a strong pair of hands grabbed her by the shoulders and entreated her to get up and leave the room. She obeyed, but not before casting one final look over her father's body, lying prostrate on his bed under a sheet. And she would bet money that she had glimpsed a bulge in the sheets, a suggestion of her father's erect manhood and further proof that he had not yet departed this life entirely. Outside the room, the cold air stung her cheeks. It was there that it hit her that her father had died. She would always recount that in the moment before he passed – he, who throughout his life had held the entire family captive, starting with his mother and siblings, to his wife and children – had belched those final four words with which he had freed his daughter from the plaguing sense of weakness that only a woman is capable of suffering, a torment she thought she would have to live with for the rest of her life. That evening, she felt a quickening like she had never experienced before.

On the day of his death a silence fell over her father's house for an hour, and then everyone set about being busy. Up and down they went, boiling the sheets, scrubbing the stairs, cleaning the pots and pans, and pulling out half-forgotten linen from mothball-scented chests in the turret. She, too, got caught up in the frenzy, and yet the girl Dolores, her still-red cheeks from the flush provoked by her father's words, rushed off and closed herself in her room. She always recalls her first coming like this. Go tell her saintly mother, God have mercy on her, that it was not to pray for her father's soul that Dolores had shut herself up in her bedroom in a hurry that day, but to indulge in wanton self-gratification with the help of, for the first time, a cigar that she had stowed safely away in the small drawer of the sottospecchio. For Dolores, it was the beginning of a guilt-free journey of sensual pleasure and enjoyment, in the spirit of her father's whispered cautions before his death. And although she was still a child, she was aware of how quickly her heart had started beating. And, like the pounding of her heart that day, the pealing of the bells was getting louder now, as one bell joined another, tolling faster and more zealously.

The high-pitched notes reminded her that she had not shed a single tear – not at the hour of agony of her father's death, nor in the days that followed. She had merely looked on in curiosity at the behaviour of her father's nearest and dearest who had gathered by his bedside. She studied and memorised their behaviour: the gushing tears, the desperate sobs, the laments of loss. Then came the pursed lips, and she understood how a restrained grief should look during the burial. She stroked and fingered the mourning outfits. The black silk veils on the heads of the women and the crêpe on the arms of the men excited her. The sombre incandescence of black-on-black drove her wild. She could not get over the lacework with which they decorated the candles and the embroidery on the pall with which they covered the coffin. Her father's death turned out to be more of a life lesson than her aunts could ever have hoped, as they deliberated over what to do with this child and her sister. Now that Giovann Battist no longer had a hold over his sisters to make them care for his children – as he had asked them to do when his wife had caught pneumonia and died, leaving the girls behind with their father when they were still little – the situation was ripe for them to take things into their own hands. Giovann Battist's siblings inherited his house. Their father's dying wish, it was revealed to the young girls at last, was for them to become nuns, and the family lost no time in kicking them out of their own house and sending them off to the convent. Neither Dolores nor her sister had any doubt that this was just one of their lies. The last place their father had wanted to lock up his daughters was in the convent, but Dolores rejoiced at the idea that she was getting rid of her narrow-minded aunts for good.

Dolores had no time for languor and no patience for

idleness. From childhood she had always been assiduous, nimble, hard-working. Work never slowed down, something always cropped up. She liked to say, 'the moment I stop, I die, then I'll surely rest.' You would think she did not know what quiet and respite were – she was always on the go, never stopping to rest, her arms and legs at it from dawn until dusk. The memories of those first days at the convent also reminded her of the words of the saint of Avila, and even in her old age she continued to proclaim her happiness at the appearance of the nuns who were so good, so diligent, living so measuredly together.

During her first weeks at the convent she was made to wash, scrub, hang, dry, starch, iron, fold, dust, polish, stack. Then it occurred to her that she could do even more than all that, and she set about stitching anything ripped or with a hole in it with a needle and thread, until she showed them that she could also draft and fasten, cut and sew. And then, as tends to happen, one thing led to another and the work picked up instead of letting up. Sor Rodolfa showed her how to hold the drum in her lap and to embroider using silk threads. Sor Ċensina took her up to her room and taught her to weave cloth on the handloom with a jacquard. Sor Imelda lent Dolores her lace pillow and bobbins and, in no time at all, Dolores learned to thread lace like the kinds she remembered from her father's funeral. Dun Ġwann was so delighted by this lacework that he asked Madre about it. Before you knew it, the young Dolor was receiving every kind of commission: for a chalice pall or starched amice, a ciborium veil with a tiny cross embroidered into it, or a long lace sash for embellishing the alb that sits underneath the chasuble, the priest's outermost vestment. As the village festa approached, Dun Feliċ wanted in on it too, and took her to meet Sunta and her offspring, four girls and three boys, who were engaged in creating the decorations and dressings for the church all year round. From them she learned to recognise one type of damask from another, and to embroider with threads of silver and gold; how to ruffle the tassels, change the feathers of the flabellum, make the covers for the chandeliers and fix the fringe onto the canopy. She was gifted with the eye for embroidering neatly in miniature, the patience for labouring carefully for long stretches of time, and the heft for working at least twice as hard as everyone else.

But now her vision had started to fade, and neither her glasses nor her magnifying glass were enough. Sometimes she would rub and rub her eyes, impatiently. Sometimes she felt like ripping them out of their sockets, giving them a good polish and popping them back in, in the hopes that she would finally be able to see clearly again. She would spend the best part of five minutes wiping the lenses of her glasses over and over because they still seemed fogged up. She even had to block the bright light from the lamps in her room with pieces of tulle to ward off headaches. Doctor Ghio's words weren't trivial, she knew that. But the word cataracts brought a pang to her heart every time she remembered Sunta's eyes, which in her old age had clouded over with a white film, like a drop of emulsified milk, which rested on the surface of the eye and spread out in the shape of an eight-pointed cross. It was as though all the crosses Sunta had embroidered in her lifetime had found their way into her eyes, and it took losing her sight to finally make her stop working and take a break. Dolores would well up at the thought that hers would be the same fate as Sunta's, sitting down and staring into nothing, unable to see, waiting for death to come knocking while listening to everyone around her carry on with their busy lives as usual. Life, it seemed, was merely a straight road to hell. An eye that could not see, a hand that could not do – this was what hell was to Dolores.

'These thoughts are the work of the devil,' she murmured to herself, the moment she realised that she had been staring idly out the window. She had never understood the mystery of silent contemplation. Dolores was no Saint Tereża of Avila. The bells had fallen silent, and not even a whisper of the vibrating tolls lingered.

With a jade mouthpiece between her lips, filterless cigarette lit at the end of it, Beneditta stood in the middle of the room, which could have been bursting with one-o'clock-in-the-afternoon sunlight had the windows not been obscured by dark, heavy damask curtains. Beneditta had her arms crossed and was leaning slightly backwards in a relaxed pose and resting on one leg, but with an arrogant look in her eyes as if to defy anyone who dared contradict her, and with a half-smile that implied she was on the verge of one of her characteristic obscenities. Today, for the plotting of the swearing game, Beneditta had thrown on a wide-fitting men's shirt, white, creased and shabby, that sat just above her knees. She had nothing on underneath. Her hair was long and wild. Her stance, her appearance and her behaviour attested to Beneditta's superior sense of confidence. It was Beneditta who really drove the guests wild and this, perhaps, was the reason she was Madre Dolorosa's favourite. Every now and then Beneditta would take the mouthpiece between her fingers and drag on it, as though her actions might help her get to the bottom of her thoughts. When she was done sucking in the smoke, she looked around at the other girls sprawled about here and there – on the sofa, on a chair, on pillows on the floor – then straightened up, let the smoke slowly back out and with wide, lazy steps, walked up to one of the girls and whispered into her ear.

When the first whisper reached Carmelina's ear, she burst out laughing and widened her eyes, then she got up and ran over to the settee opposite, to where Marija Assunta was, and softly repeated Beneditta's words. Marija Assunta smiled but remained as she was, sprawled out, and turned her head to the right to whisper Carmelina's words into Jeanne's ear, who then stretched over and whispered them to Marwa, who got up and whispered them with an almost-laugh into the ear of the young Nathaline, who, when she heard the words, did not giggle, smile, or leave her spot. She looked around at the other girls and became aware that she had no one to pass on Beneditta's freshly-crafted swear to other than Madre Dolorosa. Madre was seated on a Victorian-style chair with upholstered armrests covered in a pale champagne-coloured damask, the front legs bulging outwards. None of these details were visible, however, hidden as they were by the sizeable figure and elaborate layer-upon-layer skirt of Madre Dolorosa – who, as everyone said, was like a religious statue. The Victorian chair was next to the small table where Madre always sat at this time of day as they were all busy concocting a new litany of blasphemies before lunchtime, smoking a short, fat cigar and drinking a strong black coffee with a block of sweet chocolate. Madre said gently to Nathaline, 'I'm the most vulgar out of all those born from a woman,' as if to encourage her not to be shy to pass on the blasphemous words she had just heard in her ear – from Marwa, from Jeanne, from Marija Assunta, from Carmelina, from Beneditta – and, at the same time, to fill the silent, heavy void this new girl Nathaline carried with her everywhere she went. Nathaline seemed even more bashful than usual, but got up and went over to Madre, kneeled, kissed her hand, and from her bosom produced the small notebook tied with a cord that hung around her neck, which she used to use to write down what she wanted to say. She scribbled the words Marwa had whispered onto the first page, ripped it out, and handed it to Madre. She, in turn, swung around on her chair to face the girls, wearing an elongated expression of sorrow and pain across her face, and implored them to listen, each and every one of them. Madre Immacolata Concetta, who rarely participated in these swearing games of Beneditta's, was also present, quietly seated on the other Victorian-style chair beside Madre Dolorosa, her eyes closed, her mind apparently elsewhere but in reality listening to and pondering over everything. She knew she was up next, after this game, with her obscene storytelling. Beneditta's blasphemies were nothing more than kindling for Concetta's perverse mind. This time, Beneditta had embellished her swearing with a mixture of genitals, bodily fluids and saints in the correct syntactical order, which only made sense when spoken out loud. The girls clapped for her and for Madre, who raised her eyebrows to thank them and smiled coyly at Beneditta to signal the success of her blasphemy, and that they would include it in next Friday's performance, so she could move on to devising the next one. Dolores had shaken her head at the two previous rounds of swearing, the first because it sounded too try-hard, the second, because she hadn't taken to the obscene reference to Addolorata, Our Lady of Sorrows.

During her engagement, at a time before life had burdened her with sorrow and bitterness, Dolores's mother had made a promise in front of the edifice of the Addolorata of the seven daggers in her bedroom, that if her firstborn were to be a girl, she would name her after her. The firstborn had been a boy, and they buried him just two days after birth. The second boy had barely turned one month before they laid him in the ground.

When Maria Dolores finally came along, it was clear that voto fecit gratia accepit, she had made a vow and received grace, but the daggers' wounds had by this time already reached the depths of her mother's heart, and she bestowed upon her the name of Duluri, Dolores, ready-tainted with bitterness. Her mother had been plagued by an overwhelming sense of guilt after convincing herself that the deaths of her two boys were befitting punishment for her deep-rooted desire – contrary to that of each and every member of her family, and her husband, contrary to that of her neighbours and close friends, and to that of everyone else she knew and didn't know – to give birth to a daughter before a son. There was very little doubt, Madre Dolorosa would confess to anyone who would listen to her tell of her mother's tribulations and the meaning behind her name, that there was any other name in the world more suited to her than this one. Her mother had died lamenting that the only legacy she had left for her daughter was one of sorrow, despair, and the young Dolores had cried and cried until she could cry no more. While narrating these events, Madre Dolorosa would beat her chest and press the holy scapular to her bosom, exclaiming that this legacy was what had turned her into the daughter of sorrow, her heart overflowing with sadness from birth. And that she, Dolores, was the mother of sorrow, too, because she was, she asserted, like every woman and mother rightfully was and should be, always and forever, the merciful mother, the mother who empathises, the mother who takes the suffering, the pain of others into her arms, her heart, her bosom. She was the mother who shoulders it all, who feels and cries for others. She was the one who cares deeply. Not to mention that she had also witnessed her son's suffering and lost him forever. 'Is there a more cruel fate than a mother losing her only son,' she would weep, in a pile on the floor. 'Look at me,' she would continue, 'my eyes are testament to everything that I am feeling. Watch the tears well up, see the sorrow running down, cascading. Witness the passion of this woman who has suffered. My tears are a woman's tears, they are both my strength and my weakness.' Then, she would wipe her eyes – which, for Dolores, were more than just windows, they were an entire display through which she exhibited the vast spectrum of feelings of the heart – stand and straighten up, head tilted upwards but her gaze looking down, peacocking in front of the guests, receiving applause from those who had come especially for the burlesque spectacle she had prepared for them, together with the girls, on a Friday evening.

On Monday mornings, Madre Dolorosa, Madre Concetta, Beneditta, Marija Assunta, Carmelina, Marwa, Nathaline, Jeanne, and sometimes Damjan, would all be present, planning and making preparations for that week's soiree. Today they were gathered together sharing what came to their minds. One of them chose stories they had not put on in a while; another proposed repeating a more recent enactment with a twist, to make it less recognisable; someone else sat quietly leafing through some books for inspiration before making a selection; another came with the idea of creating a game or story entirely from scratch. Madre Dolorosa remained silent, listening to them babble away and say their piece, contemplating every thread they unravelled to try to make out how, by the end of the day, they were going to stitch together the best ones. The pattern design for Dolores's life had not started today, nor even the previous Monday, or the previous. In her eyes these Monday brainstorms showed, in their smallness, just how much drafting a woman must do before she is able to cut out the pattern of her life and assemble it to begin living. It had been a long time since Dolores had fashioned her own life, considered the shape she wanted it to take, modelled it on this or that woman, the ones she dreamed of becoming, but also those she never wanted to be. She took one bit from her, and one bit from the other, then cut or added what felt extra or was missing to produce the exact robe she wanted. She would say to the girls, when telling them about the pattern-making of her own life, that like Santa Tereża she sometimes wished to die the death of a martyr and that other times, she deliberately did things that did not please God. 'A good pattern design,' she would go on to say, 'is one where the right side and the wrong side of the fabric work well together, like two sides of the same coin.' She would often tell them that a well-designed garment contained hundreds of patterns buried within it – your own patterns, the patterns of others. Some designs remained visible, recognisable, despite being hidden; some, you forgot were ever there, but sure enough, there they were and would remain so, getting bolder over the years to withstand the load of the others that came after them. The foundations evolved, and it was upon these that the woman-in-progress built herself, raised by all the women who came before her: strong because she learned from their weaknesses, brave because she knew their fears, mighty because she recognised the power contained in each.

After Madre Immacolata Concetta finished telling her story, and before the girls finalised the morning's creations and left for lunch, Madre Dolorosa, her eyes darting between the girls and Concetta, informed them that this year's coronation of the Madonna on the first of May fell, precisely, on a Friday. Then, she dismissed them because today she and Concetta were going to take lunch by themselves. When Dolores prepared food for the two of them you could assume that she was in the mood to pamper Concetta and, most likely, that she had some good news to share with her. Or, it was some bad news over which Dolores had been agonising with worry. Dolores was not the kind to work hard in the kitchen; true that she was always on the go, but cooking was rarely her first thought of the day. It was enshrined in one of the clauses of the contract each girl was made to sign before entering Dolores's and Concetta's house, that it was up to the girls to decide between themselves who was going to take care of the shopping, the food preparation and cooking throughout the week. Today, Dolores was in the mood to be alone with her sister Concetta, who never turned down Dolores's cooking, especially when, like today, she was roasting fish. While the girls dined in the refectory, Dolores and Concetta remained by themselves in the kitchen. Alone together they would shed away tens of years, let them gather in a pile by the leg of the table, and begin nattering as though they had barely just turned 20, although it was Dolores who went on the most, while Concetta preferred to listen in silence. They might as well have been alone in the house, because there in the kitchen it was as though everyone else had vanished. Dolores placed the coffee pot on the hob.

They did not agree about who had first come up with the idea of moving in together. In Dolores's version of events, which should not be taken entirely to heart, she had decided to leave the convent and had begun looking for a place of her own. Sometimes she would insinuate that she had been kicked out of the convent for immoral conduct, and other times, that she had run away to give birth to Damjan in secret, and every now and again she would embellish the tale and confess that she had been snatched from her room at the convent and held captive by a group of loutish men, who had used her every which way for their own pleasure until she had managed to trick them and escape. But alone with Concetta the story was nearest the truth, as they reminisced about the days when they would dream of having their own house where they could live as they wished without the interference of anyone, a house where they could behave exactly as their hearts desired without needing to answer to anyone. And since they both shared the same dream, they could even split a house like that between them. Concetta frequently reminded Dolores that it was she who had encouraged her to leave the convent during her novitiate, and that had she not listened to her at the time, she would still be there and would very likely have become the actual Madre by now. Never mind that, on hearing these words, Dolores would pull her leg, lamenting that Concetta had made her miss out on her vocation and had thereby ruined her life, and that she would now have to suffer punishment for it in hell. Concetta would pull a face because such thoughts often creeped into her head, and this was precisely why Dolores threw these accusations at her, because she knew what a pedant Concetta was, and that her words would cause her to fret and lose sleep.

Then, the house presented itself with a stroke of good luck. They heard about it from Marie, who cleaned Concetta's parents' house, as well as some of the other large houses, including that of the Sciberras brothers. The four brothers, who were all single and had lived good, long lives beyond their 90s, had died in succession over the space of a few months, and the empty house was put up for rent. Concetta had thought to enquire about it before going to see it. She found out from Marie that the four brothers had all been born and died in the house, and that their father had bought it when he married their mother. And she heard, also, that he had been a boorish man, and that one fine day he up and left his wife and children, vanished from the country and never returned. Marie's words had sparked Concetta's curiosity and she made up her mind to go and visit the house.

Dolores, who adored empty houses, had gone with her. More than once she had experienced strange and confusing dreams about buildings, especially if she recently heard about a new place or entered a new building for the first time. In the dreams the insides of the buildings were much bigger than they appeared on the outside. As soon as she found herself in one room, another would appear directly behind it, and the same went for the floors, going up and going down, each room, each floor decorated in a completely different style to the previous. She would never forget her dreams the night after using the newly installed lift at the convent of the Dominicans – for the very first time. She had spent the entire night going up and down in the mechanical box, the floors multiplying the more she tried to reach the roof or the cellar. Every time it came to a halt, she opened the door and peered out. On one floor she saw nothing but gilding; on another, everything was the colour of blood; a third was decked only with wood; and the next, everything had been draped in damask as black as darkness itself.

In the Sciberras house there was no lift, but Dolores saw it there again in a dream. The house appeared at least three times larger, the garden seemed to have no beginning or end, and in her dream she adorned it with trees so tall they disappeared into the sky, and flowers of every colour. You could bet that over the years everyone who came to visit had heard the description of the house from Dolores's dreams – because perhaps it was how she had wanted it to be – before she had even visited it. 'The interiors of buildings have always fascinated me,' she would say to them, and then she would treat them to nostalgic recollections from her childhood and what a joy it had been, while playing with other children her age, to build monasteries and dream of becoming a nun, or living the life of a hermit and maybe – and why not? – dying a martyr. Then, she would go back to describing the first time she had found herself in this house.

It was not a small house, at the very least it had three floors with a wide entrance and rooms on either side of it. At the back was a sizable garden laden with flowers and orange trees. In the centre of the house was a courtyard, which you could go straight towards as soon as you entered through the front door, by walking along the entire length of the entrance hall and crossing the large room that during the days of the Sciberras brothers had served as the dining room, and that today everyone knew as the guest room. When you went through the door leading into the courtyard, you found yourself underneath the porticoes, which could only be found on that end of the house. Opposite was a large statue of the Madonna propped up on a pile of rocks. When they came to view the house, Dolores quickly realised that it was much smaller than she had dreamed it, yet as she drifted through from one room to another, she was taken aback by its beauty, and she was itching with eager anticipation to begin the renovating and decorating, to give the house a fresh look not far from what she had imagined in her dreams. For the very first time, she said, she could get to work drafting, trimming and sewing damask curtains for doing up her own home, reflecting her own taste in the colours and the quality of the threads and fabrics. Over here, I will place a jardinière with mirrors and shelves for plants; I want the piano over there, I have always wanted a piano in the house; this room will be blue for the Immaculate Conception, and this one black, for Our Lady of Sorrows; this, here, will be the library, where I want a bust of Edmondo De Amicis; this floor will be for the bedrooms; I want a four-poster bed, and I will make all the linen myself with embroidered edges; this bathroom must go; and this room I will keep for weaving, if I can manage to bring the loom through this door.

Concetta had interrupted her to remind her that they would be living there together, and the house would be hers, too. But Dolores waved her arm to brush her aside, as if to say yes, that was so, and then carried on examining every wall and every corner of every room on every floor, listing all the work she was planning to carry out on each and every one of them with her very own hands. Concetta was not plagued by the same work malady as Dolores, and neither was she obsessed with decorating and embellishing as she was, and so they quickly agreed to disagree, and the rental contract for the house was passed on to them in a short space of time. Finally they had found a way to free themselves from the shackles of their fathers and to take the reins of their lives into their own hands. They now held the keys to their own house, where they could re-enact the roles of the sisters Marta and Marija to their hearts' content, as they had often done when they were little. Only women would be allowed to live in their house. From now on, men would only be present as guests, a very important detail for both Concetta and Dolores. A guest, they had agreed, was someone who could enter the house only with their express permission and who, during his visit, had to accept to follow the rules they imposed upon him. 'The right to ownership,' Madre Dolorosa told the girls repeatedly, 'must never be handed over to the men or the guests, and I must stay vigilant to never again call anyone my master.' In her father's house the women had outnumbered the men, and yet he had ruled over them all. In the convent they were all women too, each responsible for the other – until, that is, the priest turned up, and they would all start pissing themselves, even if he was only a fresh-faced novice. This was for the first time, and above all, her house, and in here, men were to have no entitlement. Never mind that it would be at least another ten years before they opened its doors to the girls, and after that, to the guests. Because, before anything else, Dolores wanted to erect a bell tower on the roof of the house.

GILBERT AHNEE was the editor-in-chief of both *La Sentinelle* (2010–2013) and *Le Mauricien* (1996–2009), Mauritius' leading newspapers. He now works as a freelance writer. *Exils*, his first and only novel, was published by Editions du Centre de Recherche Indianoceanique in 1989.

ARIEL SARAMANDI is a British-Mauritian writer. Her work has appeared in *Granta* and *The White Review*, among other publications. *Portrait of an Island on Fire*, her debut essay collection, will be published by Fitzcarraldo Editions in Spring 2025.

STEFANI J. ALVAREZ is a transgender woman who, from 2008 until 2022, was a migrant worker based in Jubail and Al-Khobar, Saudi Arabia. At the annual Philippine National Book Awards, her *Ang Autobiografia ng Ibang Lady Gaga* [The Autobiography of the Other Lady Gaga] (VisPrint, 2015) won Best Book of Nonfiction Prose in Filipino and her *Kagay-an, At Isang Pag-Ibig sa Panahon ng All-Out War* [Cagayan, and a Love in the Time of an All-Out War] (Psicom, 2018) was a finalist in the Best Book of Short Fiction in Filipino category. Currently a writer-in-residence at the Akademie Schloss Solitude in Stuttgart, Germany, she was born in Metro Cagayan de Oro in the southern Philippines.

ALTON MELVAR M DAPANAS is an essayist, poet, and translator from the southern Philippines, and is the author of *In the Name of the Body: Lyric Essays* (Wrong Publishing, 2023) and *Towards a Theory on City Boys: Prose Poems* (Newcomer Press, 2021). Published from South Africa to Japan, France to Australia, and translated into Chinese and Swedish, their latest works have appeared in *World Literature Today*, BBC Radio 4, *Oxford Anthology of Translation*, Sant Jordi USA Festival of Books, *Modern Poetry in Translation*, and *Infinite Constellations* (University of Alabama Press). Formerly with *Creative Nonfiction* magazine, they are editor-at-large at *Asymptote*.

HAYTHAM EL-WARDANY writes short stories and experimental prose. His most recent book is *Jackals And The Missing Letters: On Animals Speaking at Moments of Danger* (Dar Alkarma, Cairo, 2023). He is a two-time recipient of the Cairo International Book Fair's best short story collection prize and was the 2022-23 Keith Haring Fellow in Art and Activism at Bard College, NY. He lives and works in Berlin.

KATHARINE HALLS is an Arabic-to-English translator from Cardiff, Wales. Her most recent translation is Ahmed Naji's brave, irreverent prison memoir *Rotten Evidence* (McSweeney's, 2023). Her translations for the stage have been performed at the Royal Court and the Edinburgh Festival, and short texts have appeared in *Frieze*, *The Kenyon Review*, *The Believer* and *World Literature Today*, among others, and in various anthologies.

VICKY GARCÍA (Laborde, Córdoba, Argentina, 1986) lives in Buenos Aires where she studied Letters, as well as Dramaturgy. García attended various literary workshops, among which those dictated by Gabriela Cabezón Cámara and Selva Almada stand out. In 2019 she was the winner of the Young Art Biennial award for her short story 'Rastros' published in the anthology *Divino Tesoro* (Mardulce Editorial).

MEGAN MCDOWELL is an award-winning translator who has translated many of the most important Latin American writers working today. She is from Richmond, KY and lives in Santiago, Chile.

HEUIJUNG HUR was born in Seoul and currently resides in Nashville, Tennessee, where she teaches at Vanderbilt University. The winner of the 2016 Literature and Society New Writer's Award, she is the author of the acclaimed short story collection *Failed Summer Vacation*.

PAIGE ANIYAH MORRIS is a writer and translator from Jersey City, New Jersey, now based in South Korea. She has translated work by Pak Kyongni, Han Kang, Ji-min Lee, and others.

SEMA KAYGUSUZ was born in 1972 in Samsun. Due to her father's itinerant military career, she lived in various regions across Turkey. Folktales, legends, and stories, excavated from various dialects and languages during her travels, remain her greatest sources of inspiration. In 2009, a literary poll by the journal *Notos* placed Sema Kaygusuz at the top of a list of 'writers who will be most influential in Turkish Literature.'

MAUREEN FREELY was born in the US but grew up in Turkey. After graduating from Radcliffe College, Harvard University, she moved to England, where she teaches at the University of Warwick. She has translated many classics of twentieth century Turkish literature as well as five books by the Nobel Laureate Orhan Pamuk, and is formerly Chair and President of English PEN.

MICHAEL LENTZ was born in Düren in 1964 and lives in Berlin. He is an author, musician, and editor. His most recent novel *Homewards* was published by S. Fischer this year and Deep Vellum will soon be publishing an English translation of his novel *Schattenfroh*.

MAX LAWTON is a novelist, musician, and translator. He has translated many works by Vladimir Sorokin and is currently working on translations of works by Michael Lentz, Antonio Moresco, and Louis-Ferdinand Céline. He is writing a new novel entitled *The Abode*. He lives in Los Angeles.

MUTT-LON is the literary pseudonym of author Daniel-Alain Nsegbe. He was born in 1973 in Messondo, Cameroon and now lives in Yaoundé, Cameroon. He studied biochemistry at the University of Yaoundé before working as a maths teacher. He currently works as a TV editor for Cameroon Radio and Television. He belongs to the Bantu ethnic group the Bassa (Mutt-lon means 'man of the people' in the Bassa language) and it is the folklore of this heritage that he explores in his writing. *Ceux qui sortent dans la nuit* [Those Who Come Out at Night, 2013] is the first of his three novels. It brought him critical acclaim when it received the prestigious Ahmadou Kourouma Prize in 2014.

RACHAEL MCGILL is a playwright for stage and radio, prose writer and literary translator from French, German, Spanish and Portuguese. Her translations of *The Desert and the Drum* by Mbarek Ould Beyrouk (Mauritania) and *Co-wives, Co-widows* (Central African Republic) by Adrienne Yabouza, published by Dedalus, were both shortlisted for the Oxford-Weidenfeld Translation Prize. Her play *The Lemon Princess* is published by Oberon, as are her translations of the Kerstin Specht plays *Marieluise* (winner of the Gate Theatre/Allied Domecq Translation Award) and *The Time of the Tortoise*. Her short fiction has been published in anthologies and online. Her first novel, *Fair Trade Heroin*, longlisted for the Linen Press First Chapter Award, was published by Dedalus in 2022.

ANTONIO DÍAZ OLIVA is a Chilean writer living in Chicago, where he works as editor and translator at the Museum of Contemporary Art (MCA). He is the author of six books, including the novel *Campus* (Chatos Inhumanos, NYC) and the short story collection *Gente un poco dañada* (different independent publishers in Latin America). He received the Roberto Bolaño Young Writers Award and the National Book Award for Best Story Collection in Chile.

CHARLOTTE COOMBE is an award-winning British literary translator working from French and Spanish into English. Shortlisted for the Queen Sofía Spanish Institute Translation prize 2023, winner of the Oran Robert Perry Burke Award 2022 and shortlisted for the Valle Inclán Translation Prize 2019. Her published translations include *The Seaweed Revolution*by Vincent Doumeizel, *December Breeze* by Marvel Moreno, *Fish Soup* and *Holiday Heart* by Margarita García Robayo, *Khomeini, Sade and Me* by Abnousse Shalmani, *The President's Room* by Ricardo Romero, and *The Imagined Land* by Eduardo Berti. Her translations have been published in journals such as *The Southern Review, Modern Poetry in Translation, Latin American Literature Today, Words Without Borders*, and *World Literature Today*. She is also the co-founder of Translators Aloud, a YouTube channel shining the spotlight on literary translators reading from their work.

YUSI AVIANTO PAREANOM writes fiction and nonfiction. He used to work as a journalist and was involved in several theatre, film, and multimedia arts productions. He is the founder of Banana Publishing and Jakarta International Literary Festival.

PAMELA ALLEN is Associate Professor of Indonesian Language and Literature at the University of Tasmania, Australia. She is a widely published literary translator from Indonesian to English.

ENRICO REMMERT was born in Turin, Italy, in 1966. He has written three novels: *Rossenotti* (1997); *La ballata delle canaglie* (2002), translated into English by Aubrey Botsford as *The Ballad of the Low Lives* (The Toby Press, 2004) and *Strade Bianche* (2010). His most recent work is the collection of short stories *La guerra dei Murazzi* (2017), where *Baal* first appeared.

ANTONELLA LETTIERI is a London-based translator working into English and Italian. She was the 2023 NCW Emerging Translator Mentee for Italian and was awarded first prize in the 2023 John Dryden Translation. Her translations, articles on literature and creative writing have been published in English and Italian magazines.

MARGARITA GARCÍA ROBAYO was born in 1980 in Cartagena, Colombia, and now lives in Buenos Aires. She is the author of several novels, including *Hasta que pase un huracán* [Waiting for a Hurricane] and *Educación Sexual* [Sexual Education] (both included in *Fish Soup*), *Holiday Heart*, and *Lo que no aprendí* [The Things I have Not Learnt]. She is also the author of a book of autobiographical essays *Primera Persona* [First Person] (forthcoming with Charco Press) and several collections of short stories, including *Worse Things*, which obtained the prestigious Casa de las Américas Prize in 2014 (also included in *Fish Soup*).

CAROLINA ORLOFF is an experienced translator and researcher in Latin American literature. In 2016, after obtaining her PhD from the University of Edinburgh, Carolina co-founded Charco Press where she acts as publishing director. She is also the co-translator of Jorge Consiglio's *Fate* and of Ariana Harwicz's *Die, My Love*, which was longlisted for the Booker International Prize 2018

FIONN PETCH is a Scottish-born translator working from Spanish, French, and Italian into English. He lived in Mexico City for 12 years, where he completed a PhD in Philosophy at the UNAM, and now lives in Berlin. His translations of Latin American literature for Charco Press have been widely acclaimed. *Fireflies* by Luis Sagasti was shortlisted for the Translators' Association First Translation Award 2018. *The Distance Between Us* by Renato Cisneros received an English PEN Award in 2018. *A Musical Offering*, also by Luis Sagasti, was shortlisted for the Republic of Consciousness Prize 2021 and won the UK Society of Authors Premio Valle Inclán 2021 for best translation from Spanish.

GHEORGHE SĂSĂRMAN is a Romanian architect, journalist, and writer living in Germany since 1983. His literary debut in 1969 was a collection of science fiction short stories, *The Oracle*, and he continues to be best known for his science fiction writing. *Circling the Square* was first published in 1975 in censored form, only appearing in its full version in 2001 after the fall of communism. Many of the stories from *Circling the Square* were translated by Ursula Le Guin in a volume published by Aqueduct Press (2013). Săsărman has written over twenty volumes in different genres and his works have been translated into eight languages. He has won numerous prizes throughout his long career, including the European Science Fiction Convention (EUROCON) Prize (1980).

MONICA CURE is a Romanian-American poet, translator, and dialogue specialist. She won the 2023 Oxford-Weidenfeld prize for her translation of Liliana Corobca's novel *The Censor's Notebook* and her translation of a second novel by Corobca, *Kinderland*, was recently published with Seven Stories Press as well. Her poetry translations have appeared in *Kenyon Review*, *Asymptote*, and *Modern Poetry in Translation*. Her own poems have appeared in *Plume*, *RHINO*, *Boston Review*, and elsewhere. She is currently based in Bucharest.

GEETANJALI SHREE is an Indian novelist and short-story writer, born in Uttar Pradesh, India in 1957, who works primarily in her native language, Hindi. For her novel *Tomb of Sand*, Shree was awarded the 2022 International Booker Prize.

DAISY ROCKWELL is a painter and award-winning translator of Hindi and Urdu literature, living in northern New England. Her translation of Geetanjali Shree's *Tomb of Sand* (Tilted Axis Press, 2021) won the 2022 International Booker Prize and the 2022 Warwick Prize for Women in Translation.

SEYNABOU SONKO was born in Paris in 1993. She studied modern literature in Montreal and Brussels. She is a writer and also makes music under the name Seynabou. *Djinns* is her debut novel.

POLLY MACKINTOSH is an editor and a translator from the French. Her translations include works by Antoine Laurain, Serge Joncour and the early French feminist Marie-Louise Gagneur.

LEILA SUCARI is a freelance writer for *La Agenda* and other print and online media in Argentina. In 2016, her novel *Adentro tampoco hay luz* won first prize from the prestigious Fondo Nacional de los Artes; it was published by Tusquets Editores in 2017, and an excerpt from the translation by Maureen Shaughnessy recently won an honorable mention from the Gulf Coast Prize in Translation. Sucari's second novel, *Fugaz*, was published by Tusquets Editores in 2019. Her poetry collection *Baldio* came out in 2020 from Pánico el Pánico. *Te hablaría del viento,* a collection of her recent flash essays, was published in 2021 by Editorial Excursiones. Her much anticipated third novel is forthcoming from Tusquets Editores in 2023.

MAUREEN SHAUGHNESSY has translated Maya folktales by Guadalupe Urbina and several Cañari legends, and she co-translated the memoirs of Carles Fontserè, the Catalan poster artist. She lived in Barcelona, Spain, for six years, has traveled extensively throughout South and Central America, and currently lives in Bariloche, Argentina.

SENTHURAN VARATHARAJAH, born 1984 in Jaffna, Sri Lanka, is a Tamil-German novelist and poet. Varatharajah's first novel, *Vor Der Zunahme Der Zeichen* [Before signs increase], was published in 2016 by S. Fischer. His second novel, *Rot (Hunger)* [Red (Hunger)] was published in 2022 by S. Fischer. Varatharajah's work has earned him numerous prestigious awards, including the 3Sat Preis, the Adalbert-von-Chamisso-Förderpreis, the Bremer Literaturförderpreis, the Rauriser Literaturpreis, the Alfred Döblin Fellowship of the Berlin Academy of Arts, the German Literature Fund scholarship, the Berlin Senate scholarship and a fellowship at Villa Aurora in Los Angeles. Varatharajah lives in Berlin. His family fled the civil war and genocide against the Tamil minority in Sri Lanka, arriving in Germany when he was four months old.

VIJAY KHURANA is a writer and translator from German. His debut novel, *The Passenger Seat,* was shortlisted for the 2022 Fitzcarraldo Editions/New Directions/Giramondo Novel Prize, and his short fiction has been published in *The Guardian, 3:AM Magazine,* and *NOON,* among others.

LAURA VAZQUEZ is a French poet and novelist who lives in Marseille. In 2023, she was awarded the Goncourt Prize for Poetry. She has written five collections of poetry in addition to her novel, *The Endless Week,* and an epic, *The Book of the Long and Wide.* For *The Endless Week,* Vazquez was a finalist for the Wepler Prize and the winner of the Page 111 Prize. Her work has been translated into Chinese, English, Spanish, Portuguese, Norwegian, Dutch, German, Italian, and Arabic. She is currently at work on her first play.

ALEX NIEMI is a writer and translator from the French, Russian, and Spanish. Her translations include *For the Shrew* and *Hekate* by Anna Glazova, as well as *The John Cage Experiences* by Vincent Tholomé. She is also the author of the poetry chapbook *Elephant.* In 2023, she received a National Endowment for the Arts translation grant, the Heldt Translation Prize from the Association for Women in Slavic Studies, and a nomination for the Best of the Net.

LORANNE VELLA is a Brussels-based Maltese writer, translator and performer. She is the author of several novels including *Magna™ Mater, Rokit* and *Marta Marta*, as well as a number of short stories, including the short story collection *mill-bieb 'il ġewwa*. She has won numerous local literary awards both for her original works, including the National Book Prize for *Rokit* (2018) and *Marta Marta* (2023), and her translations. Together with Joe Gatt, Vella is co-founder and co-editor of the online literary journal in Maltese *Aphroconfuso*, launched in May 2023.

KAT STORACE is a writer, editor, literary translator from Maltese and co-publisher at Praspar Press. She has worked in magazine and literary publishing in Malta and London, including at Faber & Faber. Her first full-length translation *what will it take for me to leave* (Praspar, 2021), a collection of short stories by Loranne Vella, was shortlisted for the Society of Authors' TA First Translation Prize 2021.

BRENT WADDEN is an artist producing abstract woven works that bring together traditions of painting, design, craft, and folk art. Recent solo exhibitions include *WHIMMYDOODLES* at Pace Gallery in LA (2023), *Night Soil* at Peres Project in Milan (2023), *René* at Almine Rech in Paris (2022), and *Two Scores* at Contemporary Art Gallery, Vancouver, Canada (2018).

CAN XUE, the celebrated writer, originally from Hunan Province, now lives in Xishuangbanna in Yunnan Province. She has been at the forefront of experimental writing in China since 1983. She has achieved acclaim in the west, where she has won or been longlisted for literary awards.

CHEN ZEPING and KAREN GERNANT have collaborated in translating contemporary Chinese fiction for more than twenty years. Their translations include works by Can Xue, Zhang Kangkang, Alai, Zhu Wenying, and many others.

COVER

Upper work:
Brent Wadden, *Alignment #13*, 2013
Painting – Hand woven fibres, wool, cotton and acrylic
on canvas 215 × 370 cm (84.65 × 145.67 inches)

Lower work:
Brent Wadden, *Alignment #1*, 2012 (detail)
Painting – Hand woven fibres, wool, cotton and acrylic
on canvas 198 × 177 cm (77.95 × 69.69 inches)

CREDITS

With support from:

Fondation Jan Michalski

Editors
Rosanna McLaughlin, Izabella Scott,
Skye Arundhati Thomas

Art direction & design
Thomas Swann

Assistant editor
Samir Chadha

Reader
Emily Wright

Proofreader
Clémence Appie Gbonon

Founding editors
Ben Eastham, Jacques Testard

Founding art director
Ray O'Meara

Published by The White Review, March 2024
Edition of 2,250
Typeset in Nouveau Blanche
Printed in the United Kingdom

ISBN No. 978-1-9160351-7-1
The White Review is a registered charity (number 1148690)

The White Review, 8-12 Creekside, London SE8 3DX
www.thewhitereview.org

THE WHITE REVIEW
WRITING IN TRANSLATION
ANTHOLOGY

ISBN 978-1-9160351-7-1

£14.99